Evergreen

BYZANTIUM
Sky Press

Byzantium Sky Press
Ellendale, DE, 19941

ISBN 978-1-955872-06-5 (paperback)
ISBN 978-1-955872-07-2 (ebook)

First Byzantium Sky Press Paperback edition, July 2022

Interior design by Crystal Heidel, Byzantium Sky Press

Manufactured in the United States of America

Body of book is typeset in Adobe Garamond Pro
Title and Chapter Title is typeset in Timberline
Author name typeset in Montserrat

Evergreen

A NOVEL

ANNE CROWN

BYZANTIUM
Sky Press

Dedication

For my beautiful and talented daughter Nicole.
You are my heart.

Acknowledgments

Writing, like many creative endeavors, is often solitary, but I have been fortunate to live in an area where writers and artists support and encourage each other.

I am lucky to belong to an extensive group of talented writers and authors right in my own backyard—the Rehoboth Beach Writers' Guild. I have been an active member and participant in the guild since its inception in 2004 and find it to be a wonderful resource for information and friendships.

If it hadn't been for the guild, this story likely would still be in notebooks buried in a box in my office. Although I have always written, the many offerings and opportunities provided by the guild inspired me and gave my ideas a voice. To this day, it remains a unique and rewarding experience to interact and share ideas with other writers who understand the need and desire to sculpt words into art.

To Maribeth Fisher, founder of the guild, writer extraordinaire, author and teacher, I owe my gratitude for her guidance and feedback on everything on the written page. To those writers in our non-judgmental novel group who met faithfully for nearly three years and listened, critiqued, shared their stories, and helped in the birth of this first novel, I offer many thanks.

Francophile and Paris resident Mimi Horne made sure I had accurate locales in and around Paris. The communications staff at *Condé Nast* helped verify the magazine's office locations during the period of the story. My appreciation to Peggy Raley-Ward, owner of award-winning Nassau Valley Vineyards and Winery, for sharing her expert knowledge of wine and winemaking.

I am especially grateful to very special lifelong friends—Amy Klass Coyle, Chrys Chiappa Dudbridge, Janis Levins Dunlavey, and Sonia Inez Vicinanza—who took the time to be my focus group and be brutally honest about my writing and story line.

To professional editor Susan Sutphin whose invaluable comments and encouragement kept me moving forward.

To Crystal Heidel at Byzantium Sky Press for believing in my story and her willingness to publish it. Thank you for your literary insight, artistic talent, and editorial input. I couldn't have done it without you.

Evergreen

1

Going Home

"EM, YOU'VE GOTTA SEE THIS," Katie called out.

Lost in her thoughts, Emma pressed the iron carefully around the delicate embroidery of the linen tablecloth, something she had seen her mother do many times right here in this room. So ordinary, so routine. But nothing was ordinary now—not being home at Evergreen or spending time with her sister. No, nothing would be ordinary again after having come thousands of miles to bury her mother. She used to think her entire life was extraordinary, filled with success, family, a career in Paris, and love. But now she wondered, was it really? So much had changed. She missed her mother already and her extended family.

"Emma," Katie called again. "Come here . . . please."

Her concentration interrupted, Emma turned away from the stack of linens she was ironing and sorting in the kitchen and moved toward the door to the hallway.

"What is it?"

A week after their mother's funeral, the sisters had begun to go through the big Victorian house, salvaging what they would keep and what they would give away. It was strange to be back here under these circumstances, the same kind of event that had made Evergreen their home after the death of their mother's father.

"Come look at what I've found."

The excitement in Katie's voice reminded Emma of when Katie was five and had come running into the house yelling for Emma to come see what she'd found in the garden hedgerow. Only baby bunnies, but for Katie, a great discovery, new and awe-inspiring.

"Buried treasure?" Emma asked as she made her way down the long hall with its high ceilings and mahogany crown molding—a hallway that once had been a stage for theatrical skits and whirling toes to entertain her father. She stopped at the parlor where Katie was surrounded by stacks of books and cardboard boxes.

"Well, sort of—old photographs."

Emma paused in the doorway and watched her younger sister as she sat on the floor in her capris and Ferragamo leopard sandals, rustling pages and laughing at what she'd found. As always, her little sister looked great, a fashion statement from head to toe, her long strawberry hair flowing over her bare shoulders. Was this the same skinny, freckled-faced kid who had followed her everywhere, asking her questions about how fireflies got their name, or how a bug could have lightning inside its body?

The scent of honeysuckle drifted through the loosely draped, white voile curtains filtering the mid-morning light of late April, backlighting her sister's silhouette and giving the room its own spirituality. Emma remembered her grandfather's parlor as dark, with dingy lace curtains, a worn oriental carpet over the oak floor, and overstuffed velvet furniture. The old pedal organ that had stood in the corner—the one she used to plunk on her visits those many years ago—was replaced with a cozy chintz-covered armchair. Her mother and father had turned this space into a cheery playroom for her and Katie, then later into a formal sitting room for guests. The room had had many faces, and Emma had mixed emotions about being here again. Her heart ached.

Emma watched Katie study a photo album. Her sister's eyes focused intently on the pages as her mouth broke into a smile.

"Let's see." Emma held out her hands to take the album from her sister, but Katie grasped her hand and pulled her to the floor.

"Ow!" Emma hit the rug, rocking backward on her hips.

"Sit. We'll look at them together."

Emma was glad to be temporarily removed from the monotony of sorting but wondered if they would be able to get anything accomplished. It seemed Katie was continually distracted. Emma was anxious about all the work they had ahead of them, not to mention the paperwork associated with the estate.

Katie opened to the middle of the book. "Look. Here you are with Shep."

Emma brushed her dark brown hair behind her ears and studied the photo of their collie surrounded by tall sunflowers in the back garden. She smiled. "We were inseparable." Emma pointed to a photo on the next page. "And here you are with Magic working your very first cavaletti."

They both stared at the little girl on the grey pony. "I'm very serious, really concentrating." Katie laughed.

Emma thought about how that was a time free of worry, so wonderful and so unappreciated while living it, though grateful now for having had it.

As Katie fingered through more pages, they both laughed and sighed at the childhood birthday parties, Easter outfits, and former pets—amazed at how dated the photos seemed and how much history the snapshots contained, not only of their family but also of the home itself. Once her grandfather's farm, then her father's horse farm, and later her mother's Bed and Breakfast, the house intertwined their family history—a history beyond boxes and photo albums. Nostalgia swept over Emma, and her throat became dry. She couldn't wrap her mind around the fact that she had pockets full of memories but no tangible family now to reach out to, hug, and hold—except Katie.

"Look," Katie said. "Here's dad with Beauty and Jazzy."

Emma stared at the handsome figure of her tall father with his shot of red hair standing next to his black mare and foal. Katie took after him—the Irish side—with her fair skin, green eyes, and red hair.

"He really did well with the horses."

Yes, Emma thought, it had been her father, Timothy Connelly, with his passion for horses, who had elevated Evergreen into a horse farm. He had added a handsome twelve-stall barn complete with an indoor schooling arena for dressage and jumping. The farm itself had a practice cross-country course that meandered around the entire property. Many of their horses competed internationally, and both girls were avid riders and pony clubbers. Still, Katie had been her daddy's little angel. She was only eight when he died.

Emma looked hard at the photo of her dad, realizing how special her time with her father had been and how much more time she'd had with him than Katie. Katie was a few years younger and the wild child who was into everything good and bad—like makeup, smoking, dating, and sex—sooner than her sister. Emma had been more academic, loved art, music, and of course, her horses. In fact, horses had been her passion early on and were the single most consistent connection between both of them and their father.

Her dad, a lawyer by trade, turned weekend country gentleman, had become well known for his thoroughbred breeding business. He converted his own passion for horses and riding into a profitable operation that produced some of the top show hunters and jumpers in the country.

It had been an ordinary Saturday morning until her mother answered the telephone. Emma and Katie were in the kitchen talking and watching their mother cut large slices of French bread for their toast. The kitchen was the family's favorite gathering place, large and airy, with white linen napkins neatly arranged on the red and silver formica table where the girls were sitting. Sunlight poured through an open window that looked out over the summer garden bursting with roses, hydrangeas, and lavender. Shep was napping under the old oak tree at the far end of the yard. Even now, Emma remembered how the scent of roses mingled with the aroma of bacon sizzling on the stove that morning.

They watched their mother touch her face and wipe tears from her eyes and cheeks. Emma had been scared and worried but tried to remain calm. Katie burst into tears at the sight of her mother crying. Emma remembered her mother pulling off her yellow cotton apron and wringing it into a ball and then sliding down the wall near the phone in a faint.

The news had been surreal. Her father's overnight flight from Paris to New York was missing in a sudden electrical storm. The airline was notifying the families, but there was no other news as to what had happened. Later that evening it was confirmed: Her father was dead.

Emma gently touched the photo of her father and felt her chest tighten. He had died too soon, hadn't seen her grow up, and now when she had to grieve again, she couldn't reach out to him.

"They were beautiful horses, weren't they, Em?" Katie murmured.

"Yes, beautiful," Emma struggled to hold back her tears. My father was beautiful too, she said in her heart.

Katie turned toward Emma, handing her the album. "Do you think there's more in the attic?" Before Emma could answer, Katie stood and was already moving across the room toward the back of the front foyer and up the stairway to the second floor. Emma heard the creak of the pull-down stairs. After a few moments, Katie yelled, "Em! Come on up."

Emma turned more pages in the album not wanting to move. She wanted to study the artifacts she held in her hands. She didn't like attics or dark, dirty, confined spaces.

"There's more stuff!"

Emma moved slowly out of the room toward her sister's voice and climbed to the top of the creaking steps. Her eyes settled on the sea of dust-covered boxes, lamps, trunks, carpets, and disarray before her. Sunlight trickled through the eaves' window giving the attic junk a ghostly quality.

"Oh!" Emma gasped for air.

Katie grinned. "Isn't this a treasure?"

Emma was speechless, overwhelmed by the task before them and all the stuff. Oh my god, she thought, how can we go through all of this? Beads of sweat formed over her brow. She struggled to breathe while Katie saw this as an adventure. Katie, whose energy seemed endless and spirit unbeatable, was making Emma long for calm and solitude.

Emma finally blurted out, "I had no idea. We'll have to clean this out before we sell the place or decide what to do with it."

Katie wasn't listening. She was already opening the beautiful tin steamer trunk and peering over the top edge. She reached for a folder with the word "Evergreen" written across the top and handed it to

Emma. "Here you go, take a look at this. I'm going to keep digging through the trunk."

Emma recognized her grandfather's handwriting and realized she was holding a condensed history of the farm. Her maternal grandfather, Thomas Barré, had owned property along the southern portion of Cedar Run in Virginia. In the 1920s, he and his brother Jim used their sawmill to produce the oak, pine, and hickory boards needed to build the five-bedroom Victorian farmhouse on more than two-hundred acres. After he died, their mother inherited the place, and it was here that Katie and Emma had grown up. Evergreen stood like a sentry on the highest point of the property, and stately Virginia cedars lined its long driveway.

Emma skipped down to the early history of their property and began to skim. According to her grandfather, the current land was but a small portion of the original thirty-thousand acres that once made up Effingham Plantation. Emma knew about the plantation, but simply couldn't imagine all that land. She read that by the late 1700s, only about two-thousand acres remained due heirs and owners selling it off or parceling it out. Emma's eyes shifted to a large notation at the bottom of the page. The writing was a bit faded but she managed to make out that William A. Alexander built Effingham, the Tidewater colonial manor house that still stands today. The name rang a bell. Wasn't he a descendant of John Alexander, the Scotsman after whom Alexandria, Virginia was named?

Emma turned the page. Yes, there it was in black and white: William A. Alexander, the great-grandson, with notes about his family and a brief genealogy. Emma couldn't believe what she was reading. Her family was related to the original owners by marriage. She now understood why the land was always so important to her grandfather and her mother. It was part of who they were and their family history for hundreds of years. They had been part of the land well before any of them were born.

Emma looked at her sister. "Did mom ever tell you about the history of Evergreen?"

"Just that grandad and uncle Jim built it and that the land was originally part of a plantation in colonial days."

"Well, you've gotta read this. It's fantastic! Grandad wrote down how our family is connected to the manor house and the owners in the eighteenth century. Katie, did you hear what I said?"

"Yes."

"Here's another tidbit for you. Before you were born, mother and I visited a cousin of hers who lived in the manor house.

"Really? Cool. I'll read it. Put it in the box to take downstairs, but now look at this." Katie was in junk heaven. She picked up a worn album and dusted off the leather cover, revealing the faint gold letters: "Our Family."

Emma gazed over Katie's shoulder, watching her flip through the pages of faded photographs. Many of the faces were unfamiliar, but she thought she recognized some aunts, uncles, and cousins on her mother's and grandmother's side. She wished she'd known them all. More old pictures, then pages fell from an envelope: birth certificates, a marriage certificate, baptismal records, a wedding photo, and a small key with a red ribbon looped through it.

Katie held up the key. "My, my, this key looks like a . . ."

But before she could say the word, Emma tried to snatch the key from her sister and fell forward onto the dusty trunk.

Katie looped the red ribbon around her finger and held the key high over her sister's head. "Oops. Be careful, sis. Want your *diary* key?" Katie laughed.

Emma's face reddened as she tried again to grab the key from

Katie's hand. She was getting angry. Emma felt like a sixteen-year-old being tortured by her little sister.

"Oh My God, you *had* a diary," Katie roared. "I'm amazed."

The attic dust lodged in Emma's throat. "Give it to me." She coughed. "Give it to me!"

In the next instant, Katie was on her knees rummaging through the trunk, searching for the book of secrets. Emma watched with dread as her sister dug deep and then pulled out the yellow box with Emma's name on it and removed the top. Inside were photos and memories of childhood friends, dances, letters to former boyfriends, and letters from Paris to her mother that Katie pushed aside so the little red book was in plain view.

Emma reached and strained to retrieve the key and the book from her sister. "That's private!"

"Not for long, sis, not for long." Katie grinned as she held the book up in front of her.

"Come on, Katie. We don't have time for this!"

"Uh oh," Katie teased. "I think you're worried. What is it? Something incriminating?"

God, Emma thought, I don't want her knowing about the men in my life, especially about the parties and sex in high school. But it was more than that. The diary contained the intimate moments she had shared with *him* . . . from the very beginning. But that didn't stop Katie from putting the key into the lock and turning it. She opened the book and began to read: *September 25, 1972, Last night was so wonderful. We went to the boathouse at midnight, and . . .*

That did it. Before Katie could react, Emma knocked the book out of her sister's hands. She grasped it tightly and held it against her chest.

"You can dish it out but can't take it. Is that it, sis?" Katie smiled.

"We all have secrets, Katie."

"Do we?"

Emma paused. She wanted to keep her feelings safe, private. She knew she didn't want Katie to read the diary and Emma wasn't sure she wanted to either. Opening that diary was like opening her heart, and if done too abruptly, it would shatter once again. Emma looked up at Katie. "Well, private. I mean private."

Katie smiled. "So, what do you need to hide?"

"Nothing. I just don't want to share it with you."

"I'm your sister. I'm the best person to share it with."

Emma couldn't believe the direction this was taking. She fingered the lock on the diary. "No, I don't want to share it with anyone, at least not now." Those memories still hurt. "Didn't you have a journal or diary, Katie?"

Katie laughed. "Heavens no. I didn't have time."

Emma pushed on. "Not even in college?"

"No," Katie said matter-of-factly. "Especially not then. I didn't want to keep track of my dating disasters."

"So, there was no one special?"

"Not really." Katie paused. "But I did write Kevin Reilly's name over and over again on my book covers."

"Who?"

"Oh, someone I had a crush on freshman year."

"And?"

"And nothing. We were talking about *you* and *your* love life—your recorded love life, remember?"

"Still not sharing," Emma barked. "Give it a rest; we have work to do."

"Okay, okay." Katie shrugged and gave her sister a gentle hug. "I didn't realize it meant so much to you."

Emma now had an aura of mystery about her, something to be

solved, unlocked, and explored. She remained silent and kept her diary close to her as they continued to sift through the pieces of what remained—old records warped with time; boxes of farm ledgers and journals belonging to her grandfather; dishes, linens, books, and more books. In a way, it was like walking through an amusement park in the dark, not knowing what would pop up next. She pulled more treasures from the attic—her grandfather's love letters to her grandmother, brittle and yellowed with age, and letters in her mother's handwriting to her parents when she was at boarding school, parts of their lives she had never known. She was glad to have this history, this family. At the same time, she wanted everything—well, some things—the way they had been.

Katie handed Emma the marriage certificate of her grandparents dated 1897, and Emma realized how little she knew about them. She felt as if she were finding bread crumbs along a lovely winding trail as she tried to piece together something of her family history.

Emma's memory of her grandfather was a more recent version than the one in the tintype she had pulled from the album, and her grandmother had died before she was born. Still, she didn't know anything about how they met or about their siblings. Had they met by chance? She continued to study the tintype photo cradled in her hands and thought "by chance." Isn't it all by chance? She ran her fingers slowly over the surface of the photo and knew it was by chance that she was here at Evergreen once again.

Emma tilted her head. "Do you think everything happens by chance?"

Katie glanced at her sister. "What? Why? What made you think of that?"

"Oh, that we're here again by chance . . . that life is so . . . random, so . . ." She stopped herself from saying the words, *finite, fragile.*

From the wedding photo, her grandmother's exquisite features were readily visible. But what color were her eyes? They were light— perhaps blue or green. They must have been blue like her mother's and hers. Yes, they were blue, she decided. Looking deep into the background of the photo, she spotted the faint outline of a Victorian house, which made her wonder where the photo was taken. It wasn't here—maybe a studio backdrop.

Her grandparents looked almost too serious staring at the camera. She thought about them and their lives and struggles, and whether she could have survived living in their time. A maelstrom of ideas raced through her head as she tried to imagine and envision being them. The photo didn't reveal their happiness, but she had heard plenty of stories about their love and dedication to each other. Emma let out a deep sigh and wondered if, *by chance*, she would also find someone to love her that deeply and forever.

"You and Trevor, you met by chance, didn't you?" Katie asked, as if reading Emma's mind.

Emma glanced up, startled, and felt her entire body warm at the mention of Trevor. A smile softened her face.

"Well, I certainly didn't plan on it, and I didn't plan to love him either."

"What happened, anyway?

"I'm still trying to figure that out."

WHEN EMMA AWOKE the next morning, Katie was gone, or so she thought. Emma called for her and looked around the house and then headed outside with coffee cup in hand. The spring sunlight warmed her bare feet as she walked through the gate and into the pasture. She sauntered up the hill and stood surveying the fields. For a moment, she was her mother that summer morning looking for her four-year-old daughter who had sneaked out of the house after breakfast. Emma remembered walking forever over the big hill of the pasture, past the ponies and horses, to search for bluebells near the edge of the run out of sight of the house. When her mother found her, Emma was covered in mud and flower petals and was talking to Shep, who laid beside her basking in the sun. Emma, blinded by the sunlight, was frightened by the larger-than-life figure—a giant—descending from the mountain to get her. "There you are my little one," her mother had said, reassuring Emma. "I think you've wandered too far from me."

The pink shirt in the distance brought Emma back into the moment as she continued toward the run where she found her sister picking wildflowers—blue flag iris, pink and red columbine, Virginia bluebells, and daffodils—and placing them in a large basket that sat near the edge of the water. The colors overflowed onto her bare legs and warm grass, and Katie looked like a girl of twenty with her strawberry hair flickering like a flame.

"How long have you been out here?"

"Not long enough," Katie said. "I'm beginning to see the Renaissance colors of this place. I'd forgotten them."

Emma looked at the flowers strewn in the wicker basket and thought they would make a wonderful still life or a lovely line in a poem. What was the saying . . . *art imitates life?*

"A penny?" Emma knelt next to her. "You seem sad."

Katie continued to pluck the flowers from the field. After a long silence, she said, "It's more nostalgia, I guess." She wished everything could be the same again, she told her sister. She wanted her youth back, all those lazy days of summer, her parents, her boyfriends, her pets. She wanted it even though it hadn't been perfect, even though she knew she was in a much better place now.

"Nostalgia. It's our genetic deficiency." Emma smiled.

"Do you believe the saying that *Time moves toward you?*" Katie wondered.

Emma always thought time was more elusive, hard to grasp and hold onto, but memories—memories moved toward her like the breeze swirling around them. "Don't know, but it never seemed that way for me. Why?"

"Just remembering how it was."

Emma understood by the look on her sister's face that she, too, recalled the gatherings they'd had with all the family, sometimes thirty people or more. The grownups would sit on the screened back porch and talk and laugh while the children played, trying to see who could spit their watermelon seeds the farthest.

Katie pressed the flowers close to her chest. "They're lovely, aren't they? Perfect, but they'll soon fade." She paused and turned toward Emma. "I don't want to sell Evergreen."

"I know. I don't either." Emma shifted from her knees to sit on the tufts of grass and took one of the flowers from the basket. "Did you know that if you spot the first daffodil of the season, your next twelve months will be filled with wealth and fortune?"

Katie smiled. "Really? You just made that up."

"Actually, there are several legends and folklore about daffodils and good luck, but you have to remember to always give them in bunches. A single daffodil can mean misfortune."

"And I suppose bluebells mean little girls dressed in blue or sad bells tolling."

Emma laughed. "Actually, they're associated with constancy and everlasting love. They're also sometimes called *fairy thimbles*."

"Gads. Where do you come up with this trivia?"

"Well, most flowers have some meaning—"

"Jeez. I just came out here to think about what I want to do." Katie laid back on the grass, arms spread wide like a snow angel. She smiled. "Not to philosophize, but I'd take the everlasting love."

"And do you know? What you want to do, I mean?"

Katie shrugged. "Not exactly."

Emma knew that since those early carefree days, Katie sometimes felt her life was choppy—two engagements and no marriage—but Emma understood that there was nothing worse than being too late to finally get it right or get her own life on track. But it wasn't too late for Katie at all.

"I can have my old job back in New York if I want to stay stateside," Katie told Emma.

Emma noticed the flush of her sister's cheeks and the small lines around the corners of her mouth. "Is that what you want? I thought you loved living and working in London."

"I don't know. It's just that—"

"What?"

"I feel happy here, safe, connected to something." After a moment, Katie said, "I hate being a grownup."

Emma waved toward the farm. "Neither of us wants to see this land become tract housing. We'll figure this out together." In her heart, she knew they would never sell Evergreen. After all, they truly were part of its history, land, and family.

Katie nodded. "Evergreen would be a beautiful place for horses again, maybe boarding and lessons, don't you think?"

Emma smiled. That had been their childhood dream, and *this* was the Katie she had grown up with, the inspired dreamer.

"Yes, that would be wonderful."

Katie looked at Emma. "Mom and Dad would like that, I think. They'd be proud."

Emma nodded. "They were always proud of us both."

An unexpected stream of cool air surged around them, and the sky darkened to a purple grey. Ionic charges and petrichor shocked their senses with the smell of approaching rain. Emma could see that Katie felt recharged by this sudden turn in the weather and perhaps in her future. A thunderstorm rolled over the farmland, with lightening dancing along behind. Once or twice, a bolt snapped at the large cedar trees along the riverbank.

Emma heard her sister count, "One, two . . ." after she saw the bolt until she heard the thunder. Electrical charges were magical reminders of their youth, their genesis, much like Evergreen itself, all intertwined into one lifetime. At least that's the way she imagined it as they quickly gathered the flowers and basket and ran for the house, the cold drops pelting their faces and torsos.

2

Virginia

EMMA HAD SET UP HER laptop on a desk under the window on the south side of the large dining room, where she could see the vast fields of bluebells and ox-eye daisies reaching out to Cedar Run. There was something special and comforting about being home again in Virginia. The rolling hills, pastures, and quiet were what she had needed to finish her novel.

After months of sorting, cleaning, organizing, tossing, and dealing with legal papers, time was slipping away. Emma knew she had to get back to writing. She had a deadline to meet. Her editor had given her until the end of summer or early fall to finish her revisions. She had already toyed with some chapters during the last four months, but her deadline was fast approaching. The sweetness of late summer surrounded the farm as she settled into the high-back wooden swivel chair that had been her father's. She remembered him sitting at this very desk going over feed ledgers and training schedules for the horses.

She had learned bookkeeping from him and knew how to manage her money to the cent. She had to. Although she was grateful to be on *Condé Nast*'s payroll full time, a writer's career and income could be unpredictable.

The morning light washed over her desk and across the dark floor. Emma looked out over the side garden, taking in the Virginia magnolia tree—a tree she had longed for when she lived in Paris, when each spring, the Tuileries' gardens burst forth in a palette of colors, reminding her of home. She sighed. Now she longed for Paris, seemingly never satisfied with any one place. Something was always missing.

Emma took a slow, deliberate sip of her coffee and let the sunlight warm her face. She removed her silk cardigan, hung it over the back of the chair, and began to type, excited to get back to her characters, help them resolve their conflicts, and move on. Exactly what she wanted for herself—to move on. She moved quickly back into the setting and dialogue, realizing that her writing was not that far removed from who she was. *For her, memories had been happy and exciting—worth reminiscing about.* She typed the words and then stopped, feeling as if she were writing her life instead of living it. She remembered, though, that writers write about what they know or think they know, even in fiction. True enough. Both Trevor and Katie were major characters in her novel, and she hadn't bothered changing their names. Maybe she would later. Maybe not. After all, this was fiction. She could make them say and do whatever she wanted and even throw Katie off a cliff, if she so desired. Emma smiled at the thought. She loved her little sister, but sometimes, well, she simply didn't have the patience. Katie could fray her last nerve.

Emma opened the window to let the morning air sweep across her face, hear the rustling of the magnolia, and admire the undulating branches of the Virginia live oak outside. Her mother had planted the magnolia long ago for its stately Williamsburg appearance, and Emma had begged her father to plant the live oak because it reminded her of the ones with Spanish moss draped over their branches that she had seen in pictures of southern plantations. No Spanish moss ever grew on her trees—too far north—but she dreamed of them just the same.

Looking beyond the far meadow, she thought about her grandfather and her visits to Evergreen. The two of them used to walk there among the newborn calves and heifers. It was on that very hill near the lower bank, in the spring of her fifth year, when a white bull stepped into her world—a world where her grandfather and his sheep dog had rescued her from the powerful snorting bovine racing toward her.

When she was older, she and her father walked the same fields to pick wildflowers and check on the mares and foals. How history repeats itself, she thought. Like a dream evaporating into the fine mist of her childhood, she knew she would not walk there with her own children.

Or her father.

She would be walking alone.

Emma had been deeply in love, or at least had always thought so, but she couldn't get her mind around why it hadn't worked out. It was the only thing she had ever truly wanted in her life. It was true what she told Katie: It hadn't been love at first sight, but when she finally fell, she fell hard and for a lifetime.

She focused on the computer screen, Trevor's name right in front of her, and for a moment, she was a freshman again. A freshman at that well-known all-girls college across the river from Georgetown. Gads, had she only been nineteen when she met him? A babe, young, impressionable, and still innocent. It was the first fall mixer—when the Catholic boys' and girls' colleges were thrown together, mixed, shaken, and blended until something happened. Maybe a panty raid a week later, a pregnancy in the spring, a dance, a date, a relationship . . . Smoking was in then; drinking was a big pastime. Even now, she could smell the back-to-school scent of fall when turtlenecks were enough to take the chill out of the air and weekends revolved around football and cheerleading.

She felt a pang of desire. Being here in her childhood home meant she could almost touch the past. How she wished she could go back to those times of "firsts"—first graduation, first car, first date, first love—but time kept moving forward, sometimes too fast to even catch a breath let alone find happiness.

Emma reached along her bra strap to unlatch the safety pin holding the key she had placed there for safe keeping. She opened the middle drawer of the desk and reached for the compartment in the back, pulled it out, and slid the red book into her hands. Smiling, she inserted the key into the cover, clicked it open, and then slowly flipped the pages, searching for the correct date: *September 8, 1971*. A Friday night. Funny how she still remembered it after all these years.

A clear, starlit night for my first mixer. The entire area near the tennis courts and inside the smoker was filled with twinkle lights and throngs of girls and invited guys from Georgetown. Monica and I went together, but she hung out in the smoker mostly, dragging and puffing. I pushed my way through the crowd and headed for the food and sodas.

She looked up from the book, picturing that night. She had been so excited to go to the dance, changing her outfit five times before settling on her new orange dress.

I wore my orange dress with the large cap sleeves, round neckline, and big buttons down the front. My fake white beads looked so fashionable. I wore my hair down with the ends flipped up.

Emma studied the words she had written in tight neat letters, controlled and exact, and felt a twinge of sadness. Maybe she had tried too hard to control her emotions the way she'd controlled her penmanship. She glanced at the calendar on the desk, studying the date—August 15, 2002. It had been so long ago, but in her mind, just yesterday. Where had those years gone, evaporated into the cosmos? Was this some joke God played on the human race, making them think they had time to do everything and that youth would last? Emma leaned forward in her chair and continued:

Bodies came together and swirled around each other to some piped-in rock and elevator-like music. I don't know how he found me in the crowd, but he did. He introduced himself.

Emma fidgeted with the gold chain around her neck and began to read the next paragraph describing him, but she didn't need the ink on the pages to tell her what she saw in her mind. She knew exactly how he had looked that night—so preppy and sharp—a navy blazer, a blue button-down shirt tucked into his khaki pants, and Cordovan loafers on his sockless feet. He wasn't strikingly handsome, but there was definitely something about him that was charming and endearing. It was the boyish grin and Irish eyes that Emma remembered most.

He was a good talker and seemed to take an interest in me and my studies, especially my love of languages and philosophy. We talked for a while and danced once to Roberta Flack's, "The First Time Ever I saw Your Face" before some other guys came up and started talking. He was a good dancer. I danced all night but not with him. He got lost in the crowd, but near the end of the evening, he asked for my phone number. Neither of us had anything to write with or on, so he memorized it—or at least pretended to. I doubt if I'll hear from him . . . but I'm curious. I think I'd like to get to know him.

How plain and simple the diary entry was. No magic, no sparks, only a random event. Not how she remembered it. He was taller than she, with warm brown hair and green eyes. She reminisced about his devilish grin, the few freckles across his nose. Sexy in a boyish way. She loved his smile.

She did indeed hear from him a week later and within three months was head over heels. How could she have known then that they would be in and out of each other's lives for decades? Maybe it was all tied to a singular moment, she thought.

She thumbed through the book, looking for more insight into their beginning. She realized he had tried early on to get to know her and figure her out, but she had resisted. He took her to nice restaurants, the theater, and called her a couple of times a week. He wanted to make sure she was looked after. Once when he was sick and couldn't take her out as planned, he'd asked his best friend to fill in for him.

She read several more entries. He had said he "never knew what she was thinking." At the same time, he found her "amazing" but "puzzling." "You're the only girl I've dated this long and still don't really know," he'd told her more than once in the first few months of dating. Emma now knew that to be true and that it had frustrated him. She felt sad about this. She also knew, though, that it hadn't been about him but her fear of her own feelings. Feelings unknown to her; feelings she had when she was with him and without him. Sexual desire that never went away. A desire in conflict with her upbringing.

Trevor had asked her what she wanted in life and how he might fit into her plans.

But she had kept him at a distance, fearing she would get hurt or that he was not sincere. She knew she had been afraid to get involved too soon. She had wanted to finish college, have a career and travel, and had thought the timing was all wrong. Eventually she convinced him she was right.

Emma looked out the window again, noticing the clouds moving slowly across the cerulean sky. How young and foolish they had both been with each other, not knowing what to do or how to treat each other. She hadn't had the wisdom or sophistication and lacked self-confidence and openness. So, she followed friends' advice: "Don't let him see how much you care." "Play it cool." "Be mysterious and aloof." She did and she was. Well into their relationship, she remained afraid to commit or make a mistake. Now, Emma regretted not being herself, not letting him get closer or know how much she cared. Mark Twain was right: "Youth is wasted on the young." She knew this firsthand. She and Trevor had both been too young, emotionally insecure, and unprepared for a real relationship and what it meant.

Emma read through several entries until she got to one of the last ones from her sophomore year.

I've been accepted at the Sorbonne for independent study, sort of my own junior year abroad. I'm excited to study at Georgetown's Institute of Languages when I return. I'll graduate a year later than my class, but I'm really excited about going to Paris. I can't wait to learn French. I'll miss him, but the year will go by quickly, and then we can be together.

Junior year, 1973, a long time ago, she thought. Her mind wandered to Paris, where she had relied on museums, art, and music for consolation. She had been able to rekindle her interest in art. She hung out with young carefree artists and musicians whose ideas of love lasted for one night or a few hours. Many were American students who had come to the city to become famous artists but instead ended up on the streets at Montmartre, cranking out mediocre art for tourists.

If she had been smart, Emma thought, she would have stayed stateside, close by, and would have been there for the senior parties and Trevor's graduation. But she didn't. She wanted to learn French. She was serious about her studies; he studied some but partied more. She learned while in Paris that he had won a scholarship to Duke to study law, an option he decided on after dropping out of pre-med freshman year. He couldn't handle the dead bodies, organs, and blood. She had no idea when she would see him again. They didn't write other than the one pathetic missive she had sent him early on from Paris saying goodbye. She wanted him but didn't want him. Either would have been overwhelming. She wanted him to say, "I love you, don't go, stay here with me." She had almost called him once from Paris but didn't know what to say exactly: "Absence makes the heart grow fonder" or "out of sight, out of mind." The latter probably. Perhaps, she thought, being away might give her courage, independence, or maybe she could learn to live without him.

This had been the way she handled her emotions—she ran. It had taken Emma years to acknowledge this, although she didn't know why she reacted this way. Loving someone forever was hard. Maybe she didn't have the energy for it, or maybe it was the possibility of deep hurt that she held closest to her heart, not the happiness she searched for now. She wanted to be able to run toward love, not away from it. Maybe she could change. Maybe she already had . . . maybe.

AFTER HER OWN graduation from Georgetown two years later, she remembered how happy she had been to live near campus, take a course or two, and work in downtown Washington, D.C. She had been lucky to get a job with *Condé Nast* as a freelance writer, which meant she could stay in touch with her friends and travel occasionally. She loved being close to the Kennedy Center, the art galleries, museums, and great restaurants that the nation's capital offered, but the best part was she was closer to New York. Trevor had finished his law degree and was back in Brooklyn working as a public defender.

She loved him for that. He could have gone corporate and chased the big bucks like so many of his friends. He had said he didn't need the money. He had plenty of his own, inherited from his maternal grandfather. But for Emma it was the fact that he thought he could do more good this way. She also believed that he wanted to succeed on his own. Of course, she never doubted that.

From time to time, when Emma had thought about Trevor and the criminal fraud and corruption cases among officials in the borough, she realized that he was damn good and could have made it as an actor if the legal bug hadn't gotten to him first. He was naturally theatrical. She had been in the District Court during one of his arguments when he threw money and other objects in the courtroom to prove a point. She was consumed by his wonderful way with words, his passionate demeanor, and strong, forceful approach to "winning." He could mold an argument like pastry dough and had the tenacity of a hitman going in for the kill.

At the time, they both had seemed happy in their careers and took to the friendly skies every couple of weeks to spend a weekend together, trying to maintain a long-distance relationship, so much so that a psychic had thought Emma was an airline stewardess. It was difficult being apart. He hadn't asked her to move to New York, although she would have, and once had sought employment there with a book publisher. Perhaps it was more exciting to keep that burning passion alive instead of settling for the everyday routine of living together. For Emma, her heart knew it wouldn't change whether they were together or apart. It was the same life continuum for her. He was a rising star, though, and Emma believed that for Trevor, his career came first. She had accepted that for now.

When the chance came along to return to Paris for a one-year assignment, she knew she had to go. It had come so quickly, and was an opportunity of a lifetime. She would be working for the magazine as a full-time writer, and it would be good to be back in Paris, living there as a grownup, not as a student. She and Trevor weren't exclusive, although she had wanted that. She had thought he loved her and wanted her to be happy. He'd wait for her. She'd only be away for a year. He let her go.

Emma sighed. She put the diary on her desk, reached for her coffee, and gulped a swig of cold, sticky, and stale caffeine that hit her stomach with a thud, suddenly giving her a chill. She pushed her chair back and headed for the kitchen. Time for a fresh pot.

The rich, bold aroma of French *Verlet* tickled her nose, a smell that put her in Paris again, at café Le Relais Odéon on the Left Bank, in Saint Germain, where she used to stop on her way to the office. Whenever Trevor was in Paris, they went there together. Had her first overseas stint with the magazine really been in 1977? It didn't seem possible. Those memories were frozen, timeless in her mind.

She knew now how lucky she'd been to see him in Paris that year. He had wanted to be with her and had made an effort to occasionally carve time from his busy schedule to see her. On weekends during his stays, they'd read the paper and sit for hours, watching young and old share a kiss, a cigarette, a pastry. She could still see him placing his newspaper on the red bistro table in the corner where they always sat. He would put two spoonfuls of sugar into what he called "French tar." Emma always had espresso and a warm buttery croissant, with *confiture*, that only the French knew how to make. Now she began to salivate and felt a sudden pang in her empty stomach, hungry for something rich and well deserved. She laughed out loud at the thought—*rich and well deserved*—*yes*, indeed, he was.

She poured a cup of coffee, took a piece of gruyère from the fridge and some bread from the counter—lunch—and headed back to her desk. The warmth of the afternoon sun lit up the entire dining room, creating an impressionistic blur of purple, green, red, and yellow below the open window. Like a Seurat or Monet, she thought, where colors vibrate within and next to each other in warm saturated light. Giverny, Monet's home and garden, was one of her favorite places.

She remembered how she and Trevor had stayed in nearby Vernon one weekend at a lovely Bed and Breakfast, La Villa Geraldine, right in the historic district, across the street from the fine arts museum. Their room overlooked a garden. A Queen mahogany sleigh bed covered in white cut linen faced a working fireplace. The morning light gently massaged the walls, soothing their huddled bodies. They ate every morning in the solarium—coffee and a full breakfast for Trevor; *Mariage Frères* tea and a croissant for her.

She bit into her almost sandwich, washing it down with coffee, stared at the computer screen, and read the last line of type: *She felt caught between the past and the present, stuck in her head about what could have been.* She leaned back in her chair, wondering if she was stuck in the past. Here she was in Virginia, eating bread and cheese, and drinking Parisian coffee. How French was that! She laughed at the irony. Maybe she was always there . . . maybe the past *is* always present.

Emma looked blankly at her keyboard, trying to cleanse her mind of these thoughts. She needed to write, keep moving forward. She lifted the coffee cup to her lips, swilling the steamy liquid. She began again. Her fingers moved rapidly in rhythmic determination, creating a dissonant harmony with the birds outside. The light shifted, casting long shadows across the room. Emma reached for the desk lamp, pushed the button on its round brass base, and kept writing.

3

Working in Paris

IT SEEMED LIKE ONLY yesterday when Trevor had retrieved the green bottle, popped the cork, and read the note: "Welcome to Le Meurice."

"I think we need to celebrate," he told her. "It's not every day we're treated like royalty in Paris."

It was Emma's first international assignment for *Condé Nast*, and the management of iconic Le Meurice, one of Paris's premier hotels perfectly situated near the Champs Elysées, knew that she was doing a story on five-star hotels in Paris. The hotel had a long history of accommodating royalty, aristocrats, artists, writers, and celebrities. Even Salvador Dalí lived here off and on for years. Everything was comped: the room, the champagne, the special chocolate and fruit basket, the robes, all phone calls, everything. Emma smiled gleefully, delighted that she was in the City of Light with the love of her life on her first big all-expenses-paid account. She glanced around the room, staring at the elegant classic French décor, and twirled onto the beautiful balcony high above the rue de Rivoli near Place Vendôme, where she could have a continental breakfast each morning. The "Marco Polo Suite," described as the hotel's "perfect hideaway for couples in love," was located under the eaves of the hotel with a fantastic view of Tuileries Garden. She studied the swathes of dusty pink fabric cascading from the ceiling to the parquet floor and caressed the white linens consuming the bed near the arched window. A ceramic and gold-plated claw-footed tub rested prominently on the bathroom's Portuguese marble floor.

Hideaway indeed, she thought to herself. This was heaven.

"I'm glad you're here," she told Trevor as he poured the champagne into their glasses. "This is surreal. I've dreamed of this."

Trevor handed her a glass and took her hand. "A toast: To us, to this moment, and to being together."

She took a sip of champagne, then laughed. "Pinch me!"

"I have a better idea." Trevor pulled her close to him and pressed his warm open lips onto her mouth. Emma felt her knees give way.

TREVOR STAYED WITH her that night, and the next evening he fixed her dinner at his family's apartment a few blocks away. The apartment, a small penthouse, had been purchased by his maternal grandfather, a financial wizard, years ago. He had been there often as a child and young man but had never entertained anyone there. She was the first. Emma thought it was very traditional, old-school French in its décor and could use an update, a woman's touch. But the views were extraordinary. They soaked in the heart of the city from his balcony overlooking the Louvre and the Seine, watching the people below hugging their coats and jackets to keep the wind at bay. The sounds of the city drifted up to their conversation—voices, horns honking, engines racing, and police whistles guiding traffic. It was like no other city. She felt sometimes that Paris existed just for them—for two lovers—a place where time didn't matter.

SHE WAS HAPPIEST waking up next to him and hanging out in and around Paris. They enjoyed early morning coffees and croissants at the corner café near his apartment and special visits to the Musées d'Orsay and l'Orangerie, where they could focus on their love of the impressionists and post impressionists. They took short day trips to Chartres and Versailles and, of course, Giverny. Emma loved Monet's pink and green country house surrounded by beds of multitudinous blooms of all varieties, the rose allées, famous water gardens, and the Japanese bridge. It was like living in one of Monet's paintings. His garden was his true masterpiece—his passion. In fact, he had said, "I perhaps owe having become a painter to flowers." She wondered if she had that kind of passion for writing or for anything for that matter. Even Monet considered his life a failure. Surely, we are too hard on ourselves, too critical. She knew she was at times, but with Trevor, she saw the long-distance relationship as one generating more longing. That's what she had wanted to believe.

THE CHILL OF the whistling wind pressed black coats and hats close to the skin, as umbrellas turned inside out from wind shear. But Parisians drew their warmth from the cafés and daily life of the city.

As the last of winter swept into March, an early spring would soon reveal itself in the Tuileries gardens and park. Often Emma would brown bag it there, waiting for the awakening of the beautiful spring flowers, and amuse herself as an onlooker of all things Parisian. She was lucky to be here in fabulous Paris and thankful that Trevor had been able to visit every couple of months or so. Perfect.

Today Trevor was taking her out to lunch. When he arrived at *Condé Nast*, she was running around frenetically trying to find her assistant, Jean Pierre.

"Where is he?" she yelled, nervously pushing her long hair off her face.

Trevor noticed her carrying a stack of papers and a book entitled, *Make Everything Better*, which to him meant dysfunction with a capital D. Thank heavens he knew it had nothing to do with him, or at the very least, he excused the notion from his head.

"Hi honey. Give me five minutes and we can go," Emma said as she swept by him. "Go in and sit down. I'll be right . . ." her voice trailed off, as she hurried down the hallway, her shapely figure vanishing into a blur at the far corner and disappearing into a black hole somewhere.

In her office, Trevor walked around the bright orange sofa to take in the magnificent view of the Champs Elyseés and the Place du Concord. Bright daylight bounced into the room, almost blinding him as he stood at the window watching the people and the traffic bustle around the plaza below. Horns honking and French voices yelling out "Move it—idiot!" made him smile. Just like New Yorkers but on a smaller scale and, according to Emma, with a lot more class.

Around the room were photographs and art displayed like tiny treasures—paintings from Italy, prints from the d'Orsay, and art books stacked neatly on a credenza away from the travel magazines and articles. As he examined a grouping of photographs on her desk—him rowing for college crew, both of them dressed to the nines for the junior prom at the country club, and the two of them holding hands on Pont Neuf—he had flashbacks of the special moments they'd shared together.

In his mind, Trevor went back to when they first met. He couldn't recall what she wore only that she had beautiful sky-blue eyes, flawless skin, dark-brown hair, and forbidden lips he wanted to kiss. From the very beginning, Trevor knew she was someone he wanted to know. In an instant, she had made his heart ache, and the honest truth was it still did.

EMMA QUICKLY RETURNED and walked up behind him. "Okay, I'm finished. Let's go." She exhaled her words rapidly. "Trev? Are you ready?"

He looked up. "I was just reminiscing."

Emma looked at him quizzically. "About?"

He pointed to the photos. "Oh, where we've been."

"Hmm." Emma kissed him. "That's sweet, Trev. But for now, do we know where we're going?"

Where *were* they going, she wondered, and where would they end up? She was hoping he would catch her innuendo and say something definitive like *Wherever our hearts will take us; we'll always be together.* But those were her sentiments. Still, she waited for his answer.

As their eyes met, he noticed her sultry expression and said, "Sure." Then, with his sexiest voice, he added, "We can eat or not; your pleasure. We can go back to my place and . . ."

Emma put her arms around him. "You know that you're all I want in the world, but I'm truly starved."

≈

"*MONSIEUR, MADEMOISELLE, voici votre table.*" The head waiter directed them to a quiet spot in the corner. A few moments later, the aroma of fresh *bouillabaisse* and French bread went straight to her stomach. The place was filled with the typical lunchtime crowd and rapid-fire French conversation. "No strike this week," she heard one man say. But they all knew *les grèves* were a way of Paris life.

Emma leaned forward in her chair as Trevor held up his glass and said, "*A notre amour.*" Only he could make a simple toast turn into a romantic gesture about their love. His boyish smile and laughing eyes made her heart leap. She listened intently as he talked, hearing only his voice over the background noise of *les garçons* carrying their trays and taking orders, knives and forks gliding over china, and crystal glasses singing soft melodies. No matter where they were, it was only the two of them, alone in the crowd.

On Monday, he would fly to New York but return in July for a long weekend, and then they planned to travel south to Provence well in advance of French vacation time. Emma didn't want to think about his leaving, not today, not now—not ever, truth be told.

"You know, Em, visiting you here in Paris is so much better than I had anticipated." He took another sip of wine. "What I mean is, there are a lot of miles between us, but I'm happy this worked out for us."

Why wouldn't it? she thought. Of course, it worked and would work, she told herself, but perhaps he wasn't that sure. They still lived in different cities, were tied to demanding jobs, and didn't live together.

Emma trained her eyes on his and leaned in closer. "If you mean you're worried about the long-distance thing, I am too. But when you're here, nothing else matters." She reached for his hand. "I think our love can withstand the separation, don't you?"

"I hope so, Em. I hope so." He raised his brow.

Not exactly the words she had hoped to hear, but they were his words—honest. She knew in her heart that nothing would change *her* mind. Nothing.

4

Returning to Georgetown

ON THIS SLEETY FRIDAY, Emma watched the late afternoon news. She couldn't believe how quickly another year had slipped by. Back in her row house apartment, the TV screen fluttered a hypnotic repetition that made her quietly doze off. It had been a long week of matriculation and angst about why she should punish herself again with coursework, but she was determined to take some grad courses, maybe complete a master's, and focus more on writing, especially fiction.

She had lived at Thirty-Fifth & Q Streets since her senior year. It was only an hour and fifteen minutes from New York via shuttle, and she hoped to be able to see Trevor a little more even though they were in separate cities. New York would have been better, and she would work on that, but for now she would get paid for writing near her home town. The stint in Paris had proven that she could handle the demands of big assignments. She was full-time staff writer now, moving up quickly. She loved her time in Paris and knew she'd go back again one day.

She pulled the afghan up around her neck, waiting to see the news, but her eyelids shut out everything around her. She had had a late lunch at her desk and then stopped on M Street before coming back home. It had taken her longer than she had hoped to trek up Wisconsin Avenue, window shopping along the way. She had visited Pappagallo's—her favorite shoe store—and bought some hand-made Belgian chocolates at Leonidas.

She was tired. After the news, she turned off the TV and switched on the radio. "Ring of Fire" by Johnny Cash came on, and Emma began singing, "I fell into a burning ring of fire; I went down, down, down, and the flames went higher." She thought immediately of Trevor as she began to twirl around the room to the strum of guitars. "Love is a burning thing and it makes a fiery ring." The song reminded her of the heat generated between them. She glided to her room, pulled a red cocktail dress from her closet and a red teddy from the lingerie drawer and put them aside for the suitcase. She wanted to be sexy for him this weekend. She retrieved the small box of chocolates from the bag on her dresser and hummed back to the living room.

Emma sat in front of the tall Palladian window. The backlit street lamps cast ghostly, long dark fingers across the cobblestones. She unwrapped a large dome-shaped truffle, savoring the aroma of the dark chocolate, and took a bite, letting the burst of hazelnut crème explode on her tongue and in her mouth. Chocolate, so sensual and so decadent as to be forbidden. No wonder women hid these damn things from themselves, she thought, and suffered the guilty pleasure of succumbing to their temptation.

She could write an article about chocolate being a worthy cause for all women, a substitute for men, for sex. Well, *sometimes*. She thought about Trevor and how sex with him was passionate and new each time. She daydreamed about his naked body pressed up against hers, his wet, deep kisses, his laugh, his smile, his voice. She wondered how many times a day she was in his head disrupting legal arguments, briefs, and client meetings. Probably hardly ever, she thought. Men have that ability to compartmentalize their emotions and separate their personal lives from their work. Sad but true. Somehow, she hoped he was different.

She knew there was passion bubbling beneath that legal façade and remembered that night at the historic 1789 having dinner with some of his friends and business associates from New York. She didn't remember anything about the restaurant's quintessential French cuisine or Federal style interior, but only that she and Trevor could barely contain themselves, sitting next to each other, touching each other under the table. He whispered into her ear, "Do you feel it?" meaning that hot magnetic pull between them. Emma was so overheated she had to excuse herself from the table, go to the ladies' room, and put cold water on her face and the back of her neck. She wasn't sure they would make it through the meal without ripping off their clothes. No man before or since had ever made her feel that way.

Some of their best and worst times were in Georgetown. In college, they had gone to the loud drunken parties, dances, and get-togethers. She remembered the rowdy boat house debacles near Key Bridge, holding his hand and weaving through the crowd when the lights went out, reaching for Trevor in the dark and not finding him, someone grabbing her ass, being frightened until the lights came on and then finding him, and holding onto him tight for the rest of the night. She had loved the evenings strolling up Wisconsin Avenue after dinner at Filomena's, picnicking in the park near Dumbarton Oaks where he told her she had beautiful "chocolate brown hair," holding her tight and kissing her cheek while dancing at the Crosstown Lounge, squeezing her hand during "Finian's Rainbow" at Trinity Theater, drinking beer at the Tombs, drinking more beer and listening to music at the Brickskeller or the legendary music clubs like the Cellar Door and Bayou. Georgetown was a part of who they were, who they had been.

Soon she'd catch the shuttle and, in a couple of hours, would be with him in time for a late dinner. She had been too excited to eat much for the last couple of days. Endorphins rode the waves of her stomach like the high seas in anticipation of seeing him. The actual flight to LaGuardia was short, but getting to and from the airport took another hour on each end. Emma was running late and knew she'd likely get into some Friday airport traffic, so she had called Trevor and left a message on his machine. She grabbed her coat and the notepad she used to jot down story ideas, and headed for her car. The air was chilly but clear. She turned on her radio and drove onto M Street to get across the bridge and speed to National.

Emma hurried along the crowded airport corridor to the gate, arriving just in time to board. She settled into her seat and tried writing down some ideas, but was too excited at the thought of being with Trevor after almost a month. Her heart was pumping, adrenaline rushing. She tried to relax, breathe deeply, and not think too far ahead.

5

Brooklyn

WHEN EMMA LANDED, she looked for Trevor but didn't see him anywhere. She had been waiting for him near the gate for almost twenty minutes when a young man came up to her.

"Are you Ms. Collins? Are you waiting for Mr. Kinney?"

Oh my god, Emma thought, something has happened. "Yes, I'm Emma."

Evidently, Trevor had been called into a meeting with the district attorney at the last minute and had sent Henry, a junior law clerk to pick her up and take her to Brooklyn.

They pulled up to the brownstone on Clinton Avenue. Henry helped her with her bag, unlocked the door, and built a fire in the fireplace before leaving. Emma set about getting the pot and water ready for some coffee when she heard Trevor's voice ring out. "Hi Babe. I'm home."

She practically ran across the room, threw her arms around him, pressed into him, and gave him a deep, wet kiss. When she pulled away, she noticed his eyes were half open and a little red. How are you? You look tired, Trev."

"It's been a long day, and I could use a drink and something good to eat—"

"Let's eat in tonight," Emma interrupted before he could finish his thought, gesturing to the fire Henry had started when they first arrived.

Trevor smiled. "You're just what the doctor ordered. How's my girl?" he added.

"Right now, perfect."

And she was. She put her arms around him tightly and kissed him again, not wanting to let go.

SATURDAY MORNING EMMA awoke satiated. Lying next to him evoked simultaneous ecstasy and peace. A broad brushstroke of morning light flooded their naked bodies. Her eyes studied the long contour of his back, noting a mole on his right shoulder and the small freckles at the nape of his neck. She felt calm, safe. She glanced at the photo of the two of them on the dresser, the one taken one summer on Fire Island. She edged her body closer until she fit perfectly into his shape and dozed off again.

She awakened an hour later to the sound of running water and the smell of coffee. She rolled over onto Trevor's side of the bed, the sheets still warm from his body. She sat up and threw her legs on the floor, headed for the bathroom, and opened the glass shower door.

"Want company?"

He held out his hand, and she stepped into the shower, pressing up against his warm, wet chest. She soaped up a sponge and began washing his chest and then his back. She loved bathing with him; it prolonged their intimacy and led to wet lovemaking. They couldn't get enough of each other, but today he seemed lost in thought. Work, she assumed, but wanted to know for sure.

They dried off with the soft Egyptian cotton towels hanging on the door and put on some casual clothes.

"A penny?" Emma queried. "What are you thinking?"

"Uh, it's office stuff—a case—last night," Trevor explained.

Emma knew not to press too hard. He'd tell her what he wanted her to know. She knew when his eyes didn't meet hers that he was trying to figure it out.

In the galley kitchen, Emma pulled a blue ceramic cup from the shelf, poured her coffee, and held the pot for him. Trevor reached for the cream from the fridge and handed it to her. Even early in the morning, his boyish good looks made her happy. She loved his hazel-green eyes and his smile. She could forgive anything with that smile.

They sipped their coffee in silence, still waking up. She couldn't help but notice how immaculate his place was, almost unlived in. Even the walls had a fresh coat of blue-grey paint. The glass cabinets dictated compulsive organization. The stainless steel fixtures and appliances made it look high-tech and professional even though she knew he mostly ate out and catered all of his parties. Copies of the *New York Law Journal* and the *American Journal of Criminal Law* sat on the dark-grey countertop; incoming and outgoing letters and bills sat neatly arranged in a gun-metal basket. A small calendar hung near the door and a single photo of him and his friends at the shore was tacked on a small bulletin board near the phone.

"Well, what's on the agenda for today?" she asked.

"We can do whatever you want, but first I have to check in with the office and maybe make some calls."

"On Saturday?"

"You know what it's like, Em."

"I do?" Of course, she knew. Deadlines and changes had wrecked her weekends more than once. She was just simply unhappy that this had to fall on their weekend.

She moved into the dining room. Trevor tucked the newspaper under his arm, followed her and pulled out her chair. They sat down in front of the French doors leading to the patio. In another month, it would be spring and the little blue crocuses around the brick wall would be blooming.

She turned to face him. "I thought we planned to spend the weekend together."

"And we will, but first—"

"When did you know about this, Trev?"

"Only last night."

The morning light fell like golden marigolds across the table, landing on their arms. He took her hand, making her heart pound deep in her chest.

"Look, I'm disappointed too, but let's make the best of the time we have. It shouldn't take too long."

She knew his boss was demanding and that Trevor was hard-working and conscientious. She hoped he could indeed resolve things with a few calls and not go into the office, but she wasn't holding her breath. This was who he was now. Take it or leave it, she thought. She felt resigned but a little sad that his time wasn't his own and certainly not hers.

She squeezed his hand. "I understand."

"That's my girl." He smiled, leaned into her, and pressed his lips gently against hers.

6

Too Little, Too Late

WHEN EMMA THOUGHT about that weekend now, it was like so many others lost deep in the recesses of her mind. There were the flights to New York and D.C., stolen weekends here and there for three years, forever, it seemed. She wanted him, only him, *full time*, not in bits and pieces. But as a rising judicial star, his time wasn't his own, nor was hers, and it had been too hard to sustain a long-distance relationship as the weekend trysts became fewer and fewer. She wanted more.

And she thought that Rick would be the one to give her that. Emma had finished her coursework and was in the process of completing her thesis. She had met Rick one Saturday afternoon in front of the Georgetown University bookstore. They had bumped into each other, literally, her books scattering onto the sidewalk. He was tall, not as tall as Trevor, and good looking, sort of a "poor man's" Paul Newman with black hair and brown eyes. He was a medical resident at GU hospital. He was not too complicated and liked to party. She liked his friends and especially his family. His mother was a native Virginian and his dad a professor from Maryland. Locals, like her parents. He spoke a couple of languages, including French, which appealed to her.

For the two years she dated Rick, she had pushed Trevor deeper into the corners of her mind by tuning out her heart. Their visits became nonexistent, with occasional calls on her birthday or holidays. Time and distance had separated them. She felt as if he had forgotten about her. She dated several men off and on, but not seriously. She was having fun while she waited for Trevor to come back to her, or so she thought.

Rick had been there for her. There when she needed to talk, when she was sick, and to celebrate every holiday. That became important to Emma. He had nursed her through the flu one winter with chicken soup he made himself. He cared. He was a friend, but her feelings for him were not the same as those she had for Trevor. Rick was loyal. He was handsome. He didn't make her stomach flip, heart race, or entire body ache with desire. But he had asked her to marry him. To *marry* him. That's what she wanted; that's what she needed, she had thought then. Something Trevor hadn't done. She thought she could learn to love Rick.

Besides, somehow Emma hoped that being engaged would jolt Trevor into a more meaningful reality, one focused on her. She should have known better, but at twenty-nine, she felt she wasn't getting any younger, and practically all of her friends were already married. It was just time. She got engaged. Of course, she had wanted to tell Trevor herself how she felt but never did. Too late, she thought.

SHE WOULD NEVER forgive herself for that irretrievable day that set the final spiral in motion. Six months after she got engaged, Trevor had come to D.C. on business, and they planned to get together at the Tombs for lunch. She knew he would be waiting for her.

As she turned the corner and began walking down Thirty-Sixth Street, she saw him in the distance standing on the cobblestone sidewalk in front of Sam's deli talking to Skip, a former classmate who was now an ortho surgeon at GU hospital. Her eyes carefully scanned Trevor's body, and his informal blue shirt and khaki slacks took her back to that first night at the mixer. She could hear her heart beating in her chest. She felt like an undergrad again.

In that moment, despite the engagement ring on her finger, she knew she couldn't marry anyone but him. She would break her engagement, she decided, as she watched him walk inside the bar. She walked across the street to meet him, excited that she had resolved her dilemma, her heart.

As she opened the door to the Tombs and started walking downstairs, stale smoke hit her face and the din of student voices pierced her ears. Oh my god, she thought, was this happening? What year was it? Sophomore year? Déjà vu. She felt herself walking in slow motion, her legs floating easily on air in a hurry to move forward, but her legs were moving slower. It was like treading water with ease. She was drifting in a fog-like dream. Suddenly, she could only hear her heart beating loudly in her head, drowning out everything around her. She tried to catch her breath, choking on the dense smoke burning her eyes. She was excited, terrified, unsure.

She stopped at the foot of the stairs, her eyes scanning the crowded and dimly lit room of bodies crammed into tables, booths, and stools around the bar. Her vision adjusted slowly, first to the photos of crew members on the wall, the oars over the fireplace, and then to the crowd at the bar. She watched the bartender top off a beer and place it in front of a guy seated on a stool in front of him. She stood in the middle of the foray of patrons entering and exiting the collegiate caverns for what seemed like forever. She watched Trevor take a long swig of beer and then ask the barkeep for another. His shoulders slumped slightly over the beer mug as he lit a cigarette. God, he never smoked, she thought.

Emma wondered what his reaction would be to seeing her. She frantically tried to remove her ring, but it wouldn't budge from her swollen finger. She turned it around. He wouldn't care once she told him her new plans, she thought, as she slowly weaved her way through the maze of tables to the bar. She stood behind him about to say hello when he looked up and saw her in the mirror behind the bar. He turned to face her, his debilitated eyes fixed on her. Too much to drink, she wondered?

"Trev, hi. It's good to see you," Emma tried to lean into him. "It's been a while."

His body stiffened. "Evidently, too long,"

Emma thought that was a sign he'd missed her. She smiled. "Yes, I agree. It's been too long." But I've thought of you almost every day since we last saw each other, she wanted to say.

"So, you're engaged," he snapped. No hello, no kiss, nothing. It was Skip. Skip had told him.

Emma started to answer but was cut off.

"Let me see the ring," he demanded in a distant, aggrieved voice.

Emma didn't know what to do. She slowly held out her left hand for him while he examined the ring in a dismissive way. "It—it—was his grandmother's," she mumbled, as if to verify its worth, her worth. Then Trevor spoke the words that still rang in her ears.

"Get out," he said angrily. "Go on. Get out."

"But, but—"

"Go on. Marry the guy. I don't care," he added as he downed what was left of his beer.

"But—I—I don't—" she muttered, her eyes tearing. But he wouldn't let her speak and say she had made a mistake, *loved him*. She was dizzy with rejection and disbelief.

She began to back away, turning and stumbling through her tears. What had just happened? She didn't understand. She was dazed. Why hadn't he begged her NOT to marry? *He doesn't love me; he doesn't want me,* she thought to herself.

Emma stepped backward, crying uncontrollably, her lips quivering. She looked at him again, but he had turned away.

"You, you don't understand—"

"Go on. Get out," he repeated.

The words sent shocks of anger through her. Who does he think he is? "What the fuck—I *will* marry the guy," she sobbed to herself walking away from him. "The guy who cares, the guy who loves me, and the guy who is *always there* when I need him."

Emma left the bar, confused, with tears streaming down her cheeks, her sobs choking her. She couldn't catch her breath. It wasn't supposed to turn out this way. He didn't care? He didn't love her? How could that be? She wanted to shake the last few minutes out of the cosmic universe. She felt sick to her stomach. She called Rick as soon as she got home. He comforted her. That damn bastard. He understood how she had felt about Trevor all along, but under the pretense of consoling her, he took advantage of the situation to pull her in. A better man would have confronted Trevor or told her to, she thought later.

In her heart, she knew that's what *she* should have done, but she didn't have the wherewithal then. She had felt beaten and alone. And she would learn that Rick needed to *control* the situation, control her, have her to himself. He wanted no competition. It took Emma a long time to realize that Trevor had been surprised, angry, and hurt. She had been dumbstruck. She hadn't considered any of that—only that *he didn't care, he didn't fucking care.*

7

The Wedding

IT WAS A CLEAR WINTER'S day when she donned the candle-light satin gown, adjusted the delicate tulle veil, and stared into the bedroom mirror. The vision before her was pale and out of focus. She felt nothing but a slight chill. She was numb.

She had gotten this far and continued through the motions. She put on the new pearl earrings her father had given her mother for their first anniversary and her grandmother's pearl necklace. Would Trevor call, would he show up at the church? She had wanted to phone him after she had her hair done that morning, but couldn't bring herself to do it. It had been almost a year since their fateful encounter. She didn't want to be humiliated with more rejection.

She stepped into the cold morning air, deaf to all around her except the crunch of the limo's tires over the snow-covered ground. The grey gesso-like sky seemed rough around the edges. As they approached the church, she felt as if her heart had stopped, her mother's words still echoing, "It's not too late to change your mind." Oh god, if she only knew. Maybe her mother did know, as Emma did with all of her heart. She didn't want to marry anyone but Trevor. She hadn't known how to get out of the engagement, she didn't know how to get out of the wedding, and for years, wouldn't know how to get out of the marriage. She didn't want to hurt anyone, and Trevor had said, "Go ahead. Get married. I don't care."

She believed him.

He was the first to teach her to leave.

The walk down the aisle and the ceremony were a blur. She only remembered that no one objected at that most critical part, but she hesitated, waited for Trevor's voice. There was only silence until Rick declared, "He's not coming." What? Why did he say that? That should have been her cue to flee and run as fast as she could out of there and away from him, from everyone. She was paralyzed, couldn't think straight. Where was her courage? Rick knew what Emma refused to acknowledge—it was Trevor she loved. Rick jabbed her in the side with his elbow when she couldn't form the words "I do." But she did. The words had been forced out of her, exorcised like some demon from her very soul. She had always sensed that Rick knew it had always been Trevor, but at that moment, he had something to prove—that he *would* marry her no matter what. He wouldn't be left alone, not at the altar, not ever.

LATER EMMA REALIZED she had been delusional. Trevor hadn't known when or where she would be married. Deep down, though, she hoped somehow he would find out and pursue her like in one of her romantic fantasies. How absurd. She had to have been out of her mind. The sad part was that Rick obviously knew he was her "second choice," but his ego didn't let that stop him. She never told anyone that her heart had been broken, that she had felt doomed to marry someone she didn't love. Why had she let her word mean more than her heart?

After sleeping with Rick on her wedding night, she had locked herself in the hotel bathroom and cried. She had wanted to run, to leave, but she had given her word, taken a vow. She had been trapped in her own snare: wedded and bedded to a passionless life.

BACK THEN, SHE hadn't analyzed why she married Rick, but she had played over and over in her head Trevor's final words, "You know you shouldn't marry anyone but me." He had told her that during a phone call a couple of months after their meeting in the Tombs. Still, he wouldn't commit, wasn't ready, and didn't ask her to wait for him. He had let her go, thinking she loved someone else. She had let him go, thinking he didn't love her.

With Rick, she was miserable from the beginning, before her wedding day, but she knew she had to make the best of the bed she had made. Punishment for making the wrong choice. It was the Catholic way and the notion that women should suffer, didn't have many choices, and should marry and procreate. She tried to make it work. She worked on her marriage, tried counseling, positive thinking, and doing more things together. They traveled to South Africa, the Virgin Islands, New Orleans, Quebec, Rome, and other faraway places to instill romance into their relationship. She even tried to learn golf for him, but she was a tennis gal and found golf slow and frustrating. The truth was that she and Rick had very little in common. His college partying had turned into professional-level, late-night drinking at bars, which had led to affairs with two of the hospital nurses. Not that it mattered much to Emma because she would see and sleep with Trevor throughout her marriage. Only he could keep her soul from shriveling up and disappearing.

AN ACCIDENTAL ENCOUNTER had brought them together several months after the wedding. She had been in New York for a week at the main office and attended an event at Gracie Mansion. It was a typical New York cocktail party with celebrities mingling while the press looked on skeptically. Emma didn't think much about the hand that slid slowly over her elbow, but the "hello" threw her off guard.

She knew that voice too well and remembered the words spoken to her not long ago. She hadn't known how to respond, whether to walk away and not look back, or touch his hand and welcome him back into her life. She hesitated and then started to walk away, but his hand pressed firmly on her arm.

"Stay. Please."

The words rushed at her, bringing back those times in Brooklyn when he had asked, "Can you stay?"

There was always a reason why she couldn't, or so she had believed, out of loyalty to her job, her husband, or a new lover. All had always been the wrong choices. She regretted not listening to her heart when she should have.

Emma stopped and turned back. She smiled. "Hello again," she replied. She wanted to feel estranged from him, not know him, not want him, but her heart wouldn't let her. Her heart had always been true. It was her head that didn't listen or trust and that had fought hard to suppress what her heart yearned for.

"What are you doing here?" they both asked simultaneously.

Emma laughed, remembering how easily they fit. "I'm here with my editor who is covering the mayor's re-election. And you?"

He smiled. "Well, it's New York. I live here." He paused waiting for her to laugh. "I work for the mayor now."

"Really? Out of the frying pan into the fire," Emma replied.

"I try to keep a low profile."

"Yes, I can see that," she said sarcastically.

"Are you here for long? Where are you staying?" He reached for her hand.

"Another couple of days. I'm at the Roosevelt."

"Have dinner with me."

Emma felt flushed, warm all over. The crowd was closing in on her. "I need some air." She moved through the crowd to the front door and main portico. Outside, she took a deep breath and stood quietly looking at the gardens and East River. "It's very southern, don't you think? Out of place for Manhattan."

Trevor stood next to her with his arm around her waist. "There are a lot of things out of place," he said pensively.

Emma turned and looked at him. "Trev, would you get me some water?"

"Of course. Are you okay?"

"I feel a little lightheaded."

"Okay." He started to walk away and then turned back toward her. "Will you still be here when I come back?"

Emma nodded. "I'm going to sit in one of these big chairs. I'll be here."

Trevor headed through the crowd and returned with water and

some cheese and crackers. But he didn't see her. Panicked, he walked around the large porch until he spotted her at the far end, off in a corner, sitting with her head against the back of the green wicker love seat.

"Here," he said, handing her the water. "I brought you a little something to eat if you feel up to it."

That was thoughtful, she thought. She was hungry but not sure her stomach could handle it now. She needed to calm down, relax. "Thank you."

Trevor sat beside her and watched her sip the entire glass of water slowly, deliberately. "Feeling better?" he asked.

Emma smiled. "Thank you. I really needed something in my stomach."

"Dinner then?"

"Not tonight," she said. "I think I'll call it a night and take some Tylenol and lie down. It's been a very hectic few days."

"How about tomorrow?"

Emma hesitated a long while, knowing she should refuse him. She should. She must. But she couldn't. "Okay. Tomorrow."

"Do you need help getting back to the hotel?"

"Oh, I'll be fine. Thanks."

He kissed her hand. "Until tomorrow," he said, as he rose and went back inside.

"Tomorrow," Emma repeated.

8

The More Things Change…

A STACK OF CLOTHES lay on the bed in Emma's hotel room. After an hour of going through her travel wardrobe, she still hadn't decided what to wear. This should be easy, she thought, but nothing about seeing him had ever been easy—except for the passion. That had not changed. It was only dinner, she decided, and plucked the short black dress with the keyhole bodice from the pile. She looked in the bathroom mirror at her pale complexion, warming her cheeks with a delicate blush and going over her lashes once again to make her blue eyes stand out. It was almost 7:00 p.m. as she hurried out of the room and down the hallway to the elevator. She never saw the flashing button on the phone, and even if she had, she probably would have ignored it. Only Rick would be calling to check up on her, which he did every morning and every evening. He was four hours away and the marital chains still clung to her.

A black Lincoln picked her up in front of the hotel, but not Trevor.

"Mr. Kinney?" she asked. The driver said, "He's waiting for you," as they drove out of Manhattan to Brooklyn. God, had she known she was going to his brownstone, she might have made some excuse. Now she was the fly heading into the spider's web, a lovely spider at that, she thought. What did she expect? What did she want? Isn't this what she wanted, remembered, dreamt of? To be alone with him again, in bed with him. Yes, she told herself as if she were already there, enveloped in his arms, his entire body.

He greeted her at the door with a kiss on the cheek. "I hope you don't mind the surprise of dinner here. I've made your favorite pasta."

Emma smiled. "No. It's like old times." Old times she couldn't forget, when she felt alive, in love, happy. She had felt alive in the moment, but alone afterwards. No commitment, occasional weekends. Isn't that the part she'd forgotten? Or had she? Maybe she was used to suppressing the not-so-good bits.

A waft of olive oil and seafood swirled around her. "You made pappardelle and shrimp?"

He nodded, escorting her into the kitchen. "And I added your favorite mushrooms, garlic, basil, and the usual light béchamel sauce."

Emma looked at him amazed. There was a large fresh salad, Italian bread, and chianti on the nearby table. As she glanced beyond the dining room to the outside terrace, she saw the charming table for two with the fat wine bottle adorned with a dripping candle in the center, and thousands of mini-lights throughout the garden. She couldn't believe he had gone to all this trouble. She tried to remember the last time he had made dinner for her. Paris. It was probably Paris.

"When did you have time to do all of this?"

"There wasn't much to do really. The lights have been there for a couple of years. Do you like it?"

"It's lovely. Can I help?"

"No," he said, pulling her close to him and kissing her gently. "Well, there is one thing you can do for me. Stay with me tonight."

Emma kissed him. I'm married, she thought. I have a piece of paper that says so, although I never wanted it or really agreed to it. I'm married, she repeated to herself, but to the wrong man. She didn't answer him.

"Let's have some dinner," she said, carrying the chianti and salad out to the terrace. Let's see how things go, she said to herself, smiling.

≈

WHY HAD IT BEEN so easy to fall into this pattern again, into his arms, into his bed?

So it began again—long talks on the phone, surreptitious meetings, and flights between New York and D.C. to ignite their clandestine love. Down, down, down . . . again.

All that mattered to her was seeing him, being with him, loving him no matter what. They spent time together in New York and Washington as often as they could, as well as a few days at Fire Island when Rick was away at some medical conference. She had talked with Rick on the phone while Trevor was lying next to her or was in the shower. When she was with him, she removed her wedding ring, trying to absolve herself of her one critical mistake.

By her own admission, Emma had married too young. It was something Trevor would say to her over and over again. But he never asked why, and she never offered. It was easier to ignore the past and enjoy the moment without regret or overanalyzing their mistakes. Any other resolution might have destroyed them both. He hadn't been ready, and she had feared he never would be. Her biological clock had been ticking in the recesses of her mind. But she had been too emotionally immature to know what she wanted or what to look for in a lifelong commitment. How do you know what you want, when you want it, and when it's right? Not at nineteen, not at twenty-nine. Maybe not ever.

She now knew, though, that Rick was just obsessed with no one else having her. His version of love was not what Emma dreamed of. There was no partnership, no give and take. It was all about him and what made him happy. Emma couldn't hold onto that, and from the beginning of her marriage, it started to eat at her gut. She followed his lead and drank too much wine too often. She lost weight and developed an ulcer. A marriage under false pretenses, his drinking and her continuing to sleep with Trevor, slowly drained her. The weight of lies and deceit was killing her soul. She had lost her horizon line.

She had never told Trevor why she married Rick. Hell, she hadn't told Rick either. But the misery of being between these two men was dragging her down. She needed to think. She needed to fix this.

Both relationships were like trying to fix a broken watch without the right tools. How do you mend hurt feelings, depression, and loss? Time, Emma would say, resolved all, but that was only partially true. And Trevor was always present, a phantom who would show up unexpectedly, full of love, as if nothing had ever happened. Maybe love is episodic at best—like rain, innocent and refreshing—but hard to hold onto, Emma thought.

After more than five years of marital hell, she called it quits. She needed to be on her own, to be set free. She got a divorce. A divorce would make everything right, she thought. It would erase her mistake. She could begin again. It would take her years, though, to know that two wrongs never made anything right.

9

One Last Time

THE FIRST YEAR OF her divorce, Emma soon learned that old habits die hard. In spite of being single, their routines hadn't changed. In fact, she traveled more for the magazine. Trevor was a rising star working for the mayor and both were married to their work. He spent his time in Manhattan and the Hamptons. She rarely got to New York. Instead, she spent half her time in Paris and half in Washington, D.C.

He had never asked her to move to New York, and she wasn't sure he would have had time for her even then. She was too damned independent for her own good. She didn't let him know how much she needed him. Occasional phone calls and infrequent weekend visits meant they were growing apart again. They both were in and out of other relationships and hadn't reconnected for more than a year. It was about timing. Or was it? Was it too damn hard to commit? Too complicated?

She had always wondered, and the idea of resolution had been in the back of her mind for a long time. He had never left her thoughts; it didn't matter who she was dating or sleeping with. They never measured up to her feelings for him. She decided she wanted to know why he had sent her away all those years ago. She wanted to be free of doubt and innuendo. Had he not wanted her because she had married Rick and a divorce couldn't make it right again? She had consistently had these thoughts, but had never asked because she believed there had been too much to risk.

And it was more than that. She wanted to believe she could put away the past and work things out in her life and reunite with Trevor. She wanted to tell him that she had never planned to marry Rick, had never loved him. Maybe when she was married, she was safe for Trevor and he was for her. No need to have a real relationship when she was with someone else. She had to know.

While she was in New York on business three years after her divorce, she called him. They decided to get together for dinner in Brooklyn near a friend's apartment where she was staying. By chance, he was living nearby in Park Slope, close to where he had grown up. Kismet perhaps. After some small talk, they set up a day and time to meet. It was the phone call, that reconnection that had revived her, at least for a few moments. She hadn't paid much attention to his reference to "we" did this, "we" did that, until he told her he was married. She clutched the phone with both hands to keep steady on her feet. She was light-headed and weak. Disbelief poured over her as she fought the nausea rising in her stomach. She slid slowly down the wall of her room, landing softly on the floor in a lump of bent flesh and limbs. There was a long silence. She was in shock. Why hadn't he called her and told her? Why would he? Hadn't she done the same?

"Emma? Are you there?"

She wished she were somewhere else, someone else. She held back her tears and a weak "yes" slipped through her quivering lips. She paused, trying to make sense of this, to distract herself from the moment. Then, without thinking, she said, "Can you still meet for dinner?" Wait! Why was she going to do that to herself? Was she so crazy that she would punish herself by seeing him, knowing it was over. *It was over.* Eating was the last thing she wanted to do, but she needed to see him, ask him, find out why, and tell him why she married Rick.

Trevor didn't hesitate. "Yes. As luck would have it, my wife is away."

What? She hadn't planned on inviting his wife, but thought it was an odd twist of words, of fate, the way he said it. Another double entendre, mixed message, or was she just grasping for meaning in his words. Still, she would meet him, see him, and tell him what she needed to.

After she hung up, she cried for three days until there was nothing left.

THE WARM NIGHT air hung gently around her as she walked down President Street to Union. She tuned out the few people and little traffic of the early spring evening as she thought about seeing him again and what she would say. It was different now. He was married. Everything was different, but her heart tossed aside that reality and beat faster with each quickened footstep. She hesitated outside the restaurant and looked inside. She could see him sitting at the bar, his back to the door. Similar moments and meetings flashed before her and flung her back to college and everything since. It was as if she were in the last moments of her life. She was on the outside looking in.

Married or not, every emotion—excitement, joy, fear, disappointment, sadness—whirled inside her. Could she really do this? What came to mind was the bad advice she had received from her girlfriends all those years ago: "Stay cool; don't let him know how much you care." She was good at hiding her feelings, and she knew she wouldn't cry, couldn't cry. She had drained herself of all her tears, tears she had saved for a lifetime.

She took a deep breath, opened the door, and forced a smile. He turned and met her gaze. He looked the same, except for the rimless spectacles that lay across his perfect Celtic nose and a few new smile lines. The same boyish grin was there, and years of emotions danced on the edge of Emma's nerves. It was as if they had never been apart. It was as if they were twenty again—just beginning, everything new.

He put his arms around her and gave her a kiss on the cheek. "You look wonderful, Em. I'm glad to see you. What brings you to New York?"

Emma hesitated for a moment, wondering whether she should tell him the real reason she was here: to see him and reconnect. But things had changed now. Bad timing.

"I had a literary agent to see in the city."

He was delighted to know she was doing well at the magazine but would learn over dinner that the agent she was meeting with was for a book she was writing, a love story. But she didn't tell him it was *their* love story or what could have been their story.

She was more interested to learn about his life, although he wouldn't say much about his wife or how they had met. Emma drank a little too much wine at dinner, hoping to be able to finally tell him how she felt and that she was sorry for screwing up, but the words wouldn't form on her lips. She believed now it only mattered to her. But he had never asked her to marry him. She stared into his hazel-green eyes pondering how to ask, how to beg the question. She lost herself in his smile and was swept back to his brownstone on Clinton Avenue and the touch of his body against hers.

When she finally posed her question, she asked, "So, are you deliriously happy?" She couldn't ask *why not me?* It hurt too much. Instead, she focused on him. She was a coward where he was concerned, a romantic one at that. That was her big, important question? She knew that loving him had made her incredibly happy and, on occasion, equally miserable. Now she wondered whether that same passion was there for his wife. That was it. She wanted to know more about his wife than why he hadn't asked her. She was afraid of the answer, the truth. She liked thinking that she had been his one true love.

His answer surprised her. He took a sip of wine and thought about it for a while. Then he looked at her and said, "I'm content."

Content? What in the hell did *content* mean? Weren't you content after a satiating meal, getting a promotion, or having a cigarette after sex? God, wasn't he crazy in love—heart-stopping, passionate, impossible love? The words were screaming in her head but she couldn't form them on her lips. She didn't get it. Maybe she had different standards, greater expectations, and more passion when it came to him. Maybe it was his way of saying, it wasn't like what was between "us," but I'm satisfied enough. Emma had a hard time with this. How could he have settled? Maybe it was the need to be "steady," no more roller coaster feelings, none of the ups and downs and twists that had kept them from the straight path to marriage.

Emma felt as if she might explode and dissipate into the atmosphere. She wanted to yell at him and tell him he had made a mistake. But she couldn't. Hadn't she done the same? She had settled. When she thought about her own marriage, though, she had to admit she was never passionate or content. Before it even began, she wanted it to be done, finished. The stupidity of it all. At the time, she thought the engagement had been the right thing to do—the next step as a couple. Emma now knew that to make friendship turn to marital love simply hadn't worked. She had been afraid to listen to her heart. She had never considered her own sacrifice: her happiness. *Damn—damn!*

THAT NIGHT AFTER dinner, he walked her back to the brownstone apartment. Emma kept her emotions close as they talked about old times, college, Paris, and mutual friends. In all the years they had been together, neither of them had discussed marriage and now was no different. Emma believed they were both afraid to face the reasons. Perhaps neither of them felt as if they deserved each other and had no reason to stand in the way of what or who could make them happy. Did they love each other so much they could let go, or not enough to hold on to? It has been said that "love only happens when two hearts are ready." Maybe that was it. Trevor hadn't been ready when she had been; when he had been ready, she hadn't been. Two hearts, some of the time ready. No wonder it fell apart.

MONTHS LATER, THEY got together one last time in D.C. and had dinner a couple of blocks from the White House at Dominique's, one of their favorite places. Emma was dressed in an absolutely stunning, short black silk cocktail dress and had let her long dark hair fall seductively over her shoulders. She wore the same pearls she'd been married in, thinking appropriately of now laying them to rest with everything past. She waited at the bar and was being chatted up in

French by the charming bartender when Trevor walked in, his eyes searching the room for her. She turned toward him just as he leaned in next to her.

"Wow, you look gorgeous." He kissed her on the cheek.

"You look good yourself. Didn't know you were wearing Armani these days." Emma smiled.

Trevor laughed. "Are you hungry?"

"Always."

She examined his lightly tanned complexion, the remainder of a summer on the water, probably at the Hamptons. She noticed a slightly receding hairline, but other than that, nothing had changed. He looked great and she learned over drinks that his career had put him on a path to move up in the courts as a judge.

Midway through entrées of duck and bison, Trevor reached into his pocket and took out a photo. "I have some news." He handed the photo to Emma. Emma studied the black and white image in her hand, not sure what to make of it. She used to think that everything was black and white, cut and dried, with little grey in between. But time had brought that into focus. Now she believed most things were grey with some black and white around the edges, like the photo she held now.

"I'm going to be a father." He smiled.

"What?" Emma looked at him in disbelief. Oh my god, she thought. She reached for her wine, then her water, hoping to keep her mouth and throat occupied so she wouldn't scream or throw up. It was a sonogram, a goddamn baby! His baby, not hers, not theirs. Emma would never be a part of it. She was more than devastated. This couldn't be real. A sonogram like her own, the one from early on in their relationship before she knew what she wanted. She should have told him about her miscarriage, their almost love child; maybe it would have made a difference. But it was old news, just as destructive and filled with loss. Too late now.

Silence grew between them as Emma tried to think of what to say, what to ask. She was dumbfounded. Her mind was racing. She wanted to be happy for him. She couldn't speak. She wanted him to be happy but *was he* really? Her emotions were on a rampage. She wanted to slap him. She did the only thing she could in the moment. She excused herself, went to the ladies' room, and threw up.

Several minutes later and a little paler, Emma returned to the table. "I ordered some coffee. Would you like something else?"

She fixed her eyes on him. Yes, I would, she thought to herself. I'd like to start over, go back to the beginning. Why couldn't the two of them have merely loved each other and been happy? Why had they made so many mistakes with each other?

"I'm sorry," he whispered. "I wanted to share this with you. I never really planned it. It just—Emma, are you okay?" Trevor waited for an answer.

Hell no, she wasn't okay. But she knew she'd started her descent into regret with her own stupid marriage. And now this. Deep down she knew he'd make a wonderful father, but she'd given that dream away too. Emma forced a slight smile. "I will be," she said. There was nothing more to say.

LOVE. HOW TO FIND IT? How to keep it? Do we choose love or does it choose us?

She still loved him and always would, but time and distance had changed the equation. She couldn't go back. A year later, she moved to Paris, although nowhere was far enough. He was always with her.

10

Paris Again

EMMA REMEMBERED HER first time in Paris and her exciting one-year assignment with *Condé Nast* thirteen years ago. Had it been that long? The passage of time catches us all unawares, she thought. Things with Trevor had been good then. Paris, the most romantic city in the world, had been their own special paradise, a place for just two lovers. Now the time she had was time to heal.

Often, on her way to work, passing Le Meurice Hotel, she remembered the night she and Trevor had celebrated her new job in the fabulous Marco Polo suite. She could still hear the champagne cork pop and feel Trevor pulling her close and kissing her. Reliving that scene in her mind made her feel warm and weak all over. Maybe that's why she was comfortable in this city. It brought back happier moments. Maybe it was Paris, or France, that was the love of her life.

As a senior writer, she had been happily living in the city, getting accustomed to Parisian life, speaking French, and working hard.

Paris had everything—beauty, culture, great food, history, romance, and charm. She relished seeing, feeling, and breathing in the Louvre, Royal Palace, Arc d'Triumph, place du Concord, Eiffel Tower, and Notre Dame.

Her small one-bedroom flat on rue Vaugirard with its tiny bare-bones kitchen was all she needed, but the balcony was worth the cramped quarters. Facing the Luxembourg Gardens on one side and the Sorbonne on the other, she felt connected to the history and edgy character of the Latin Quarter neighborhoods, where writers of the Lost Generation—Hemingway, Fitzgerald, and Stein—used to gather at Café Les Deux Magots and Café de Flore. Plus, she could hop the metro to her office near la Madeleine.

It was good to be back at the main office where she had begun to develop a circle of friends. Some were old acquaintances at the magazine and others were new ones she met on her trips outside the city and south through Provence—her favorite spot. Provence had a slower pace where the important thing was to live and enjoy whatever you were doing in the moment. The Provençal mountains, valleys, fields of wheat, lavender, sunflowers, and vineyards made her smile and daydream. She had begun thinking about maybe working from a home office there and only coming to Paris on occasion—something of a dream.

Early next year she would go to Provence again to do a story on French chocolate. Emma knew that, for most, France was about the wine and cheese, cafés, baguettes, and croissants, but through interviews with some of the top chocolatiers in Paris, she also had learned that chocolate was one of France's gourmet secrets. She had read that the French regarded their chocolate-making tradition with such esteem that they had their own Academy of Chocolate and Candy Making. Each year, the Academy recognized and rewarded an individual dedicated to chocolate making. Who would have guessed that forty experts oversaw the vocabulary of chocolate making and edited the national dictionary of chocolate terms—abaisse, finish, artisanal and more.

She had spent days researching newspaper articles on chocolate, French chocolatiers, and the upcoming trade show in Marseilles. Paging through the books of the Academy's pristine library with its wall-to-wall volumes on chocolate, she imagined she could smell the chocolate escaping from the pages of recipes and dictionary of chocolate terms.

Sitting at the large mahogany table reading *L'Histoire du Chocolat*, Emma easily imagined Anne of Austria bringing the delicacy from her native Spain and handing it to her new husband, King Louis XIII. She could see the king sigh with delight at this decadent, delicious discovery. Perhaps Anne had told him how the Spanish had brought cocoa from the Aztecs, who loved its restorative and aphrodisiac-like properties. Maybe it was chocolate that gave the French their reputation as sensuous lovers, she mused, as she paged through a stack of books.

Emma read how France's own industrial revolution had brought chocolate to the masses in mousses, cakes, candies, and hot chocolate. But the pièce de resistance was the annual Salon du Chocolat. Not even the New York City Chocolate Fair Emma had once attended could compare with the over-the-top exhibits, entertainment, classes, tastings, demos, and competitions of the Salon.

This year's Salon was in Marseille during the week of Valentine's Day. More than 100,000 visitors had come to taste twenty-five tons of chocolate made by more than seventy masters. The crowded Parc Chanot convention center put Emma front and center into the world of chocolate—white chocolate, milk chocolate, dark chocolate,

chocolate-filled macaroons, chocolate with ginger, fennel, lemon, orange—every flavor and color imaginable. Throngs of fashionistas hovered around the models wearing dresses, hats, and shoes made of chocolate! *Mon Dieu!* Did shoes dipped in and decorated with chocolate mean always staying at room temperature or below? She laughed. It would have been a waste of Jimmy Choo's!

As she wandered through the exhibitions, Emma saw chocolate baking, decorating, spraying, injecting, and ice cream dipping. She passed up the chance to try on chocolate makeup or have a chocolate facial for fear she might lick herself to death or pass out from the fumes. Lovestruck couples sampled chocolate cupids, chocolate hearts, and heart-shaped pretzels covered in ganache. The rows of extraordinary sculptures of nudes, mansions, the Eiffel tower, and life-size swans made her realize that chocolate in any form was a creative process—an art. Spurred on by the music of Edith Piaf, the smells and colors of chocolate, and the sounds of people tasting, licking, chewing, talking, and applauding fueled her own desire for a taste.

She stepped around the corner of a curtained space and happened by a booth where an older woman was doing a truffle demonstration. Emma loved truffles, especially the ones with rich caramel or hazelnut cream filling. A small crowd had gathered to watch, and Emma stopped at the far end of the counter, hoping she might get a sample or two.

Throughout the demonstration, a young man in a chef's jacket stared at her as she watched the woman quickly whip up the confections with the skill of an artist sculpting a piece of clay into a delicate masterpiece. Pristine, all in white without a drop of chocolate on her or her counter, the woman seemed to be one with her chocolate—a singular love affair. Emma again glanced at the young man who flashed a smile her way. She blushed and focused on the demonstration, wondering who he was—another chocolatier? The woman laughed as she stirred the rich gooey mixture with a large wooden spoon in a rhythmic fashion, hypnotizing the onlookers around her. The crowd oohed and aahed as she beat and then dipped her spoon into the large bowl. The aroma of deep, rich chocolate rose and fell with each swirling stir. Emma inhaled the scent on the upbeat, then moved in closer and picked up a sample from the counter.

"*Bonjour, mademoiselle.*"

The man who had been watching Emma was suddenly next to her. He rattled off something in classic French at break-neck speed, and although Emma's French was good, she got lost somewhere between the chocolate in her mouth and the chocolate of his eyes. And his smile. She froze and slowly pushed the bite of truffle around the inside of her mouth with her tongue, feeling the burst of the dark, bitter sweetness. Emma smiled as she swallowed and felt her body respond to the taste of the aphrodisiac.

"*Bonjour. C'est delicieux.*" She held out her hand. "*Je m'appelle Emma.*" She wasn't sure why she was telling him her name.

He laughed as he squeezed her hand. "René. The son of the best chocolatière in all of Provence—Margarite Girard!" That was it; he was her son. Emma and René stood facing each other, staring and smiling, still holding hands.

Margarite glanced up, chuckled, and then said, "It's the chocolate. It makes you lose your senses. And sometimes your heart."

Emma could feel her face flush in tune with the rest of her anatomy. She laughed. "*D'accord.*" Of course. Yes, that was surely it, she thought. The chocolate was making her feel this way because she hadn't had this reaction to anyone or anything in a long time.

Emma let go of René's hand and turned toward his mother, who was about to finish up the batch of truffles. She explained to Margarite that she was a writer with *Condé Nast* and would love to interview her and get some quotes for her story.

"I have demonstrations back-to-back until the evening, but—"

"I'll be happy to talk with you," said René. "If it's okay?" He glanced at Margarite.

Oh, god, Emma thought, what a come on.

She looked at Margarite, who nodded and said, "He knows as much about the business as I do. Please talk with him; he'll get you whatever you need."

Everything? Emma thought.

The journalist in her was feeling put off. She'd rather interview the main source of the story. She knew that it's always about the story, but there was something about him. The eyes? The smile?

She looked at René. He smiled. "There's a café nearby."

They moved quickly through the throngs of people, exhibitions and demonstrations, large chocolate sculptures, cooking classes, singers, and dancers, away from the sounds of the loudspeaker, announcers, and voices that encircled them. Three floors above the harangue of vendors and visitors was a large café. They settled into a cozy table near the window overlooking the Gulf de Lion harbor, so named for its potentially violent sea and surprising winds. The coastline stretched well into the distance, with a telephoto view of the Cathedral of Marseilles glistening in the bright afternoon sun. Emma opened her purse and pulled out her notebook and pen.

"Thanks for doing this. I won't take up too much of your time."

"My pleasure." He motioned to the garçon. "Let's order first."

Emma laughed. She loved the French. Everything was done around food and drink. Two of her favorite pastimes. She sat back in her chair, opened her notebook, and took a good look at his longish brown hair and deep brown eyes. He was handsome, with an olive complexion and a seductive smile. More of a Mediterranean than French look. She figured he was closer to Katie's age, maybe a few years younger than herself, and was glad she had worn her new black and red jacket. It was sophisticated, yet youthful.

Two espressos and two croissants later, Emma learned that René, who spoke perfect English with an ever-so-slight French accent, owned a vineyard near a small village not far from Saint Saturnin in Provence, where his mother had her chocolates and bakery. He had one sister, and his father was a butcher with an operatic voice who casually entertained customers when they came to his shop.

He'd been to the States—New York and California—many times for both the wine and chocolate businesses and split his time between Paris and Provence when he wasn't traveling abroad. He seemed an unusual combination of sophistication and down-to-earth. Emma enjoyed talking with him.

As the tables in the café began to clear, Emma redirected the conversation. "I think we should talk about your mother and her chocolates, don't you? It's getting a little late."

"And just when we were getting to know each other." He took another sip of coffee.

She watched his hands—no wedding ring—then searched his face for a line or a wrinkle somewhere. But nothing. A mere babe. Still, she found it exciting and flattering that a younger man seemed to find her appealing.

"So your mother had a passion for chocolate early on?"

René nodded. "From my grandmother. By age seven, my mother had learned the basics for truffles and won ribbons at local fairs."

Seven, Emma thought, remembering how her own sweet tooth and passion for chocolate had begun with her mother and grandfather. Her mother always made a very special fudge for Christmas,

Easter, and Thanksgiving. It had some mystery ingredient that made everyone crave more. Her grandfather repeatedly bribed and showered Emma and Katie with Hershey Kisses, along with every kind of penny candy you could think of—Smarties, Mary Janes, Tootsie Rolls, and Bullseyes.

"And you?" She raised her chin. "You learned early on too?"

René turned toward her. "As a child, the shop was magical for me. My mother and grandmother would mix an alchemy of chocolate smells and textures from family recipes, but mainly I was the taster." René laughed. "I tested all of their creations."

Emma chuckled, realizing that chocolate was as much in his veins as wine.

Her mind wandered to the idea of his vineyard, and the conversation slipped back to wine and which ones would best complement chocolate.

He smiled at her. "Chocolate is a lot like wine, with its own bouquet, color, and taste. It can be bitter, sweet, dark, fruity, aromatic. I like Cabernet Sauvignon or Franc with dark chocolate. Port is also good."

"White chocolate and champagne are two of my very favorite indulgences," she teased.

"Oh, they're excellent together. Mainly because white chocolate has no cacao—it's not really chocolate—so it's not affected by the acidity of the champagne."

"I think I knew that somehow."

He looked into her eyes. "But I can think of more romantic pairings."

"I'm sure you can." She blushed and turned back to her notebook.

After another fifteen minutes of talk, René pulled a small portfolio from his jacket and handed it to Emma.

Emma flipped through the slick promotional pages, bio, and awards detailing Margarite's chocolaterie, wondering how often he'd used this marketing approach to meet women.

"May I keep this?" she asked.

"Please." He stood. Then, checking his watch, he explained he needed to get back to the booth. He didn't ask for her card or number. No "may I call you" or "see you." Nothing. This surprised her. It made her all the more curious.

Emma extended her hand. "Thank you so much. I've learned a lot about chocolate and wine today."

"You're most welcome." He kissed her hand. "Au revoir."

"Au revoir." Emma waved as he walked away.

THREE WEEKS LATER, René left a message saying he had received a copy of her article and was happy to know it would be published in April. He left a phone number, but she didn't call back and was surprised when he called again. His voice made her feel nervous as she paced at her office window, watching the March winds push against the Parisians on the streets below.

"I'm sorry I didn't call," she said. "I've been really busy and—"

"Too busy to have dinner with me Friday?"

There it was, right in front of her, the question, a date. She didn't know how to respond. He was too young, she thought, too different from what she had been used to. What would they have in common anyway? She wondered.

She hesitated. "May I call you back?" Sort of the standard put-off reply, stalling until she could make up her mind. Why? What was she afraid of?

"You can call me back, but will you?"

Emma felt her throat tighten. "Of course." She was holding back, fearing what she might say, what she might want.

She promised to call.

Still clutching the phone, Emma listened to the dial tone ringing in her ear like the signal of an alarm—a warning—to take it slow and play it safe . . . or maybe take a risk?

SHE REACHED FOR the brass door handle, walked into the small bistro, and surveyed the red-covered tabletops, garçons, and customers. Eight o'clock. René wasn't anywhere to be seen. Feeling a little conspicuous, she hurried over to the bar and squeezed in between two couples sipping their wine and munching on aperitifs, remembering how once she was stood up by Rick near the end of their marriage when he had wanted to talk. She had made a decision, graciously, she thought, to come and listen, but knew she had nothing more to say. He never showed and left her waiting at Mr. Smith's in Georgetown for two hours.

Safe for now, she thought. Maybe she was a little crazy for agreeing to have dinner with René. Maybe she needed crazy in her life right now. He was too young for her and really not her type. No "little bad boy" in this good guy. Nothing would come of it. It was only one dinner. It didn't matter. Her heart was already numb. Just as she was about to order a drink, she felt his hand on her arm, turned toward him, and started to speak. Before she could, he said, "It's good to see you. You look beautiful."

"Thanks." She smiled easily, staring at his lips. She liked that he appreciated the two hours' worth of trying on outfits—settling on a little black dress that clung perfectly to her shape—and changing her hairstyle repeatedly, until she gave in and let it fall naturally to her shoulders. Besides, he cleaned up pretty well himself. She eyed his tan turtleneck, black slacks, and leather jacket. His slender build made him appear taller than his six feet. His waist was probably the same size as hers, she thought.

She looked at the snug sweater covering his shoulders and chest and imagined perfect biceps, perfect abs, and probably perfect everything else. She felt her stomach growl and had to laugh at herself—a cougar on the prowl, hungry tonight—she thought jokingly!

But he wasn't like that—not out to score—at least not right away. He was genuinely interested in listening to her and learning about her. He shared her passion for art. He was an avid reader. He knew everything there was to know about wine. He was a skier and a hiker. She could visualize them at some chalet in the Alps or hiking the Luberon. Never mind that she hadn't skied in ten years, hiking made her feet hurt, and she would prefer sitting around a fire reading a book.

René ordered a bottle of red wine and the two of them relaxed and waited for the appetizers. The smell of the warm bread produced a gnawing in her stomach. She pulled a piece from the basket and studied his face. Over the clanging of silverware and crystal, she watched his full lips recount his last visit to Napa and its wineries, how he had studied at the London Business School but had gotten his real education in the vineyards. He seemed so young to have accomplished so much. Here she was at thirty-eight not sure of where she was going next.

What were those lips like to touch, press against, devour?

Emma gave herself an imaginary slap and then gave him a cursory personal history of how she had grown up in Virginia, lived in the District of Columbia for most of her adult life, and began working for the magazine stateside when she was fresh out of college, trying not to divulge her age. Age never came up and he seemed less interested in that than in what she wanted out of life, something she was still toying with.

René raised his glass. "A toast to us, a beautiful beginning. Santé!"

Emma nodded. "Cin cin." Their glasses touched. She watched him take a sip and thought about being twenty-nine again. By then, she had been unhappily married and emotionally immature. René was neither. To a new beginning, she told herself. She leaned back in her chair and wiped the last taste from her lips.

He reached for her hand. "Thanks for having dinner with me."

Emma felt her heart flutter from the warmth of his touch and knew there was some physical connection. She smiled. "I really enjoyed tonight."

As they were leaving, René casually mentioned that he had a renovated flat in the Marais district, not far from the rue de Rivoli, close to tonight's restaurant. She wondered if this was his standard modus operandi for first dates—a restaurant near his place, lots of wine, and then? Maybe he did just want to score. She didn't want to be right about this. She expected more of him somehow. Would he invite her back to his place?

It didn't happen. She felt a little foolish, wondering what it was she really wanted. Instead, they took a leisurely after-dinner stroll through the neighborhood. The Marais—home to Mozart and Victor Hugo— was one of the most picturesque areas in Paris.

"And Marais means swamp?"

"Literally, marsh," René said. "But you can see that it is a beautiful, elegant part of Paris. What I love the most, though, is its bohemian, artistic, and cosmopolitan qualities all rolled into one."

"It's beautiful," Emma noted.

The streets shimmered in the fine mist falling around them, and colorful store signs and windows sparkled as they walked along rues Charlot and Bretagne, a part of Paris Emma hadn't explored much. She loved the blending of the old and the new, the eclectic shops, diverse restaurants, and lifestyles. They stopped and peered into the window of an antique store.

Standing there staring at the objects d'art seemed all too familiar to her. She had done this with Trevor often and now with this young Frenchman. Maybe history does repeat itself. No, Emma thought, this is different. We talk; he's truly interested in me. Emma's subconscious had made a startling discovery—did she think Trevor hadn't been interested in her? She exhaled slowly, her eyes tracing the cases and old treasures seated high in the rear of the window before settling on a delicate diamond and sapphire bar pin slightly hidden by an old pocket watch.

"Look, René," she said. "That's a lovely art deco piece, don't you think?"

René followed Emma's long fingertips to where she pointed. "The tiny pin? Yes, it's *recherché*—exquisite—like you."

Emma smiled at him, recalling Trevor's own words to her so long ago about her elegant taste and beautiful hair.

As they continued to walk, notes from the strings of a classical guitar spilled onto the sidewalk from one of the local bars, adding to the unmistakable ambiance of Paris. Emma decided then that she needed to explore this area more. She had only been to Victor Hugo's house and the Palace des Voges, but she thoroughly enjoyed walking these eclectic neighborhoods tonight with René.

At the end of the evening, he didn't make any moves on her. He didn't try to kiss her or mention another date. Was he gay? He was good looking, dressed well, and was in great shape. For now, she was flattered he had asked her out—an old woman almost forty. She knew he was someone she would like to get to know better. Maybe he would call her again.

11

A Weekend in Provence

MANY DATES LATER and for her birthday in June, René invited Emma to come to his village for the weekend. She was excited about going home with him. She had never stayed with any boyfriend's family, not even while dating in high school, and only Trevor had stayed at Evergreen that one Thanksgiving when they were in college.

When René was in his village, he lived in an apartment in his parents' home. Emma felt uncomfortable that he didn't have a separate flat away from his parents, and the age difference still bothered her. She would be thirty-nine in a few days, not in her early thirties as René had likely assumed. She smiled at the thought, though, of looking younger. Still, was she "young enough" for him? Nine years wasn't really that much of a deception, she had convinced herself. Besides, he was French; he probably wouldn't even care.

Midday Friday, they took the rapid rail TGV to Marseilles, a quick three-and-a-half hours for the six-hundred-mile trek. René and Emma spent the time talking about Paris, drinking wine, and kicking back in their upholstered and comfortable high-back seats. She felt relaxed and safe with him, feelings that had long escaped her.

Outside the train window, small villages and vast countryside blurred by, and she remembered the drive she had made to Provence with Trevor way back when. She felt oddly out of place with time as she glanced at the young beautiful Frenchman sitting across from her, casually reading *La Revue du Vin de France*. She loved his Tom Selleck dimples and jawline, his European chic style: slim-cut Armani jeans, Bruno Magli slip-on loafers, and a black silk stretch tee. Was this really the present—her present—or was it still her past? Like time, the sleek train kept moving forward, carrying her into the future.

In Marseilles, they picked up René's BMW and drove another forty-five minutes to his home. His village was in and around the Petit and Grand Luberon mountains, near Gordes, Bonnieux, Menèrbes, and Lacoste. Emma filled her eyes with the Provençal landscape, taking in les Apilles and Mt. Ventou mountains as they sped down the highway without speaking, enjoying the beautiful earth-colored and white houses with red tiled roofs, the mountains, and wheat and lavender fields. This was too much to absorb, she thought. She could only take it in little breaths and small doses for fear of losing herself altogether. Provence did this to her—made her hold her breath, anticipating the next beautiful vista.

It was late afternoon when they arrived, but the sun wouldn't set for another six hours—one of the best things about Provence. As they pulled up the winding cobblestone road and into a small garage next to the house, she took out her compact and put on fresh lipstick. She couldn't help but notice the tiny lines around her eyes—thirty-nine. She didn't feel almost forty. She took a deep breath, surprised that her hands were shaking.

René laughed. "They will like you with or without makeup!"

Emma looked over the exterior of the four-hundred-year-old house with its yellow ochre façade, which René told her had belonged to his paternal grandparents. She noticed the tall, sky-blue, double shutters at each window. René took her hand and tugged her toward a wrought-iron gated archway wrapped in pink damask roses.

Her heart became calmer as she intertwined her fingers into his smooth, warm hand. A stone path meandered through a garden of lavender, geraniums, and roses. Tall pink and purple hollyhocks stood like sentinels on either side of the front door.

Emma stopped. "René, this is beautiful." She felt the warmth of the sun on her face and the touch of a light breeze. "It's like a fairytale garden." The floral scents reminded her of her mother's flowers, especially her roses, at Evergreen. The knot in her stomach loosened.

"It's my mother. She has a green thumb."

"Yes, she certainly has." Emma thought of her mother's garden and wondered if only mothers were capable of nurturing a living, growing thing—much like children and love. Emma had no garden; no children, but she wanted both. And love, she always wanted love.

René carried her overnight bag as Emma followed him upstairs to the back bedroom. At the top of the landing, the golden glow of western light flooded the room, drawing her toward a pair of tall open doors.

She moved closer and stepped onto the small balcony overlooking the back of the house, breathing in the vista of the valley stretching toward the Luberon. The lavenders, golds, and greens vibrated towards her, swept across her body, and radiated around her.

"My god! This is like an impressionist painting!" she exclaimed, although she wondered if even Monet or Cezanne could replicate such natural beauty.

René nodded. "It's a beautiful view."

In the distance she could see rows of vines.

"Is that your vineyard?" She had no idea he had so much property.

"Tomorrow we'll take a tour." René stood next to her with his hand on her back. She felt like she could stand there forever. The view, this man, exciting her. Beyond the valley, she saw more wheat and lavender fields, more colorful houses spread over hundreds of acres of farmland. She imagined writing here surrounded by this beauty and tranquility.

René pointed to the left. "That field over there is a sunflower farm. In July, they will be in full bloom as far as the eye can see."

Emma imagined the thousands of yellow bonnets standing in perfectly spaced rows. Would she be back here in July? Would she still be seeing him then? Would they have slept together? Could she hope to get over Trevor?

"You must come back to see it," he added, as if reading her mind.

"I'd like that."

He took her hand and led her down the narrow winding stairs, through the compact black and white kitchen, and into the dining room with its large, rectangular, oak farm table. Emma stopped to take in the fresco walls with their randomly scattered, hand-painted fleur-de-lis color notes. At the end of the room, tall French doors opened onto to a stone patio and pool, both situated high above the valley.

They stepped out onto the cool grey stones and watched the afternoon winds push the clouds out of the cerulean sky. René put his arm around her waist and pulled her closer. "Over there is Rousillon—with its ochre quarries." He gestured toward a small mountain. "You can see the lights at night." She could feel the warmth of his body and her heart rising in her chest.

It was almost too romantic for her to comprehend. Emma stared at the shapes and symphony of colors arrayed before her. She stood perfectly still, hoping this moment would last and that he would keep holding her, touching her.

René turned toward her. "Are you hungry?"

Emma moved in closer and pressed her lips against his as she gave him a quick wet kiss, a reflex, an impulse. As she looked up at him, she whispered, "Something to eat would be nice."

"I'll get some wine and cheese." He trailed his hand down her arm, then walked back inside to the kitchen. She watched him disappear through the doorway. His derrière in those jeans, she thought, those broad shoulders . . . She wished she could be alone with him tonight.

She sat down at the table, letting the summer breeze sweep across her. How long ago had it been since she and Trevor had come here? Fourteen years.

She looked out over the valley and knew that just beyond Rousillon sat Bonnieux, where they had stayed one full week in a small house up the hill near the old church that overlooked the cedar forest. The second floor bedroom sat high above the village with a view that placed them almost at the top of the mountain, closer to heaven. They had been in Marseilles, St. Remy, and Aix and had spent several days in and around the Carmague, where they had taken long walks along the shore. She remembered how the flamingos cast lapis silhouettes against the setting sun and how Trevor had stopped abruptly to bend over and pick up a lavender shell.

"This is one of a kind, simple, delicate, and beautiful to see and touch. Like you, Emma." His words had transformed into a gentle kiss on the lips. Oh, he definitely had a way about him. He had her heart then and perhaps still. Powerful memories of her wish for an unfulfilled dream had left her wistful for him, again.

"Red or white?" René called out.

"Red, definitely red." Provence was noted for its reds and rosés. She loved them both.

René brought out bottles of Mourvèdre and a rosé, along with a platter of cheeses, grapes, French bread, and some yellow linen napkins. He set the blue glass plate on the edge of the wrought iron table and then wiped down the table with the blue-checked cloth he had carried over his arm.

"At your service," he said, laughing. His eyes pierced her gaze, making her blush.

She grinned and looked out beyond them to the pool, yard, and valley. A charming stone wall surrounding the property was interrupted by a tall iron gate and broken steps to the right of the house. Red bougainvillea swayed back and forth over the entryway. She eyed the plate before her.

"You're lucky to live in such a beautiful place."

"I'm lucky you're here to enjoy it with me!"

Emma, lost in his chocolate-brown eyes, reached for his hand, "Thank you for thinking that way; it means a lot."

And it did. She could belong to someone again.

After a moment, he said, "I hope you like triple cream brie."

"My favorite." A man after her heart and stomach.

He sliced the skinny centime baguette, lathered it with cheese, and held it out to her.

She looked at his hands and fingers, masculine yet refined, like those of an artist, or an artiste of massage, a master of touch, perhaps. She imagined him massaging her neck and back, touching her throat, arms, and breasts. His arms were athletic, hairless, with just enough muscle showing. Perfect, she thought, suddenly aware of the warmth of her own body and of her hunger.

With one pull, René easily released the cork with a slight pop. He poured the red into her glass, then his.

"Let it rest for a while," he said.

Emma plucked a few grapes and tried another cheese—Cantal— then picked at a piece of bread, studying him as he held the glass close to his nose, closed his eyes, and inhaled the bouquet. She examined his long dark lashes and wrinkle-free brow. He made her feel young. She could see his expression change to one of delight as he drank the wine. She pressed her glass to her lips and took a sip. "Mmmm, wonderful." She turned the bottle to read the label. "I haven't had Mourvèdre before. It really goes well with the cheese."

René watched her read the label. "So, you know something about wines?"

"Only what I like—not much about the grapes or the process." She turned the bottle around and reached for another grape. "Well, I do have a factoid from a food magazine." She popped the grape into her mouth.

"What's that?"

"That Provence has France's oldest vineyards and the rosés are the oldest French wines. Something about the Phoenicians introducing grape growing in Marseilles about twenty-six hundred years ago." She took another bite of bread and leaned back. "Am I right?"

"Exactly. Here's one for you." The afternoon light was shifting now and swept across the side of his face, highlighting his dimples. "Did you know that it takes thirteen-hundred to fifteen-hundred hours of sun to produce ripe fruit and that Provence averages twenty-seven hundred to three-thousand hours per year?"

"Okay, you win." Emma grinned.

"How did you get into this anyway, the wine?"

René's expression changed, not growing serious so much as intense.

"Be careful," he warned, "I could talk about wine forever." He held up his glass and swirled the wine. The light hit the glass, revealing the brilliant, clear red color of the liquid. Almost alizarin crimson, Emma thought, earthy and sensual. He took a slow deliberate sip.

She couldn't get past his lips and mouth. They were sexy, easy to touch and press against, full and sensitive, ready to burst with passion. Passion. The word unfurled inside her. She could see herself reaching across the table and putting her mouth on his.

"The vineyard began with my grandfather, who bought eighty hectares, about two-hundred acres, in the forties."

She could hear him talking but was having difficulty focusing on his words instead of his lips. "So, more than fifty years ago." She held her glass close to her lips and breathed in the fruity aroma. "It's been in your family a long time." She took another sip.

"Yes, but a blight in the fifties nearly ruined us." He looked down at his glass of wine. "I can't imagine growing up without this." He sighed. "Anyway, we started over. We brought in new vines from the Côtes du Rhône—like the red you are drinking—and grafted it to hardier stock."

"When did you get involved?"

"Before I was born." He smiled. "My mother worked the grapes up until the day I was born. I began walking the rows with my father when I was ten, about the same age he was when he learned from his father."

Emma conjured up images of father and son walking and working together in the vineyard just as the grandfather and father had done. Nostalgia overcame her, and for a moment, she could see herself walking with her grandfather and father looking after the yearlings at Evergreen. She could almost feel the rich green pasture beneath her feet and smell the moist air from Cedar Run.

"Little by little he showed me what to do. He showed me how to spot diseases and—"

"How?"

"How do we spot them? Have you noticed the rose bushes at the end of the rows of grapes?"

"They're lovely."

René laughed. "They're lovely, but they're there for a reason. Grapes and roses get the same kinds of diseases. Roses act as an early warning for fungus—mildew."

An early warning. She wondered if she needed an early warning. A warning to watch out for her heart because she was feeling more and more attracted to him.

"I thought they were there for decoration." She smiled

"You're probably not alone," René added. "I don't think most folks even notice or think about them."

The sun was beginning to cast long amethyst shadows along the rows of vines. Purple and green, "nature's lovers," Cézanne had once said.

"You love doing this, don't you?"

"Can you tell?"

She nodded.

"It's in my blood—much like your love of writing and art."

"It all sounds wonderfully romantic—grandfather and father and son, all working the vineyard—like an old movie script. I can see it," she said.

"I guess you could look at it that way." René paused. "But working the land, growing something, is labor intensive. As you know, you must do everything yourself. It's a big gamble."

"But look out there." Emma pointed to the valley, smiled, and reached for his hand. "That's all yours!"

René looked at her, and wrapped his fingers around hers. "These rows represent about sixty-five hundred bottles."

"Of reds?"

"Those are the grapes that thrive in our soil and climate. The mountains make a big difference in both those things."

Emma looked at the fading blue violet peaks in the distance—the Luberon—so beautiful. She noticed that as he sipped his wine, he was studying her, almost as if seeing her for the first time. She had a sense, though, that he had always known her. There was a relaxed familiarity between them where words didn't matter. Emma knew that feeling well.

"Tomorrow we'll take the horses and ride through the vineyard," he said. "You know how to ride, don't you?"

She arched an eyebrow. "Riding is in my blood."

"I thought you were a city girl."

"My father raised thoroughbreds."

"I thought he was a lawyer."

"He was." She laughed. "But horses were a passion with him." She smiled, folding her napkin. "We had jumpers and hunters. When we were older, my sister and I showed our horses throughout the country and were both avid fox hunters."

"Isn't that pretty brutal?"

"Absolutely, if you actually catch a fox." She glanced at him, enjoying the surprise she'd seen in his eyes. "But mainly we went on 'drags'—hunts where the scent was dragged for the hounds to chase."

"Ah, so no live hunts?"

"Oh, we've been on some but never caught anything. We went for the chase."

"So you were just a happy thrill-seeker!"

She looked into his dark eyes and felt a wave of desire move through her. Was she a thrill-seeker? Is that what attracted her to him? The thrill of the chase, the hunt?

"I do like thrills." She flicked her eyes at him and he laughed. Quickly she steered the conversation back to horses. "It was definitely thrilling to gallop through the fields and jump fences to follow the hounds. It was my childhood dream."

René took her hand. "And what are your dreams now?"

Emma laughed. "Ah, those are secrets." She squeezed his hand. She felt young. It made her happy to know that René was so interested in her.

"I'm very patient," he replied.

Emma swallowed hard. She didn't know what to say.

"Patience is good," she said softly.

LOST IN HER thoughts, Emma didn't hear Margarite walk through the garden to where she and René were sitting. "*Bonsoir, mes enfants!*" she called out. René stood and kissed his mother on both cheeks, then pulled out a chair for her. Emma, still deep in thought, jumped, somewhat startled, "*Oh, Bonsoir, Madame Girard.*"

"So you were daydreaming, my dear?" Margarite smiled. "It's easy to do here in paradise, *n'est-ce pas?*"

Emma nodded. "It's beautiful. The gardens, the view, the house. It's all perfect."

She studied Margarite, who was maybe in her mid-fifties, a rotund woman with a girlish face and pink skin like the women in Renoir paintings. Her black hair, with a few strands of grey peeking through, was pulled back and up in a bun, with a white silk flower perched high off to the left side of her head. Definitely a Mediterranean look, thought Emma, but she sensed more—a warm, caring woman with a daring sense of style. Emma felt drawn to her right away.

"It's good to see you again. I'm glad you could come for a visit. And René is taking good care of you?"

"*Merci, moi aussi.*" Emma was delighted to be invited. She assured Margarite that René was looking after her. René offered his mother some wine, but she said she was going to rest a few moments before beginning dinner.

"It will be simple tonight. Mussels and salad," she told them. "But I will make sure there is something chocolate for dessert." She laughed as she stood and walked into the house.

12

Dinner with the Parents

THE SUN WAS BEGINNING to set behind the Luberon, casting an amber light across the terra cotta floor and distressed wood table. Floral linens of red, blue, and yellow lay under rows of candles centered on the table. A few cicadas had begun their song but were unable to compete with Jacques' booming voice.

Jacque sang out, "Welcome, Mademoiselle Emma." He declared in heavily accented English, "We are so happy to have you with us."

Emma reached for his hand, and Jacques leaned toward her, kissing her on both cheeks, his barrel-chested frame bumping her stomach. He stepped back, swept his dark brown hair from his youthful face, and took a long look at her. "*Trés belle, René, trés belle.*" Emma blushed. Jacques arrived shortly after Margarite had gotten up from her respite and had brought pork tenderloin from his shop for dinner. Kitchen utensils clanged in the background, and the smell of briny seafood, pork, and chocolate wafted throughout the house.

Emma glanced around the dining room, admiring the paintings and furniture surrounding the long table set with faience plates from various regions of Provence. She loved everything about this old house—the uneven walls with their hand-stenciled fleur-de-lis, the sloping tile floors, the rustic wood sideboard with the marble top, and the rooster chandelier over the table. In spite of its age, each room was filled with light that could only be snuffed out by heavy, blue wooden shutters during the day and awakened by subtle candlelight at night. The simple treasures placed randomly around the room— the pottery, the family photos, the dried artichoke blossoms—told a story of family, of belonging.

Emma was comfortable here.

Jacqueline, René's younger sister, tied a red and yellow apron around her slim waist as she approached Emma from the kitchen, kissed her on both cheeks, and said, "I'm so glad you could come for a visit. René has told us so much about you." Emma knew immediately from Jackie's creamlike complexion and blue eyes that she was a younger version of Margarite.

"Thank you. I'm happy to be here." Emma smiled, remembering what it was like to be twentysomething when you knew everything but nothing. When you were self-assured but constantly doubted yourself. So young. She realized she was almost twice Jackie's age.

"You're so lucky to be a writer and an artist." Jackie beckoned her toward the kitchen. "My talents are in the kitchen. I hope to study at the Cordon Bleu in Paris in the fall."

"I'm sure you'll be great at it."

Emma followed the aroma of the pots on the stove. It's good to have a passion and a plan at so young an age, she thought, unlike most of us who don't even know what we want to do as adults. Emma had never really had a plan. Although she had started to write when she was in high school, she'd always thought of it more as a diversion, a way to put down on paper her fantasies and dreams, and from there, she latched on to whatever came up. After all, it had landed her in Paris as a writer, something of a fairytale itself. Except, of course, there were regrets. She wondered what would have happened if she had pursued her love of horses, drama, or art? She knew Trevor was her biggest regret. She might have had four children by now if she hadn't married Rick. Four is what she had wanted. Emma watched Jackie check the pork in the oven.

"So, Jackie, what do you like to cook?"

"Mainly regional meals. Unlike Mama, I don't bake, but I like to prepare the more traditional desserts like crème brulées, mousses, and some fruit tarts."

Emma smiled. "I look forward to tasting some of your signature dishes."

"You won't have to wait too long." Jackie pushed her black hair behind her ears. "The pork dish is mine."

"It seems you're well on your way to becoming a chef. It looks wonderful." How could she lose with Margarite's pastry expertise, Jacque's knowledge of meats, and the family's wine. Emma could hardly wait to savor the cooking tonight.

Emma heard voices behind her and turned toward the dining room, where Margarite was placing a large pitcher of water in the center of the table. "May I help?" Emma asked.

But before Margarite could answer, René motioned to her. "I could use your help with the wine."

Emma laughed, knowing she was no wine expert. René uncorked three bottles, one for each course, and handed them to Emma, his fingers lingering as he touched hers. She placed the bottles near Jacques' seat at the head of the table.

"Allons manger," Jacques announced as they all found their seats at the table.

The sun moved toward earth, dimming the room with an orange hue of twilight. Jacques passed the mussels to Emma.

"René has told us you are a writer and an artist. How wonderful!"

"I love it, especially traveling and meeting people." Emma looked at René. "I wouldn't have met René and Margarite if I hadn't been doing the story on chocolate."

Jacques looked up from under his bushy eyebrows and smiled at Emma. "We're glad you did."

René nodded, tapped his glass lightly, then raised it. "Santé" echoed around the table.

Silverware clinked rhythmically against the ceramic plates. Jacques said, "I'm an artist too. I carve meat while singing *Figaro, Figaro!*" He let out a roaring belly laugh.

Everyone giggled, except René, who declared, "You should hear him, Emma. He could be on the stage!"

"I'd love to hear you sometime."

"Come by the shop, anytime." Jacques' ebony eyes twinkled. "I'll put on a performance worthy of both Beaumarchais and Mozart!"

Margarite glanced at her husband with that "enough already!" look in her eyes.

How different Jacques was from her own father, Emma thought. She never remembered him singing a note unless at church with the family. He had a great sense of humor and a passion for life but never drew attention to himself, even when he deserved it. Still, he was a family man like Jacques, and Emma could compare René's family with her own. She felt a void in her heart. She missed them.

Emma spooned some of the mussels to her mouth, intermittently wiping the broth from her lips and sipping the Piquepoul wine. The garlicky brine tickled her nose. When she turned toward René, she saw him watching her every movement. He smiled with his eyes. She felt a little embarrassed and remembered the first time she watched him at the chocolate salon. He was a handsome young man drawn to her as well. Here with his family reminded her of how Trevor could not keep his eyes or hands off her during their cozy family dinner at Evergreen that Thanksgiving all those years ago. She glanced at René. They were similar in some ways—tall, handsome, smart, fun-loving, and successful—and the sex. She couldn't compare that yet but only knew her adrenaline flowed freely when she was with Trevor. He had excited her more than any man. René calmed her. Maybe she had fewer expectations of him. Maybe that was a good thing. Fewer chances for a broken heart.

She wanted to shake herself for even thinking of Trevor while sitting here with René and his family, but she couldn't help it. He was always with her. Sometimes, she was better at blocking his memory, but at this moment, she could see him chatting up her mother about her fabulous cooking, especially her corn pudding and oyster-chestnut stuffing. He had recounted stories about oyster dredging on the Jersey shore near his family's beach house.

René leaned over and whispered to Emma, "A penny? Are you still with me?"

Emma smiled. "I was thinking about family and how lucky you are to have yours."

He squeezed her hand. "I am lucky for more than that."

She felt the warmth of his touch, but her heart didn't race.

Later, as she lay in bed listening to the night noise of the whispering tree limbs and a lone nightingale calling, she thought about her family and Evergreen. She missed Katie and made a mental note to contact her to see when she could come to Paris.

The moonlight illuminated the room, forcing her to get up and walk to the window and pull the shutters. Instead, she opened the tall doors to the balcony and looked out. The valley was awash in a bright, almost white, light that made the fields, houses, and vineyards a sleepy silhouette of dreams. An ultramarine curtain of stars hung low over the valley, glistening and winking at her—the Hamptons at night. A melancholy swept over her. She sighed, turned, and closed the tall shutters, leaving the doors open and hoping the cicadas would lull her to sleep.

EMMA AWAKENED EARLY the next morning to the sounds of children laughing and running along the cobblestones. Barking dogs aroused her from a deep sleep. She rubbed her eyes, adjusting to the daylight, focusing on the room.

For a moment, she didn't know where she was. The aroma of breakfast quickly brought her back to René's house. How lovely—someone was fixing coffee and baking bread.

René stood near the stove with his back to her as she walked into the kitchen. Emma greeted him with a cheery "bonjour." René turned toward her with coffee pot in hand. She walked over to him to retrieve a cup, and he leaned forward and kissed her. He whispered, "We're alone. They're all at work."

She laughed nervously. He put his arm around her waist and pulled her close. His lips touched hers with such passion that she felt her body burning.

"René, I'm not comfortable—it's your parents' home."

"When?" He brushed his lips along her neck. "I know you want to."

He was right. She wanted to a great deal of the time, but something kept stopping her. Was it the age thing? Or Trevor's constant presence? She didn't know.

As he continued kissing her neck, Emma felt herself losing control. She gently pushed him away, looked deep into his eyes. "You're right. I find you attractive and sensuous, but there are things about me you still don't know."

"Let me find out." He brushed his fingers down her arm.

She stepped back. "I'm not sure I want a committed relationship at this point."

René laughed. "Well, what about just sex?"

Emma was surprised and disappointed. She wasn't sure she wanted that either. But if that's how he really felt, why hadn't he been more forceful or demanding of her?

René grinned. "Emma, I'm kidding—*une blague*—a joke!"

Now she was confused. Right now, she wanted coffee.

"You shouldn't joke like that—I might have gone along with it," she said coyly, trying to make him wonder a little. You have to love the French *joie de vivre*, she thought.

He glanced at her with those gentle brown eyes and sighed. "Let's have that coffee and just enjoy the day. Remember, I'm going to show you the vineyard today." He stroked her hair. "I am a very patient man."

Hell, he must be, she thought. She remembered how she and Trevor had no patience or resistance to each other.

He set a plate of warm croissants and jam on the kitchen table and reached for the coffee pot.

"I make a wonderful omelet."

Emma looked at his chest, barely hidden under his shirt, and ran her hand up his arm, retrieved the coffee pot from his hand, and poured herself a cup. "I'll have whatever you're having. An omelet sounds perfect, but let's eat in the garden."

She walked out of the kitchen with both cups in her hands. "Come on. I'll come back and help you in a few minutes. Let's enjoy this gorgeous morning."

René picked up the croissants and followed behind her through the dining room outside to the terrace and table near the back of the house. His silhouette blocked the sun from Emma's eyes as she turned toward him. "I like patient." She smiled.

13

The Vineyards

"BONJOUR, MONSIEUR RENÉ," the workers called out as René and Emma rode by. They didn't seem overly surprised or concerned that she was there. An old habit perhaps? She didn't know, didn't care.

Emma couldn't remember the last time she was on a horse—ten years ago maybe—a few times in Central Park, but other than that, this passion of hers had faded to the back burner. Trevor had been her passion, but he had never fully appreciated her love of horses, although he didn't dislike it or dissuade her like Rick had. Besides, Trevor was a city boy and would have rather played golf than get on a horse. Rick just didn't want her out of his sight.

Today, she felt as if she were back at Evergreen riding the hills with her father. She could hear him say, "Star has a beautiful foal this year. That filly has potential. I know it." Potential. Emma wondered what her own potential was or could be, and ultimately, who might fit into it. Would she have to go it alone? Would she ever see Trevor again? Her father would love it here, she thought—the sun-drenched valley, the cloudless blue sky, the mountains. It was perfect.

She couldn't believe she was actually here with this handsome young Frenchman who enjoyed riding and being with her. She looked out over the vast rows of the vineyard, too many to count, and felt as if she needed to pinch herself—out of the magazine spread in her head and back to the present.

"What are they doing?" She pointed to the men bending around the vines.

"They are thinning the grape clusters."

"Why?"

"To make the remaining fruit more concentrated at harvest."

She was curious now about the growing process, wondering how many man-hours and grapes were necessary to fill a glass. She had once read that there are about six-hundred grapes to a bottle, or one hundred grapes to a glass. "And when do you pick the grapes?"

"We'll hand pick at the end of summer."

"Is it true that some producers harvest the grapes under moonlight for optimal quality?"

He smiled. "Yes, but we don't. You read that somewhere, didn't you?"

Emma laughed. "Maybe."

On the other side of the vineyards toward the mountains, he led them into a clearing. She noticed a lone stone bench near some red bougainvillea, and they slowed to a halt.

"Let's rest here awhile." He swung his leg out of the saddle and down to the ground, holding her horse's bridle so she could dismount.

"Is this part of your fields?" She wanted to know if this remote place was his or something he had happened across.

"No. I found this one day, by chance. I come here sometimes to think, but today we're going to sit for a few minutes and have something to eat."

Something to eat? He thinks of everything, she thought, realizing he'd probably brought others to this secret rendezvous. She was hungry and glad for the food.

"Do you always carry food with you when you're out here?"

"I usually have something to eat but no wine when I'm in the vineyards. Horses and alcohol don't mix."

My god. Guess he'd be shocked to know that practically everyone carried a flask when fox hunting. In the fall and early winter, riders were up and out at 5:00 a.m. to gather before the hunt. Brandy or whiskey helped warm them before the long trek of looking for the fox. A big breakfast followed the hunt, with all kinds of food accompanied by liquor, champagne, wine, and coffee. It might be fun to take him fox hunting and see how he does, she thought.

He pulled two bottles of water out of a small saddle bag, handed them to her, and rooted around for the ham and cheese sandwiches wrapped in a linen napkin. Emma felt well taken care of with him. He seemed to plan ahead and think about what she might want or need. She liked that. Trevor was more spur of the moment, more spontaneous. Emma preferred a happy medium—sometimes spontaneous, sometimes not. She was just learning about René, and so far, he surprised her. He was unassuming and generous. For someone younger, he was more mature than either she or Trevor had been when they first met and dated. Maybe he was her age after all.

The early afternoon sun massaged her back and shoulders as they sat side by side on the bench. Who would put a bench way out here in the middle of a field? She was sure René had done this and perhaps liked the idea of a little mystery.

"So how long have you been coming here?"

"A couple of years. I discovered this spot one fall when riding."

"Really? You mean your family didn't put this here?"

"An ancestor maybe? It's quite old, but no one knows really. Does it matter?"

"Curious, that's all. The writer in me likes to gather information, find the story within the story, so to speak."

He laughed and touched her thigh. "Curious or suspicious?"

She knew she was skeptical in general, but suspicious? Did she need to be suspicious?

"I don't think even my father knows of this place," he added.

Emma took a bite of sandwich. She looked at his arms and the side of his face. His smooth, tanned youthful skin almost compelled her touch. She stroked his hand. "I'm glad you brought me here. It's peaceful. It reminds me of home."

She noticed his perfect profile—a modest French nose, not too long or wide, long black eyelashes, well-spaced tame eyebrows, and full lips aching to be kissed. He looked almost too good to be true— like a slick, airbrushed model. Airbrushed to perfection. Maybe she wasn't looking or didn't want to see the faint scar that ran behind his right ear to the nape of his neck, partially hidden by his hair and shirt. A childhood injury perhaps. A minor flaw. If there were others, she hadn't found them yet.

He turned to face her, brushed a few crumbs from her lips, letting his fingers linger, touching her mouth, and then leaned in to give her a wet kiss. She kissed him back with restrained passion, keeping herself in check, being slightly guarded, remembering how she and Trevor had made love in an open field after picnicking one summer near Middleburg. No hesitation, no thought, a chemical reaction, exploding, naked on the grass. She could see herself lying naked next to René on the valley floor, but then what? After sex, what would their relationship be? She didn't know how it would work. She thought too much. They sat for a while soaking in the sun and the landscape.

She imagined herself with him in the vineyard, walking among the sun-washed vines, carrying their dark-haired baby girl while their four-year-old boy ran ahead of them laughing and waving his arms in the air. She could see the scene of a love story in the vineyard unfolding like a vintage film in warm sepia tones. Sepia, the color of low-light intrigue, mystery, and romance. She rarely thought of her life as anything but full living color: bold, obvious, dynamic. But when she saw herself with René, everything was sepia.

"Shall we?"

"What?" What was he asking her? Could he read her mind? Did he see them lying naked in the field? Walking together in the vineyard with their children?

René laughed. "I was going to say continue on. What did you think I meant?"

She grinned. "Oh nothing. Maybe make love on the bench?"

"Well, at least you're thinking about it, but I prefer a nice soft bed surrounded by candles and rose petals."

Who was this guy? Maybe he was saying what she wanted to hear, but it was her preference too. She could see them together under the soft silk sheets of her bed. She smiled to herself, then stood up and took the reins from his hand.

"Okay, let's go." She winked.

As they rode on, Emma noticed a long, narrow path a few hundred yards ahead.

"Where does that go?"

"Up the mountain—"

Not waiting for René to finish, Emma squeezed her legs around the girth, asking her horse to trot. "I'll race you!" Her horse began a steady canter toward the path, but René passed her at a gallop, leaving her behind in a small cloud of dust.

He shouted at her, "What's the matter? Slow horse?"

Emma's competitiveness wouldn't rest with that, and no one had ever won a race against her—not Katie or her father. She squeezed harder with her legs, stood slightly in the saddle, and pushed her horse hard into a flat-out gallop to catch René. The race was on. Surrounded by the smell of summer and the wind in her hair, she remembered the times she and Katie raced through the fields at Evergreen and Cedar Run. But this was better—new territory, a new adventure, a new beginning. She was young again.

Rounding the small turn in the path and moving faster, she had René in her sights, both of them laughing until the path narrowed into dense trees and thickets. They slowed to a trot and then rode side by side up the hillside. Almost breathless, she felt like an athlete who had sprinted a mile. They both settled their horses to a walk.

"What's that up there?" She pointed to the top of the mountain. "I thought I saw some color, something . . ."

René looked up. "Maybe the chapelle?"

"What chapelle? Where?"

She couldn't imagine why there would be a chapel in the middle of nowhere. She searched the landscape but saw nothing but mountains and a small olive grove farther west.

René looked at her and then pointed to the left. "Beyond those trees at the top of the mountain. The chapelle de Croagnes."

"Croagnes?"

"A hamlet. The chapel is now a private home."

"A home?"

"It's a small chapel hidden by tall cypress overlooking an olive grove. You wouldn't notice it unless you knew it was there."

"Really?"

"It was built in the seventeenth century and used as a chapel for three centuries. It was abandoned for decades."

"And then a real estate mogul, from Britain I think, came up with the idea of converting it into a café or small B and B?"

"Nearby hamlets wanted to preserve the structure and got permission from the archdiocese to deconsecrate it."

"Interesting story." Emma was already thinking ahead to a possible magazine article. She could come to Provence for longer periods. She could scout around for a house while doing her research. Perfect, she thought to herself. I have a plan.

But her enthusiasm was way ahead of her. Excited, she asked, "Can we ride there?"

"We could, but . . ." He reminded her that people lived there and they wouldn't be able to go inside and look around.

"It's a long way up, but I know a short cut, an old walking path."

In an hour, they reached the top of the mountain. Emma stopped and looked behind her.

"It's magnificent." She had a complete panoramic view of the Luberon, the fields, and villages. She could see beyond Rousillon almost to Bonnieux and René's village. She took a deep breath, sucking in the fresh air and not wanting to release it all at once, exhaling slowly like a yogi. "This is heaven. Whoever lives here is the luckiest person on earth." She was elated to know this even existed. She wanted to find out more, do some digging about who lived here, how long ago the chapel was purchased, and for how much. "It's lovely. Let's walk a little closer."

"We shouldn't intrude," he said. He motioned for her to follow closely behind him. They entered a clearing below the chapel in the fourth row of olive trees. Emma traced the outline of the structure with its cream-colored, hand-cut stone face, lovely terra cotta roof, and a small bell tower at the front entrance. There were several full plain windows, no stained glass. It reminded her of a tiny New Mexico mission church—utilitarian yet charming.

"Do you know who lives here?"

"Why? Do you want to buy it?"

Of course, Emma would leap at the chance but realized it was probably out of her reach.

"I'm sure I couldn't afford it." She glanced his way and smiled. "But I wouldn't mind a modest summer place in a small village."

René smiled. "I'll remember that."

The sun began to push against the horizon, shooting through the olive trees, down the mountain, and casting long shadows across the vineyards.

They meandered down the mountain at their own pace, Emma following behind him, turning for a moment to look back at the chapel—someday, maybe, she thought.

14

Waiting for René

EMMA SAT AT THE SIDEWALK table of Café Deux Magots on the Left Bank not far from her apartment, waiting for René. The clear skies and warm September sun made this a perfect early fall day. By noon, the café was almost full, with waiters in black darting in and out, scurrying like ants, jotting on their notepads, and wielding drinks and food. A garçon hovered over a young couple, barely twenty, in the far corner, pouring their wine. The couple was holding hands and looking at each other with goo-goo eyes. They seemed out of place with the outsized voice of Edith Piaff blaring in the background. The café seemed too passé for their young hearts.

A crash of plates and silverware near the bar directed Emma to another table where a blonde in her early fifties dangled a long cigarette holder from her vermillion lips and played with the petit chien at her feet. She fit. She was part of the genre of a typical French retro café. A classic white ashtray imprinted with *Gitanes* was ready to catch her fading embers. Emma wondered if someone would be around when her embers faded.

Emma swirled her glass of red wine, inhaled its bouquet, and took a slow sip. She laughed at herself, knowing she'd picked up this habit from René. She could still see them riding through the vineyards in early summer—racing, laughing, taunting, and joking like kids. She looked forward to seeing him.

She sat under the green and white awning like she used to when had waited for Trevor. She had cherished those Saturdays in Paris. Sometimes they would go to a concert or bike in Vincennes Woods, picnic in Luxemburg Gardens, wander the afternoon at Les Puces flea market, or visit nearby galleries and antique stores. She appreciated their similar tastes and relished how excited he would become over some unusual find, like an early French painting, table, or special book. Emma recalled the particular day Trevor had found an old eighteen-karat agate cameo hand-carved with a portrait of Marie Antoinette. Turns out it was one of Georges Bissinger's prize-winning works from the 1867 Paris Exhibition. Trevor always had an eye for excellence. He bought it for her because of its flawless beauty. She deserved it, he had said. She wore that beautiful brooch to formal parties, the opera, and to work on her black suit. It always got rave reviews. Now it lay in a silk-lined box in the back of her lingerie drawer, pushed back as if in the recesses of her mind. Maybe it was time to retrieve it and wear it again. After all, her weekends were shared once again. Something that beautiful was meant to be seen and admired. She could almost hear those words coming from Trevor's lips.

Sometimes, their Saturdays had begun at La Grille. From there, they walked around rue Montorgueil, with its shops, cafés, and restaurants. Emma could imagine the hundreds of red, white, and blue

French flags lining the streets that Monet had once captured on canvas. Emma would buy a croissant at Stohrer's, then stand outside looking at her reflection in the window like Audrey Hepburn had in *Breakfast at Tiffany's*.

Trevor liked being in the heart of things. René, on the other hand, seemed to like out-of-the-way places, although Emma couldn't be sure he was always like that. His sense of adventure and romance seemed somewhat planned, less spontaneous than Trevor's. These two men were polar opposites. Maybe it was time to try something different, a departure from what she had known. Maybe they would fit.

She played with the red carnation in the small vase in the center of the marble table. A large shadow reached towards her, causing her to look up and cover her eyes from the sun. She could barely see the silhouette towering over her. The waiter was back?

"Hello, mademoiselle. Would you like something very French today?

Emma sighed. She knew it was René. "Mais oui. Could I have it now, please?"

René slid his hand up her arm, leaned over, and planted a large kiss on her lips. "You like? Mademoiselle?"

Emma laughed, glad to see him.

He sat down, tossed back a couple of peanuts from the small dish near her, and ordered a glass of Merlot.

He looked terrific and remarkably relaxed for having spent the last ten days in the States. They grazed on shrimp salads, brie, and bread while they caught up.

After lunch, René and Emma walked hand-in-hand to the marché along rue Mouffetard, one of the best open-air markets in the city. Wine shops, cheese shops, clothing stores, cafés, restaurants, brasseries, and bars crammed in and around the streets and alleyways. People had been coming here to do their daily shopping since the Middle Ages. The sun-filled cobblestone streets meandered through a maze of every imaginable food display. Farmers brought spectacular fresh fruits and vegetables for their stands—blood oranges, mangoes, figs, and more. Emma could find every cheese made in France at La Maison du Fromage, including her favorite triple cream brie. Sometimes she would buy a wedge and a baguette and sit in the tiny garden at Saint Médard church, understanding that this was the way to live. The lovely little church with its Watteau paintings and Gobelins tapestry was built in honor of St. Mèdard, the patron saint of winemakers, brewers, and farmers. The pulse of Paris throbbed in and around the market, with its street musicians and dancers, boutiques, shops, restaurants, and cafés overflowing with French conversation, and the clanging of glasses and silverware. She loved it here. She never felt alone or like an outsider.

After an hour or so, René headed to a small bookstore on the corner across the street, while Emma picked up some camembert cheese, French bread, oranges, and strawberries for a Sunday brunch she was to share with some friends. Later, he caught up with her, carrying a couple of newspapers.

"Let's grab a café. I want to show you something," he said. They ordered coffees, and René began telling her about his trip to the States. After spending most of his time in California talking with growers and agents, he had spent a few days in Manhattan. He had contacts there and shops that were interested in carrying his wines. One vendor invited him to an art opening where he featured René's wine.

"I never thought about how the bold colors and oversized canvases seemed to fit with the wine. It was interesting."

"Congratulations. That's fabulous!"

René smiled. He took out a copy of *The New York Times*, opened to the arts and entertainment section, and handed her the page with the ad for his wine and a brief description of the art opening where it had been featured.

Emma listened to René describe the evening and shared his excitement. She took a sip of café and read the small article in the paper. "That's wonderful! I used to go to all those artsy events when I stayed in New York."

René folded the paper back to the front page. "The odd thing is I met someone there who knows you."

Emma's eyes widened as she held her cup firmly in both hands. "Really? Who would that be?"

"Trevor Kinney."

Emma's heart began to drum in her ears. How is this possible? What were the odds? What was the connection? Her face whitened and she couldn't speak.

"Do you know him?" René asked.

After a long pause, Emma said, "Yes, I know him." She hesitated. "From college."

Her mind was reeling, and she felt light-headed, dizzy, sick to her stomach. "Was his wife with him?"

"He was with some attorneys and an art critic. I never saw his wife."

How in the hell did my name come up? She wondered, but was too stunned to ask. She waited for René to tell her the answer.

"Actually, the art critic was the connection because he was with someone from *Condé Nast*. Nathan somebody."

Nathan Kaplan, Emma thought, one of the senior editors she had worked with in D.C. when she first went to the magazine. Holy shit! It was a very small world.

"When I told them I lived in Paris and knew someone at the magazine's office here, well, your name came up." He paused. "Mr. Kinney seemed particularly surprised and taken aback, especially when I told him you had been out to my vineyards in June. He asked about you."

Emma's heart raced and her hands began to feel clammy, even cold. The cup slipped from her hands and the coffee splashed into her lap. René was moving toward her with napkins, trying to help her, but she couldn't hear him. She was numb all over.

"Emma, are you okay?"

"I'm sorry, René. I don't feel well. I need to go home and lie down." Go home, lie down, curl up in a ball, and never get out of bed. Why does Trevor have this effect on me? He's a damn ghost!

René hailed her a cab and made sure she was settled in her apartment. She just wanted to sleep, she told him. She had left him bewildered. She would have to tell him about Trevor eventually. But not today. It had been too much of a shock.

EMMA HUNKERED DOWN in her bed and pulled the silk covers over her head, throwing herself into the dark. A beautiful day ruined because she couldn't hold herself together. She should have let René stay with her, comfort her, but it was too complicated. How could she tell him that she wasn't over Trevor? Even she hadn't known for sure until her heart reminded her.

She fell into the dark abyss of dreams of water, sun, stretches of sand, and ribbons of footprints following behind. She had visions of naked bodies intertwined in passion, rocking rhythmically, and then floating, gliding along the surface of the water half asleep, refreshed. Over and over these scenes played in her head—the two of them naked, wet, and warm, huddled together in one blanket, holding onto each other as the sun slid into the water.

15

Sunday Kind of Love

EMMA HAD TO CLEAR her mind, shift her focus. At 5:00 a.m., after a restless night, she fixed herself a cup of tea. It was early, but Paris was always alive. She stood by her window, looking onto the streets still glistening from a light rain. She could hear a few buses, trucks, and delivery vans make their way around boulevard Saint Michel. The newsstand on the corner would soon lift its iron shutters. She opened the tall sheer curtains, letting the city lights flood the largest room in her loft. She loved this time of morning when it wasn't quite dawn and the sun was beginning to stretch to this side of the earth. There was a sense of anticipation, something new being created.

She walked to her desk and turned on her computer, sat down, sipped her tea, and began looking for agents and rental properties in Provence. Thousands of available properties ran several pages, so she typed in "Luberon villages." That narrowed things down to a few hundred. She sat back. Still a little too many, but she scrolled the list, looking for something near René's vineyard. Did she really think she could outrun Trevor and his memory? Could she shut down her heart by fleeing south?

The hell with him, she thought. I'm changing my life.

Between Joucas and Croagnes, she found four properties that were interesting, but each had some drawback—either too expensive, too big, or too small. She kept returning to the photos of the two-story stone building with its tall shuttered windows. A large, bright kitchen. It had a view of a valley similar to where they had ridden. It looked familiar and she could imagine herself living there. She emailed the broker to get a better idea of the exact location.

Why was her first instinct to run? This wasn't the first time, and there were all those times in between long weekends when Trevor had asked her to stay. Like him, she had been afraid of commitment. Why couldn't she exorcise him from her soul? A love like that, those feelings and emotions; she needed to hold onto them. She had them even when she and Trevor were apart—romance, passion, hurt, devastation. She could conjure whatever emotion she needed at the time; they were all there, lying and waiting beneath the surface of her being. No one had ever made her feel the way he had, and she believed no one ever could again. Maybe there is never that once-in-a-lifetime love twice.

Emma anxiously rapped her fingers on her desk while trying to find out more about the chapel she had seen with René. She needed this diversion right now. She kept looking.

René had said it was a hamlet. She searched "a hamlet." A definition popped up: "A settlement of a group of houses with a name to identify its locale." Oh, okay, so it's only about size. Then she looked up village. She knew a village had a larger population with at least a church, butcher, and post office. And so on, up to town and city, each increasing in services, amenities, and population. She realized that a hamlet could be very small, with only seven houses, but a village was usually a few thousand, and a city could have hundreds of thousands. She had learned something new. So how big was Croagnes? She typed in "hamlet of Croagnes" and got a few hits. One page said it was a hamlet of fewer than ten inhabitants, and there were a couple of photos showing cherry and olive trees, and vineyards on the side of the mountain like she had seen with René. In another photo, she could barely see the steeple of a church. She searched for "chapelle de Croagnes," then "chapel, Croagnes," and found the tiny ancient chapel of St. Madeleine. But that wasn't it. There was nothing about her chapel. Nothing.

Emma got up and began pacing and talking to herself, trying to remember how small the area had been, what the chapel had been near, what mountain they went up on horseback. She glanced at the kitchen clock. It was 5:30 a.m., too early to call any real estate agents. She sat down at the computer and tried to find agents listed for the hamlet. No luck. She was beginning to feel as if maybe it had all been a mirage, unreal, or maybe René was only putting her on. She remembered that St. Saturnin was not far from where they had ridden. She would try to find a contact there, and she could always go investigate on her own whenever she was back in Provence.

She sat down at the computer, wondering whether she was totally crazy to want a small place in Provence, and why near René when she couldn't even decide if she wanted to get involved with him? Wouldn't it be better to go someplace where no one knew her? What did she want?

Emma knew she needed to follow her heart more, trust her instincts, and take a risk. She liked him but didn't want to end up in the wrong relationship. She wanted someone who would love her unconditionally. Someone who would hold her hair away from her face when she vomited, wouldn't avoid her when she had a cold or the flu, who'd tell her when she was wrong, and still love her. She wanted a strong, handsome man of good character, someone with high values who believed in God and wasn't afraid to miss a football game or two to attend church on Sunday, although she couldn't remember the last time she was in church or had gone to confession. She needed someone who could laugh easily and have the courage to cry during times of loss and failure. He had to be down to earth and love animals, especially horses and dogs, and the farm, Evergreen. A tall order; did he even exist? She wondered. She recognized the similarities—the traits of her father. Was she searching for someone like her father, herself, or both?

She sat staring at the computer screen, hypnotized by her own thoughts. The age thing bothered her, and she didn't want to end up in another relationship about control like the one with Rick. But was she projecting way too much on René and his youth? He was mature and sensitive. She didn't even know why she was thinking this way. Fear had reared its ugly head. She didn't want to make a mistake, but at the heart of it all, she didn't want to get hurt. She was tired. Tired of thinking, wanting, looking. She turned off the computer and moved into her bedroom. She slipped under the covers and turned off the light. Alone again.

EMMA AWOKE TO A ringing and buzzing. Half asleep, she automatically reached for the alarm clock to turn it off. The noise continued. Noon. Sunday. She needed to sleep. She followed the noise to her front door and pushed the intercom. It was René. She felt a sense of blurred panic. She was disheveled, no make-up, no coffee. She tried to tell him she couldn't see him, but he insisted. Besides, she owed him an explanation. Or did she? She walked into the bathroom, threw water on her face, and brushed her teeth. She needed a hot shower, but René was at the door.

"Feeling better?" he asked. A bag of pastries dangled from one hand and he held a quiche in the other. "I know I should have called, but I was worried about you."

Emma smiled. She had to give him credit for being spontaneous. She pushed her hair back from her eyes, took the bag from him, and walked into the kitchen. She spooned coffee into the French press and plugged in the electric water kettle.

"It's okay," she said. "I do feel better, but I'd really like to take a shower."

René nodded, and she headed to the bathroom.

"I'll fix some plates," he called to her and headed to the kitchen.

Emma watched her hair dryer suck the steam off the bathroom mirror as she began to think about yesterday and what, if anything, she would say to René. After all, wasn't that why he was really here? Not to check on her, but to find out about Trevor? As she put on a pair of black cotton slacks and black and white shirt, she decided she would wait to see if or when he brought it up. Why make waves where there were none? The bottom line was she had unresolved dreams she couldn't approach and needed to keep moving forward even if no one else could understand that. For now, though, she could only take baby steps toward new beginnings. Would René let her take the time she needed to figure things out even if it meant he wasn't her choice?

Emma walked out in bare feet guided by the smell of the coffee, strong enough to widen her eyes and awaken her body. She looked at the dining room table and thought, he's feeding me again. There were two settings of juice, croissants, and jam, plus coffee and a small quiche. René certainly had a nurturing side and she liked that about him.

She poured herself a cup and said, "Thank you for doing this, but it really wasn't necessary." She'd been sick to her stomach before because of Trevor, but usually it was because she was too excited to eat before seeing him. But never had it been because she hadn't seen him, couldn't see him, wouldn't see him.

René stood at the kitchen counter, looking at Emma. "Do you feel like eating something?" He smiled. "I can warm the quiche."

Emma nodded and sat down. What he had done was so sweet. It was as if the two of them were a couple sitting down to a late Sunday breakfast and ready to read the newspaper. As that thought went through her mind, he unfurled the Sunday *New York Times* and *Le Monde*. At least he hadn't brought the paper from yesterday. They ate in silence and read the papers, looking up occasionally for one to glance at the other when each thought the other wasn't looking. By mid-afternoon, René asked her if there was something she'd like to do. Go for a walk, go to a game or the cinema, but she had little enthusiasm for anything except lounging and reading. Was he going to stay all day, waiting for her to say something to him? She got her answer.

"If you're okay, I'll let you rest."

She watched him clear the plates and rinse them off in the kitchen sink. She picked up her glass, walked up behind him, and put her arms around his waist. She pressed herself tightly into his firm body and squeezed him. "Why don't you stay?"

René took her hand, turned, and pulled her to him. He hugged her like he would never let go and kissed her deep and long. She moved in closer and held onto him. She could feel him getting hard as he picked her up and she wrapped her legs around his hips. He carried her into the bedroom and they fell onto her bed in a twisted maze of arms and legs. He yanked up her shirt and began kissing her stomach, then caressing and stroking her breasts. Their clothes were off in seconds, and he moved onto her and kissed her from her neck down to her thighs. She wanted more. She drew him into her and dug her hands deep into his back. They moved in a passionate rhythm, lost in each other, until they fell asleep exhausted, satisfied.

16

Starting Over

EMMA USUALLY BEGAN EACH day the same. She awoke with no alarm, sunlight caressing her face and shoulders. As her feet touched the warm tiles, she stretched and breathed deeply, shaking out her body from its deep repose. She steamed open her pores with a ten-minute, sauna-like shower, did her makeup, and put on the outfit laid out the night before, a habit from childhood and her mother's fastidiousness. She drank half a glass of orange juice from the fridge, grabbed her briefcase from the mahogany desk, and whirled out the door to the nearby café.

Today, though, she lay in bed watching the morning light dance on the ceiling, enjoying the warmth of his body next to her, and wondering why they had not done this every day before. She felt ageless, her body supple, and her nipples still charged from his touch. She didn't wait for the ghost of true love to reappear or guilt to flood over her. Instead, she turned slowly toward him and watched him sleep.

He was gorgeous and sexy. She moved closer and pressed into him. He had plowed the crevices and curves of her with subtle wonder and discovery, releasing her sexual urges. She smiled. Maybe she had dared to be—happy.

17

The Yellow House

ALTHOUGH EMMA HADN'T been to René's village since the summer, even in late fall, the temperature was mild and the sun-filled vineyards turned to gold, red, and bronze. It lightened her heart and gave her a sense of starting over, her mind focused on something other than Trevor.

She had started running every morning. It made her feel alive. She and René spent most weekends together when he wasn't traveling and she wasn't on a special assignment.

René knew she had been looking for a weekend place somewhere in the Luberon and had emailed her prospective rentals when he came across them. She was glad to have his support but wondered what he would think now that she had found a place to rent in his own backyard, almost on his street. So close. Was this really a good idea? Maybe it was a way of feeling safe, knowing she would be where she was wanted and appreciated. Far be it for Emma to even consider such a thing, but there it was, the reality of post-Trevor. She had been longing for Provence ever since her first time there with him all those years ago. It was an escape—beautiful, remote, quiet. Her favorite place on earth.

When Emma had first seen the old yellow house with the cornflower blue shutters, she knew she had to have it. How could she tell the realtor that this might be her last chance at happiness? The furnished house suited her. It was the perfect size, with the kitchen, dining room, study, and two small bedrooms and large bath all filling the upper level. A laundry, small guest room, a large living space and library were downstairs. The rooms needed her touch, including the neglected garden, but she loved the tall windows that opened up to balconies with the shared vistas she longed for. When she stood in her bedroom and looked out toward the vineyards and lavender, she knew she already lived here.

She looked at the rental sign now propped up against the front wall, remembering that someone had once said that a house that stands alone long enough can become either a refuge or a prison. Emma applied this analogy to herself. She knew the drawbacks of being so close to René and his family, especially if things went awry between them, but she rented it anyway. Besides, she believed that fate had intervened to bring her here under this cobalt sky, far from the everyday, as a new beginning where she could once again put ink to paper about her own truths and dreams. It was her refuge. She opened the door and went inside.

Emma stood in the center of the large bright kitchen and gazed out the window, admiring the valley, a view similar to one from René's dining room. Some of the furnishings didn't suit her, but still, the kitchen was perfect with its yellow and red décor. Old faience plates lined open plate racks in between the worn yellow cupboards above the red tile countertop and backsplash. She would add more of the pottery she had collected over the years.

She ran her hands over the pristine marble surface of the compact island she would use as a prep station. Yellow ceramic canisters for flour, sugar, and salt fit snugly in a rack on the side. She could see new pots and pans hanging from the copper rack above. She felt like a gleeful Julia Child eyeing the modern chef's stove, bigger than her own in Paris, and knew she could get by with the European fridge. She pulled back the red-checked curtains hiding the shelves of sundries under the large farm sink, then turned and walked to the yellow table and red chairs in front of the tall window with its open shutters and balcony. She pulled out a chair, noticing how the edge of the seat was worn from use. It was all very French, reminding her of Margarite's things, charming and quaint.

WHEN SHE RETURNED to Paris that weekend, Emma retrieved René's voicemail from her answering machine. He wanted to get together for dinner. She invited him over thinking that it would be the perfect time to tell him about the house. She wanted to fix something special, perhaps lobster or beef bourguignon, to celebrate his return from California and her new weekend retreat. She toyed with the idea of a Julia Child recipe she'd tried a couple of times but decided to keep it simple. She'd make him a Provençal dish that she loved—*Fruits de Mer*—garlicky scallops and shrimp and rice pilaf. Emma had retrieved all of her ingredients from the market early Saturday morning, including a fresh baguette and a lovely dense flourless chocolate cake. She was already salivating at the thought of dessert.

She had prepared her dining room table with some lovely white china and crystal glasses. The blue napkins and yellow and blue placemats added a homier, less formal touch. A vase of blue asters and yellow and white daisies brought the look of a Provence garden into her city apartment.

"Bonsoir." René greeted her at the door with a kiss. "I brought you a red and a white for tonight."

"Wonderful." Emma studied his dark, tall figure against her white walls. He always looked good. The designer jeans and fitted casual black shirt made her think of a Calvin Klein magazine layout. Wine or no wine, he could sell anything. Would she be able to sell him on her new rental? He would be happily surprised. She was excited thinking about it and how happy he'd be for her.

She had opened the door to her tiny balcony to let in some of the pleasantly mild November air. "I'll open the red and we can have a drink out here and watch the world go by," she said.

Over dinner, Emma could hardly contain her enthusiasm about the house.

"I have some news." She smiled

René looked up from his shrimp. "Good news, I hope?"

"I think so. I'm really excited about it."

When she told him, however, she didn't get the reaction she had expected.

"You're kidding?" She had his attention, but the look on his face was unexpected. He was startled.

"It was love at first sight." Emma forced a smile, worried that telling him now wasn't such a good idea.

"I don't understand." René raised his eyebrows. "Why wouldn't you want something farther south, maybe near the seashore?"

Had she told him about the Camargue? She didn't think so. Those were old memories.

"I thought you'd be excited." She cast her eyes downward.

"I'm surprised you chose *my* village."

MY? She heard an edge of anger in the word. *My.* Possessive? Ownership, or jealousy? She was surprised and confused. Not the René she thought she knew. What was he afraid of? She stopped eating and looked at him. "It's beautiful and quiet. I could work on my novel or even paint."

"Emma you can do that anywhere. What's this really about?"

She hated it when she had to analyze her own actions, justify them to someone else. Least of all to him. Trevor would have understood without hesitation. "I considered that it might not be wise to be so close to your family, but on the other hand, they don't strike me as the kind to judge or interfere. I guess I needed a change of venue, and I liked the idea of knowing someone there and that you'd be there some of the time."

She could see René's jaw tighten. "Emma, I care about you. You know that. But I don't want to feel guilty for not being there when you need me or for being there when you don't."

Emma sat up in her chair, her appetite gone. She felt stupid for expecting him to be happy. "Is that why you didn't tell me about this house, that it was available?"

"I couldn't, really, without you putting more meaning into it, could I?" His voice rose.

Was he saying he didn't want a commitment, didn't want her to expect one, or both? "We're friends, René, but we have no obligation to each other." She spoke matter-of-factly. She was in no hurry to get more deeply involved. The fact that he didn't tell her about the house left her with more questions than not. Maybe he wanted a casual or occasional relationship. Maybe he thought she was pushing for more of a commitment. She felt unsettled.

René looked at her. "I don't involve my family with my love interests."

Interests? Plural. How many were there? She reached for her wine. "Look, if you think I'm asking for a commitment, I'm not. You can date other women. I can date other men," she said sharply.

"Of course we can, but do we want to? Do you want to? I don't want you to be disappointed," he explained. "I don't want anyone to get hurt."

Was he concerned about getting hurt, hurting her, or what? The conversation was annoying her now. She straightened. "I can take care of myself. Don't worry about me getting hurt."

"Emma, I didn't mean to upset you, but I think you're already hurt. I don't want to add to that."

There it was—Trevor. Would she always carry that pain on the outside for the world to see? She thought she had been hiding it better than that.

"You want to know about Trevor? Is that what this is about?" Her heart leapt in her chest.

René leaned across the table. "Well, what do you think? I mention his name and you're sick in bed for two days."

She pulled back. "Fine. I'll tell you about him." Emma quickly went poker-faced and explained in a staccato-like voice, "It's simple really. He was the love of my life. He didn't want me. I married someone else. He married someone else. End of story."

She knew it wasn't the end of the story. The story had no ending. It was infinite and heart-wrenching. She couldn't go to a friend's wedding or watch a romantic movie without crying, seeing her own loss and mistake over and over. She thought of Emily Dickinson's words: "You left me boundaries of pain, Capacious as the sea, Between eternity and time, Your consciousness and me." She couldn't promise René anything she couldn't promise herself. She couldn't promise him love and commitment, and she wouldn't promise him loss. What did she want? She didn't know. Even when she did, she rarely chose it.

"Do you think I've never been in love, never been hurt? I'm not a monk or a saint." He swirled his wine around in its glass before taking a large gulp.

Emma's eyes widened as René raised his voice. She'd never seen him anxious or upset. She'd not thought about his past, his own baggage.

"No, I—"

René's voice strained and his eyes saddened. "I was engaged. Five years ago to a woman who lived in St. Saturnin. Our parents were friends. We dated all through high school, and after college, I asked her to marry me. A week before the wedding, she eloped with someone else."

Emma was horrified, knowing how painful that had to have been. She realized that she'd never understood how hurt Trevor must have been, although he couldn't express it. Is this why he'd yelled at her when he learned she was engaged and told her to go ahead and get married? He was hurt. She had broken his heart and didn't even know it. And he had broken hers. Years later, when she had learned he was married when they had dined together in Brooklyn, she had become depressed and cried nonstop for days. She still cried for him, but the tears had dried up, leaving only the emptiness and the hurt.

"René, I am so sorry." She squeezed his hand. "Can't we go on the way we have been and enjoy each other without worries or promises?" She wanted to move on, live a fuller life, and she felt as if René's family could be like a second family.

"I'd like to, but you have to let me in, be honest with me."

Could she be honest with him or anyone? She was barely honest with herself. She hesitated before saying, "Honestly, I was in shock that of all people in the world, you had run into Trevor. I couldn't wrap my mind around it. But he's not here. You are." Those words echoed in her head. The same words Trevor had said to her on a college date when they were talking about God, religion, right, and wrong. "You're here now, Emma, right here in front of me." He had been asking her then to let him love her.

"Yes, I am, Emma, but I think you're still emotionally attached to him or the idea of him."

Emma fingered her wine glass, avoiding his eyes. She didn't want to look at him or acknowledge that she thought he was right. She wanted to tell him not to worry about Trevor, but she couldn't. She took a drink and poured another, thinking of how a psychic once told her she was "haunted" by the loss of a great love. That was accurate. Still was. Wasn't this a reason why she needed to include René in her life even more? She was tired of being stuck in the past, waiting for something good to happen. She knew she had to make her own future. René was a beginning, a small beginning, but at least a beginning. The yellow house . . . that was a leap of faith.

18

Entre Deux

OVER THE LAST FIFTEEN months, Emma had adjusted to splitting her time between Paris and Provence. She had felt rejuvenated and inspired enough to begin again on her novel. She had spent almost every weekend and holiday here in Provence, embracing a weekend routine of writing, going to market day, church, and catching the TGV back to Paris Sunday evening.

On most mornings, she sat across an empty kitchen table drinking her coffee, insulated in the cocoon of yellow and red walls, surrounded by her favorite vases, jugs, and plates—a reminder of how she loved decorating this small space and cooking for friends and René. New and old copper pots and kettles hung over the antique marble cutting table with the handmade tiles around its edges, which had required three strong men to bring it home. The brilliant accents of Quimper plates gave the kitchen a homey, regional flavor.

She loved being able to travel in the south of France, learning about different villages and writing special features for the magazine on foods, customs, markets, and unique histories. Her research also helped with her own novel, which was set in a small village in Provence. Life imitating art and art imitating life.

In the solitude of her new house, she spent time fixing the décor and planting the garden when she wasn't tied to her computer. She felt at home knowing her mother would have approved of her flowers.

But today she was restless, stuck. The words were gone and the page blank. Emma wondered why sometimes writing had to be so hard. Why couldn't it all spill out at once and pour onto the page in perfect prose? Occasionally it did, but mostly it had to be squeezed out in bits and pieces and then woven together.

She pushed her chair away from her desk and began to pace around her small office alcove. This wasn't working. Maybe some coffee or a cigarette. My god, she was desperate and hadn't smoked in years. She needed some inspiration to be at peace and let the cosmic writer's universe hypnotize her again. She smiled. Wasn't she surrounded by inspiration and positive energy? She walked through her dining room onto the small balcony, lit a pretend cigarette, and took a long imagined drag before exhaling into the air. Her eyes traced the walls of the medieval village hugging the terraced slopes of the fertile Luberon valley, the land of castles, thriving vineyards, lavender, olives, apricots, and truffles. In the distance, high above the village, she could see a couple of old windmills dotting the upper hills that were built to catch the wind and grind flour to grain. The village lay quietly between Joucas and St. Saturnin, made up of houses noted for their charm and rustic character, old windows and doors, balconies, and thick walls. This simple beauty is what she had chosen; it was awe-inspiring, breathtaking.

To her far right, she could barely see the spire of the small church of St. Madeleine perched on a knoll in the center of the village. A quick walk from her house and she was there in the epicenter of daily life, with every lane radiating out like spokes of a wheel, so typical of Europe. A stone's throw away was the main square with its imposing fountain where the children gathered and vendors came each Saturday. Any day of the week you could find old men playing pétanque nearby in a shaded park. The intimacy of a smaller life that seemed unchanged for generations drew her in almost like being in the country, reminding her of Evergreen.

When she looked around her kitchen and dining room, she knew that any antiques dealer would relish at least some of her junk. Emma's collection of china, crystal, and clocks was French: French country, French Renaissance, and French art deco. Each piece had a special story or memory to go with it. The antique white rooster doorstop in the kitchen was something she and Trevor had picked up in St. Remy after an afternoon picnic one long weekend—almost fifteen years ago. It didn't seem like that long. The handmade oven-rack puller shaped like a tree branch with the ceramic cicada handle was her favorite find from the Apt market the first time René took her there.

There was much here that made her happy. She liked that it was only a five-minute walk to Jacques' boucherie down the hill from the church, and Margarite's bakery was another few minutes off the main square where farmers, homemakers, artists, and musicians showed off their talents and wares every Saturday. Emma loved perusing the rows of tables crowded with local wines, olive oil, lavender and lemon soaps, brilliantly colored fabrics, antiques, and cheeses. Live music played over the children's laughter and the voices asking for sausages, freshly roasted chickens, and jambon et fromage sandwiches. Margarite always had a large table of croissants, brioches, chocolate, and hazelnut truffles and typically offered some sort of chocolate demonstration and tasting. And there was her now famous chocolate oil which could be put in your coffee, in your baking, or wherever. There were many ways to use it, Emma learned.

This was the place where René brought her that first weekend, the place where his parents were married, and he was born, where Emma could let go of the past and breathe in the present surrounded by tranquility and beautiful valleys. At least that was her first impression, her reason for wanting to be here. But now there was more. The chapel had sparked something deep inside her, something she couldn't explain but needed to explore. A kind of burning desire for something she had felt years ago and was struggling to find again. Passion.

Yet the remoteness sometimes loomed in her mind. And was it such a good idea to be so close to René and his family? She hated second-guessing herself. Did she want to keep him at arm's length but still know he was nearby? Had she done the same with Trevor? Never fully commit, but know he was always available to her. That regret saddened her. If she'd only followed her heart then.

And what was her heart telling her now?

Late afternoon was already vanishing when Emma moved into the kitchen and positioned her chair next to the large window. She wanted to sit and have a glass of wine and breathe deeply. Maybe the wine would loosen up her brain and her words. In another few hours, the fireflies would appear like millions of stars so close she could reach out and grab them.

She retrieved a bottle of Provence rosé from her cupboard, poured a full glass, and looked into the fridge for some brie. In the pictures on the wall near the refrigerator, she could see her own childhood in the dark hair and light eyes of her mother. A childhood that seemed to elude her now. Emma picked up the blue envelope—the letter from Katie—she'd been saving to read, placed it carefully on the yellow tray next to the wine, cheese, and small baguette and carried everything back to the kitchen table. She missed her sister. They were so very different but had been close as children. Their love of horses, their father, and the countryside had made them inseparable.

Emma tore off a piece of bread and took a bite of brie. She thought again of Katie—tall and willowy—despite a diet of hamburgers, fries, and milkshakes. Emma could see her now talking with her mouth full, causing her to snort during a meal. She smiled. That is part of Katie's charm. She thought about that as she opened the letter and began reading, glad to know that Katie was anxious to come to Paris, the fashion capital of the world, and spend time with her.

"It's long overdue, but I'd love to visit you in Paris in June or July. I'll have some time then," her letter said. She seemed happy in the fashion industry. God knows, she had the figure and clothes for it. Emma continued reading. "My new job doesn't begin until the fall. I'll be closer, in London for a year." London. Good for Katie, Emma thought.

The fact that Katie could be here in a couple of months meant Emma would have to get her act together and finish the next two chapters of her book, an unimaginable thought at the moment. Emma had a talent for not being able to say no, but in this case, it was okay. She wanted to see her sister.

Emma folded the letter and tucked it under the tray on the table. She moved closer to the children's laughter and stood watching them kicking the ball in the narrow street and the two little Bichons yapping and scurrying around the neighbor's yard. The village was up close and personal. Intimate. In Paris, she could be more anonymous. There she could be single and no one knew or cared. She could go to the Orsay museum and sit unnoticed before Monet's painting of his garden in Giverny and study the colors and brush strokes. She loved his painting, *La Pie*, of the cottage in the snow, and Renoir's paintings of the Seine. They amazed and inspired her. She could wander the Clignancourt flea market and admire the acres of antiques or watch the bateaux mouches drift down the Seine, carrying visitors through the history and architecture of the most beautiful city in the world. There was always something to do in Paris.

Granted, there was much to do in the village on a smaller scale, but she wasn't sure what she wanted or needed the most. She was between both worlds: the city and the country, and it seemed her whole life was like this. Between the past and the present, her head and her heart, and the two men she was struggling to come to grips with. Emma headed back to her desk. She sat in front of her computer. Right now she needed to write down her thoughts. Why hadn't she thought of this before? She began to type a new chapter—The Village of Entre Deux (Between Two).

19

Emergency of the Heart

EMMA WATCHED AS RENÉ paced in the waiting room, walking in circles, counting his steps, the minutes on the clock. It struck her that time had no meaning. Time just was. It continued even when you didn't want it to. We all live in borrowed bodies on borrowed time, she thought, with short-term leases we wish we could extend. Uncomfortable hours hung in the air like clouds forming at the beginning of a storm. Emergency rooms and scientific breakthroughs burned into her brain. She waited for the downpour of bad news or the sunshine of a new day.

She knew René was wondering what would remain after the explosion in his father's heart. An aneurysm, the doctor said. An aneurysm, she had repeated over and over, while watching the minute hand of the large clock tick off slowly, methodically. Jacques had had a thoracic aortic aneurysm, and no backward glance could have predicted this; it had only happened a few hours ago. Now with his father in surgery,

Emma knew René was questioning whether Jacques would emerge a whole man, his old self, the man who had given René his childhood memories and was his role model for everything.

He had told her numerous times how his father had always been there for him—when he got into his first schoolyard fight, broke his arm doing stunts on horseback, and even when his fiancée married someone else. He believed Jacques could solve any problem and repair anything in the house—he'd installed ceiling fans in the upper bedrooms, fixed broken sinks and toilets, and built shelves to hold his library of books on food, opera, and old cars. He was a man's man with a sensitive caring side, never one to anger. Even when René had skipped school or came home too late on his first date, Jacques had not once raised his hand or voice. When all was at a low point, Jacques knew that there was a rhythm to life, an ebb and flow, and that life would renew itself clean with the next tide.

Already René was probably imagining what he'd have to do to make his mother happy without his father. But it wasn't up to him, Emma had reminded him. He couldn't fill his large shoes or heal the ache that would be left behind in his own heart, much less in his mother's. Emma felt the dingy walls of the waiting room closing in on her at odd angles like something out of *Alice in Wonderland* and decided she needed some air. She touched René's arm and gestured at the door to see if he wanted to go with her.

They stood outside the automatic doors, gazing at the avenue of plane trees and rows of purple hyacinths leading to the benches in the park beyond the parking lot. A beautiful late spring day that should have been filled with fun, not fear and death. René pulled a pack of *Gauloises* from his pocket, but after two quick drags, he tossed it to the ground and stamped out the ash with the sole of his leather work boots.

The bright sun beat down on their faces, blinding their eyes and washing away the cloudy, grey atmosphere of the hospital. In the park across the street, Emma watched a young woman with long brown hair kissing her boyfriend. A child in a red baseball cap ran after a little black dog chasing a ball. They were all so carefree, enjoying the day and each other. An ordinary day, or it should have been. She could feel René's anxiety about what else might happen today. He looked at his watch, and she knew he was thinking there must be some news by now. They headed back inside.

As they entered the long hospital corridor, a nurse said, "Your father is in recovery and you'll be able to see him shortly." Before René could ask about his condition, she had vanished into the background of white halls, white doors, and white curtains.

About thirty minutes later, René, Margarite, and Emma rode the elevator to the fourth floor to a private room. Emma noticed René's hands tense as he opened the door to the grey interior, where the silhouette of his father lay still under the white sheets. Margarite followed cautiously behind her son, her fleshy hand locked into René's palm. They approached Jacques cautiously, like children visiting the hospital for the first time. René had told Emma he hadn't been in a hospital since he was a boy visiting his mother the day his sister was born. She wondered if Jacques' room had the same feeling of isolation that he'd described he had felt on seeing his mother asleep alone in the hospital bed. Did it have same medicinal, sanitized aromas of bleach and urine that to this day made him nauseous at the smell of any disinfectant? She watched him and understood why he hated being here again. Her own throat tightened.

She glared at the medical paraphernalia sustaining his father, echoing his pulse and the blood rushing through his body. A steady rhythm of breaths and heartbeats was interrupted by the occasional musical pings of the machines. René sat on the bed next to his sleeping father and began talking to him, describing his morning at the vineyard. He told him how he'd been inspecting the vines and how the grapes would be excellent this year. He held Jacques' hand in his, leaned close to him, and whispered, "I love you Papi. You are my hero. You are strong. You are going to be fine." René wasn't ready to let go of the boyhood he had shared with his father, a father he adored.

Margarite patted her forehead with a white handkerchief and then held Jacques' hand. Her lips moved rapidly, spewing soft prayers around Jacques' head. She was calmer now but still visibly shaken by the ordeal.

Emma studied the tubes and monitors hooked up to Jacques and tried to decipher the secret code of the numbers blinking and beeping at her. How could it have been different or better? Emma had saved Jacques' life. She was so grateful she knew what to do. He was like a father to her. She loved them like family. That was it, really. She loved them all.

She moved to the opposite side of the bed. Jacques seemed to have more color and was breathing regularly. She felt her stomach relax, but when she glanced at René, she could tell he had no idea when his father might return home. She thought about how the time with her own father had been cut short, and that as an adult, she hadn't had a chance to know her father's dreams. All she knew was that he wasn't there for her high-school graduation, college prom, or wedding. No one had been able to fill that void, a loss she had been able to share with only one person, the one person who wasn't here and hadn't been in years, the one person also lost to her.

Emma saw the fear in René's eyes, a fear she understood all too well. She knew by his weak, barely there smile that he wasn't confident Jacques would return to his robust and jovial self—the man who had guided him through adolescence and into manhood. His worry made him appear younger than his years, and although it didn't register in words, she somehow sensed in that split second that the fit wasn't quite right between her and René and never would be. It had been the idea of being in love with him that had touched her heart. Maybe she had felt that way about Rick as well. Maybe she had projected on them both only the idea of what romantic love should be. Even after almost a year and a half with René, it was all too new, fresh, and unknown. She needed someone who knew her entirely—her history, her family, her passion, her longings, her dreams. It was just too hard to start over with a blank canvas, and she didn't have the energy or time for it. Disappointment flooded over her, but she was also relieved by the truth. He was dear, lovely, but a friend, only a friend.

When René glanced at Emma, her thoughts came crashing down. Could he read her mind? She wondered and then smiled sadly, realizing that he didn't know who she really was. How could he? She was still evolving and growing, searching for that happy, energetic girl who would conquer the world, write a novel, paint a masterpiece, or raise horses in Arizona. She knew she had unrealistic expectations, but she still wanted that romantic, younger version of herself to reappear. She wanted that other self to make everything all right and let her know she hadn't wasted most of her life. The thoughts tumbled through her mind as she watched Jacques's monitors record every breath he took.

IN THE LAST twenty-four hours, everything had changed. Emma had been awakened early by Margarite's screaming and crying hysterically over the phone. Emma ran to Margarite's and found Jacques in bed, blue and unconscious and Margarite out of control, waving her arms and screaming. René had been out in the field since 5:00 a.m. "Urgence! Call mobile d'urgence," Emma had yelled as she ran to the kitchen, found a sharp knife, bleach, and a straw, and rushed to Jacques' side. She checked his pulse. Not good. She felt his throat; it seemed compressed. Remain calm, she ordered herself. She hadn't done this since college when she had worked as a certified EMT part-time, but she knew it should be like riding a bike and she could do it. She wiped the knife with bleach, took a deep breath, placed her hand on his Adam's apple, and then moved her fingers down his neck until she felt the bulge near the membrane. She made the half-inch horizontal incision there, keeping her hands steady and placing a finger inside the slit to open it, then inserting the straw and breathing two quick breaths. She paused, then gave a breath every five seconds until Jacques regained consciousness and was breathing on his own. Minutes later, René ran into the house.

"We've called an ambulance." Emma looked into his worried eyes, knowing it pained him to see his father in such a state. "I had to do a trach in the meantime." Adrenaline rushed through her body as she held out her shaking hands to René.

"Are you okay?" he asked. She knew he couldn't believe his eyes. His father lay flat on his back with a straw sticking out of his throat. His color wasn't good. Panic flashed through her as René walked over to the bed, put his arm around his mother, who was standing, praying through her tears, and told them both, "He's going to be fine." From outside came the piercing sounds of the siren, and within minutes, the blue flashing lights were beneath the window. Seconds later, the doctors on the mobile intensive care unit were taking Jacques out of the house on a stretcher and placing him in the ambulance.

IN THE HOSPITAL, Margarite sat next to Jacques and kept whispering "I love you." Emma couldn't believe that one day had held so much change, going from routine to tenuous in a matter of hours. René had told her that both his parents had always been in relatively good health, but now that hung in the balance. She made a prayerful wish that Jacques would recover so that all could continue to live each day with gentle good mornings, hello's, and I love you's. She thought back to the family's black and white photos of the wedding chapel, the beautiful bride, and the handsome groom with the dark wavy hair and wide smile whose large gentle hands Margarite now grasped.

Later, Emma watched Margarite run her hands nervously over each rosary bead. Perhaps she was picturing Jacques in the kitchen singing something from *Tosca* or "La Marseillaise" with the clear operatic tones of an amateur baritone. Emma knew how happy they were and how Jacques had taught Margarite about every cut of meat and how to bring out its tenderness and best flavor. She imagined that perhaps it was Jacques' own tenderness Margarite was thinking about now, her husband of thirty years.

By late afternoon, the beeping of the monitors was the only sound coming from Jacques' room.

20

Katie

EMMA SET ABOUT STRAIGHTENING up the guest room for Katie's arrival. She couldn't believe that her sister would be here in another week.

The morning light washed through the sheer floor-to-ceiling curtains, illuminating the pale blue room. Emma dusted off the prints of Monet's waterlilies and Chartres Cathedral. Waterlilies. Giverny. She would make sure that Katie got to see their breathtakingly beauty firsthand.

She studied the watercolor near the door. A charming rendition of Margarite's patisserie. Not bad for an amateur. Emma was proud of the little painting, one of her first efforts at painting things she loved in the village.

She was proud of this room, how she'd decorated it with various objects d'art and antiques. The white-washed wrought iron bed, an obvious flea market find, topped with her mother's vintage wedding ring quilt, showed off reminders of Evergreen. The quilt was passed on to Emma when she got married, although Katie wanted it for herself. Emma was sure Katie must have fantasized what it would be like to have been born first, have first dibs on everything, known her father longer, and have been able to speak three languages.

Emma reached high into the corners of the room, searching for any elusive cobwebs. She swirled her tall feather duster around the small crystal chandelier in the center of the ceiling. She'd found this sparkling gem in a shop in L'isle sur la Sorgue on one of her first trips to Provence and had kept it in her Paris apartment, hoping to put it in a special place. It fit perfectly in this space, and it was just the touch of glam the room required.

Emma stepped away from the bed and let the glass rings of the curtains glide across the metal rod until she could push open the tall windows and air out the room. She shook out the cotton rag rug over the balcony and soaked in the tranquility of the lavender, the blue and green rock massif, the yellow and purple patches of earth. It wasn't Paris or New York. It was more like home. She folded the rug and carried it back inside, placing it neatly on the floor at the left side of the bed.

She looked around the room and knew it was a woman's room—feminine and eclectic—so unlike her sleek, contemporary Paris apartment. Eclectic, thought Emma, like her. She could pair odd pieces and make them look like they belonged. She was beginning to feel like she could fit in here, was fitting in here.

Emma loved and missed Katie for certain. Granted, she had invited her to come anytime, but was she really ready for everything that came with it—marathon exercise routines, high-maintenance face and hair that came with three makeup kits, hot irons, infusers, and dryers? And the flirting. Could she live with Katie's body gyrating toward René, Jacques, and others? Maybe she was remembering too much of her own pet peeves.

She hoped Katie would be comfortable in the house and the village. Emma did have a tendency to adapt more quickly to her surroundings, sometimes a little too much, so that locals presumed she knew more than she did, was more fluent in French, and understood their customs and traditions. They were sisters but very different. Emma remembered how as a kid, Katie often slept until noon, but made up for lost time by playing into the wee hours of the morning under the covers or under the bed. One time Emma found her at 2:00 a.m. with her flashlight shining under the bed. She was hiding and reading about sex and giggling away. She was twelve. She wondered how Katie would handle the local rooster alarm at dawn.

Emma had to laugh at herself for conjuring up these old images of the young Katie. After all, she was a grown woman now with a career. She thought about her sweeter side and willingness to help her big sister. Emma knew Katie had always looked up to her and relied on her for advice and example, but her little sister had been there for her whether it was a loss of a pony club ribbon, an injury or fall from the horse, or the loss of a boyfriend. She was there for her little sister too, helping her find her first job, helping her with her Spanish, and teaching her how to take her first ribbon in stadium jumping. They were very different but had family in common. Their love of horses, their parents, and Evergreen were ties that could not be erased.

Emma was the perpetual early bird, up as soon as the sun peaked above the earth. She had hit the morning chores running, taking notes in her head about the hen that laid the speckled egg, how sunlight changed the colors of the barn doors, and rushing to finish so she could jot down all the wonderful things she had seen. They both had curiosity about everything and loved the farm.

Emma had been shy and quiet, read Spanish and French poetry, and always had a sketch pad with her. She had had plenty of suitors like Katie, and although some of them were mercy dates and some became lifelong friends, for most of them, she couldn't remember their names. Old letters and photographs no longer brought their faces into focus. None seemed right until she met Trevor. He was fun-loving and sexy. Initially, she had felt safe with him, could be herself, and not have to worry about getting hurt. A judgment she later regretted.

Emma straightened the clothes in the closet, taking a handful of things she hadn't worn and placing them in a box for giveaways. She paused for a moment to watch the sun begin its slow descent. She wished Trevor were here right this very moment with his arms around her, holding her.

And what about René? Emma hadn't said much about him to her sister other than she was seeing someone. Turns out, she saw René more frequently in Paris than in Provence, but she occasionally had dinner with his sister when she was home and always bought pastries and chocolate from Margarite when shopping in the village. At the moment, though, she stayed in close contact with both René and Margarite while Jacques continued to recover.

Katie's radar would likely hone in on René, but she hadn't thought about René's reaction to her younger sister—her opposite, with strawberry hair, green eyes, a tall and slender build, and the ability to balance on four-inch stilettos. She's someone who doesn't overthink things and is rarely disappointed. Katie goes with the flow. Unlike Emma who, with her curves, dark brown hair, and crystal blue eyes, never wears very high heels but has high expectations and could overanalyze almost anything, including love. Maybe she should warn him. Or not. She laughed.

Emma thought her sister was beautiful; even the cheapest pair of jeans looked great on her. She could spend hours getting ready for each outing. Her nails were always beautifully manicured, and pedicures were the norm. For Emma, only expensive clothes fit her well, and she had never spent more than fifteen minutes on hair and makeup, often wearing her hair up and off her face when at the office. She had her naturally long nails done only on special occasions like the junior prom, dates with Trevor, and her wedding. She liked doing things for herself and saving her money for some little extravagance, like a unique piece of jewelry, an antique, or a trip.

Emma cleared out two drawers in the little oak dresser for her sister and created more space in the corner closet. She moved some of her clothes into her room, including the pink silk blouse and Hermes scarf Katie had sent her for a previous birthday. There weren't many fashionable shops in the village, but if Katie wanted to shop, they could go to Apt, and of course, they'd spend time in Paris.

She straightened the bed covers and moved the white wicker chair near the dresser. Emma stood back and examined the room with its uneven pale blue walls, white curtains, and accents of blue and lavender. There was a lot that reminded her of home, especially the light and the airiness of the room, but it was more of a feeling, a sense of belonging, a childhood memory of her mother. Her mother definitely would have loved this room, Emma thought. She looked out the open window. The sun was lower now and there would be another stunning sunset in the Luberon.

21

To Market

RENÉ KNOCKED ON the door. "Em, I'm here. Are you ready?"

Emma pulled off her gardening gloves and stepped near the front of the house. "Hi. I need to wash my hands and get my purse. Do you want to come in?"

René shook his head. "I'll be in the garden," he said, walking to the side of the house.

Emma hurried upstairs, washed her hands and face, changed her shirt, and grabbed her purse and keys, closing the door behind her. The early summer sky was cloud free, bright blue, with a slight breeze that cooled her skin.

She pulled her floppy hat from her purse and rounded the house, looking for him.

"You've done wonders with the flowers. I never imagined it could look so good," he said, pointing to the climbing roses and cosmos. "What are those big pink daisy-like things over there?"

Emma's eyes followed his long slender fingers toward a bed in the distance. "Oh, coneflowers. Very hardy, like a weed really."

He smiled.

Emma knew most everything in Provence had to be hardy to thrive in the rocky, arid soil.

She looked at his blue BMW convertible and waved her hat in the air. "I'm ready. Let's go."

≈

EMMA WOULD PICK up Katie in Marseille day after tomorrow, but today she had invited René to go with her to Apt to fill the larder.

On the twenty-minute drive to the market, she told him what to expect with Katie—her outspokenness, spontaneity, larger-than-life laugh, her dislikes and likes, and her overall beauty. She explained Katie was in the fashion business, a buyer for Ralph Lauren, but she could have been a model with her tall, slender build.

She looked at René. "She's about four inches taller than I am—five-ten in her bare feet."

René said nothing, focusing on the road.

"Another difference," she continued, "is she's fair with red hair and green eyes. Who'd even know we're related?" Emma glanced at René, waiting for a response. René didn't notice.

"Unlike me, Katie skated through college getting average grades, except for A's in fashion design and photography. She was a cheerleader, top volleyball player, and the popular girl who dated the jocks." Emma realized, though, that Katie had grown since then and understood what early morning and work really meant. She thought about Katie and how she would love the local Saturday flea markets here. A bona fide junkyard junkie, Katie had reveled in the old attic treasures of their parents and grandparents—items that later had become the décor for her New York apartment. Katie used to say when visiting old haunts, if you think to look under the bed, you might find a memento of someone's past. But all they ever found were dust bunnies and stored Christmas papers and ribbons. It would be fun seeing her sister and helping her enjoy village life. Emma also knew she could use some of Katie's "free spirit" attitude.

René laughed. "Emma, I'm sure I'll like her; she's your sister. I'll make her feel at home. Not to worry."

Emma paused. She wanted her sister to feel welcome, of course. René and Katie were closer in age too. She looked at him. They would look good together.

"Good," she said.

Emma watched the afternoon sun glisten on his arms. Strong, warm, and young, she tried not to stare. Would Katie see what she did? His love of family, the land, horses and everything they had in common.

"It's busy today," René said searching for a place to park.

The streets were filled with shoppers hovering over the myriad vendors' tables, some shaded by colored canopies, crammed in the center of the city, all giving way to winding narrow alleyways and squares leading to endless shops.

"It's unbelievable."

He smiled. "You know, people have been coming here since the Middle Ages. It's a food lovers' paradise."

Emma nodded. "I understand why." The streets were a kaleidoscope of colors and shapes that permeated the vast array of sundries and food. Fruits, vegetables, fish, meat, cheese, clothing, fabrics, tablecloths, flowers, herbs, perfumes, and soaps were piled on tables of hundreds of stalls, tempting shoppers and passers-by. Her senses drank in all the colors and smells of Provence. "I do so love this." It's a painting with many stories, she thought, trying to memorize the details.

René took her arm. "This way," he said, moving closer to the, strawberries, eggplant, and other vegetables and fruits.

She welcomed his hand on her arm. Emma wanted to touch and smell everything she saw. She grasped packages of herbes de Provence and placed them under her nose, enjoying the bouquet of savory, thyme, rosemary, basil, fennel, and marjoram—the essence of Provençal cooking. Her hands wandered to the cooking lavender, which she held up for René to see. He nodded, taking both and paying the rotund woman under the stall's canopy.

"This is making me hungry," she said, realizing she hadn't had any breakfast, not even coffee.

"We'll have lunch in a bit. The market closes at 12:30, so let's get what we need." He handed her some dried figs. "These should hold you for a while."

"Thanks." Emma popped a large fig into her mouth. "Mmm," she sighed and then began fingering the garlic in front of her. She looked at him hard when his back was to her, watching him select produce and fish with the precision and confidence of a master chef.

Afterward, he placed the groceries in the car. Bags of artichokes, tomatoes, asparagus, French ham, salmon, shrimp, and brie, banon, and gruyere cheeses crowded the small cooler in the trunk. She glanced at the couples and children around the vendors' stalls and in the streets, wondering how she and René looked to them. Did they think they were husband and wife filling their car with groceries for the weekend? Were they lovers? Were they too different to be siblings? Did they look happy?

"Still want lunch?" he asked her, locking the car.

She nodded.

"Come on then. We'll go to the café near the cathedral, and when we're finished, we can get the flowers you wanted."

They scurried along the crowded street around St. Anne's. Cafés and restaurants surrounded the square, and rows of buckets of every flower imaginable were lined up like soldiers at attention in front of the church.

"They're always so fantastic," she said, pointing to the tall sunflowers with blooms as large as dinner plates. Then she spotted the purple-blue artichoke blossoms. "These are my favorites." Emma realized then and there that she should come back on her own to do some sketches and take some notes and photographs she could use for future paintings and stories. "It's perfect."

René laughed. "It's a crowded market."

"It's very special. You're lucky to have it." Emma had a tendency to romanticize, but she wondered if there were things only she could envision, like the stories and art surrounding her in the moment in this market. Trevor understood her tendencies all too well, often saying she had a way of seeing things finished, or complete, that others couldn't always grasp, but that he understood. She had taken that for granted too. It had been the natural connection between the two of them, the way things were.

"Why artichoke flowers?" René asked. "You know the flowers are the sex organ of the plant, and we eat the immature flower bud—the heart."

"Look at them," Emma said, so beautiful, unique, and proud."

René shrugged his shoulders. "If you say so, but I do love to eat the hearts."

He motioned toward the café. "First, let's sit and eat." He pulled out the wobbly white iron chair from behind a small round table and helped her scoot in.

AFTER LUNCH, THEY each carried two large bouquets of sunflowers and artichoke blooms to the car. As they drove back to the village, random thoughts shot across her brain. He was Katie's age, well dressed, rode horses, loved the land, and was tall, dark, and handsome. What's not to like?

She wondered how they might get along. She cared for René but realized she didn't feel the same as he did, and the age difference still bothered her. Maybe they were friends with benefits. Or not. She thought again, they were friends.

She cradled René's bag of champagne snugly in her lap. Shouldn't she be feeling guilty about thinking of him in this way? She looked at him out of the corner of her eye, inhaling his scent, sweat, and the subtle hint of his cologne. Lemons. It reminded her of lemons. What was it her father used to wear to church on Sunday? It too smelled like citrus, lime maybe? Her father's No. 74 Victorian Lime.

Emma knew it was easy to confuse lust for love. She had done it more than once. Usually, she took her time falling in love and even longer getting over the serious ones. Maybe she needed to give it more time to develop an emotional connection or attachment.

Of course, she had known she loved Trevor within three months. This wasn't the same. Not at all. It was better than Rick, though, whom she married hoping to learn to love him. She believed she had grown a little wiser with age. She wanted a grown-up relationship, a partnership with someone who would love her no matter what; someone she could trust and love without reservation.

At the moment of this admission, Emma was jolted into the present by bleating horns and René swerving the car around the corner. She swayed into him. An exploding cork bounced off the dashboard like a start from a shotgun and struck her in the ear. Foamy champagne hit the windshield and a mist of bubbles and green glass splattered across the passenger seat and down the side of Emma's face.

"*Mierde! Imbecile!*" René pulled off the road.

"Ow." Emma moaned.

"Are you okay?"

"I think so." Her heart raced just as it had when she was eight and her pony Lucky had run away with her across the big field at Evergreen. She screamed and screamed for him to stop, and when he did, she flew over his head, landing face down in the grass. She had a broken nose. Her mother had come running to her rescue and taken her to the doctor.

René looked at her. She was shaking. He put his hand on her arm, leaning toward her. "Let me look at your face—there's glass. You may need stitches . . ." He pulled a couple of small glass shards from her cheek.

The warmth of his hand made her feel safe, but there was no way she was going to the hospital. She paused. "Let me see," she said, reaching for and turning the rearview mirror to check her face. She saw the blood first, then the line near her cheek. She touched it with her finger. "Do you have a tissue or towel?"

René reached in between the seats, pulled out a box of Kleenex, and held it for her as she gently dabbed her cheekbone. "Are you sure you're okay?" His eyes searched her face for cuts.

Emma looked closely at her face. She winced at the thought of stitches, but what bothered her more were the fine lines around her eyes and mouth. Did she look older than her age? She felt too young for age lines. Would she really be forty-one this month? Oh my god, she would be going downhill into middle age. A sense of panic ran through her. As she backed away from the mirror, she feared time really was against her. Maybe she had become desperate for love. She pressed her hand against the cut to stop the bleeding.

"I'm fine. It's nothing."

"Let me get the ice for you." René got out and looked through their packages in the back, grabbing at the bag of fish surrounded by packs of ice provided by the man at the market. "Here, put this on your cheek. It may be a little fishy, but we don't want any swelling."

Swelling. Oh crap. "What about the champagne? Do we need to get more?"

"Everything will be fine. Not to worry." René smiled.

"I guess no good deed goes unpunished," she quipped. "I've never been attacked by a bottle before."

"And a very expensive one at that," René added.

Emma smiled.

22

Emma's Birthday

WHEN EMMA WALKED into the house at 9:30 a.m., she heard the shower running and knew Katie was awake. She should never have worried about her sister being awakened by the morning rooster. Katie could sleep through anything. She'd been here for almost three weeks and had settled in nicely to a casual routine of sightseeing and shopping in and around the village. Emma tossed her mesh bag full of fresh bread and boxes of raspberry-filled macaroons on the kitchen counter.

She was looking forward to a quiet, simple birthday dinner with a few friends. It had been a long time since she'd actually celebrated her birthday. She couldn't believe she was almost forty-one. Where had her childhood gone? College, marriage, divorce . . . over. It was all too sudden and abrupt to think that she'd next be sliding down the other side of that middle-aged hump into an abyss of "maturity," another word for old age. She forced her mind to stop.

She needed to enjoy the moment. René was a terrific cook, and he'd surprise her with something wonderful; she knew it. And she was happy Katie was here to celebrate with her.

She boiled more water for the French press to make coffee for her and Katie. Emma thought they'd spend some time in Bonnieux getting some additional things for this evening. René had the wine covered, of course, but she wanted some goat cheese, Cavaillon melon, and skinny ficelle baguettes. She wanted Katie to see this lovely village surrounded by orchards and vineyards.

Emma had a special place in her heart for the 12th century church at the top of the village and the nearby cluster of Cedars of Lebanon, where she had picnicked with Trevor years ago. With an elevation of almost fourteen-hundred feet, you could see for miles across the valley floor to Lacoste and the Marquis de Sade's castle, and beyond. It was the only village she knew that had a bread museum where you could learn about artisanal bread making.

On the drive to Bonnieux, Katie prodded Emma with more questions about René, how they met, his age, did she love him, did he know about Trevor? Emma patiently filled Katie in on most things, but she understood that what Katie really wanted to know was if René was in love with Emma.

"I think you should ask René how he feels," Emma said. "I'm not sure what our relationship is at this point." She changed the subject and directed Katie's eyes to the landscape. "See that? That's Pont Julien built on the Roman road that connected Italy to the Roman territories in France." Emma drove near the old bridge. "Want to have a look?"

Katie studied the stone arch bridge. "Wow, that's amazing. It's how old?"

"Dates to three B.C., I think."

They stood on the bridge over the Calavon river and had a tourist take their photo. "There, we're bridging the past to the present." Emma grinned.

As they continued on to Bonnieux, Katie said, "Speaking of bridging gaps, have you thought about the age difference?"

Emma laughed. "Of course. But men do this all the time, so why can't women?"

"I know." Katie looked at her sister. "But how do you feel about it? This is about you."

Katie knew her well. Emma pointed to the castle on the hill. "Over there, that's the Lacoste castle of the marquis, now an historic monument."

"It's certainly high up. Lovely."

"It is what it is—the age, I mean. Let's not talk about it anymore. You can interrogate René tonight." Emma smiled.

"I barely know him. Besides, I'm only thinking of you."

Right, Emma thought.

THE NARROW, HILLY streets of Bonnieux were swarming with shoppers as Emma pulled onto the shoulder of the road overlooking the valley and the new church below. They hopped out of the car and headed for the market and shops.

Emma began her mini travelogue, entertaining Katie: "Bonnieux is one of the many historic 'hill villages' in the region, dating back to Roman times. And the cedar forest I mentioned began with trees imported from North Africa during the Napoleonic era."

"This is lovely," Katie said.

Emma directed her sister to the market and then took her on a tour of the streets and shops.

"Come on. I want to show you something," Emma said and began walking up the main street.

Katie looked at her as they negotiated the narrow cobblestone paths that kept going up and up. "Are you sure you know where you're going?"

"It's not much farther." They walked through the last stone archway near the very top and end of the road and then out into a small clearing and park-like setting shaded by huge Cedars of Lebanon. Emma stopped. "I want you to look at this view. You can see all the valley from here. The old church is over there. I'll take you there, and the new one is down below. You can almost see my village from here." *My* village, she had said. Indeed, it was hers now.

Katie, slightly out of breath, slowly turned in a circle, taking in every corner of the vista. "It's so beautiful . . . and quiet. Just like home."

Emma smiled. "I come here to think sometimes. It's naturally peaceful." She had been with Trevor the very first time she was here. "It's the perfect place for a picnic," she added, remembering how young they were back then.

"Let's sit for a while," Katie said, "I need to catch my breath after that steep trek." She noticed Emma's pensive expression. "You love it here, don't you?"

Emma nodded and sat down on the small stone bench. It was a long time ago, she thought.

SEVERAL HOURS LATER, Emma leaned forward to blow out the candles of her cake—three candles, one for each supposed decade— how appropriate, her real age unrevealed, most likely thanks to Katie.

She really wasn't that old and certainly not alone. She had her friends and Katie. Still, the one thing missing crept into her head. She remembered a very special birthday—twenty-nine—at the 1789 with a handful of friends and Trevor. She had worried then about approaching thirty. Really? Now, more than ten years later, another year dissolved into whirling smoke from the candles as friendly applause rang in her ears. She had blown away the past—decades vaporized, gone. But this was a memorable birthday, unlike some others, including last year, when she had deliberately consumed herself with work hoping to avoid the inevitable. Aging gracefully was something she might be able to do.

Katie's enthusiasm interrupted her thoughts. "Happy Birthday, Em. This is a great party. I didn't realize you had so many friends here."

Emma hugged her sister. "Thank you for helping make it happen."

"It was René. His idea. He did everything."

"Well, it's perfect. Thank you both."

"You're welcome. Speaking of perfect, your fiancé is very close to the mark."

Emma looked at Katie, knowing, realizing she'd finally expressed her interest. The seam of her lips formed a firm straight line. Emma waited before answering. "He's not my fiancé, but you're right. He's special." But he's not Trevor, she thought.

René walked over, put his arms around Emma's waist, squeezed her tightly, and planted a wet kiss on her surprised lips.

Emma closed her eyes, enjoying the moment. She heard her mother's voice in her head. "You have to follow the rules; there are rules." But Emma knew that whatever the rules were, no one would fault her in this situation with René. She felt his sensuous energy in her and knew this kiss meant more than Happy Birthday. He wanted her, and she enjoyed sex with him. When she finally could breathe, it was Katie who looked amazed, disappointed.

Emma understood all too well what her sister was thinking. He was more her type, her age. Emma realized, though, that Katie wasn't getting any younger and had broken engagements behind her. Maybe Katie was feeling pressure to find that right someone. She wasn't as tenuous about love or relationships as Emma, but she hadn't found the right man either. Between the two of them, they simply didn't pick the right men. She couldn't hold it against Katie if René appealed to her. He was, after all, a great catch.

It had been a long time since Emma had had the sole attention of one man, and she rather liked not having to explain or apologize. What do you say after a kiss like that? "Merci" didn't seem quite right and "plus encore" would have been inappropriate for now. The corners of Emma's mouth curved into a satisfied smile.

"Thank you . . . for the party, I mean. It was very thoughtful of you. Everything is perfect."

"My pleasure," he said. "I wanted to do it."

Emma pushed the knife through the multi-layered chocolate, dividing it equally. She handed him a piece of cake and watched him walk across the room to get another glass of wine. Inside, Emma sang "Happy Birthday to Me, Happy Birthday to Me . . ."

She looked intently at his physique—the perfect inverted triangle—wide shoulders, narrow hips, great ass. He moved with an air of confidence and sexiness; no swagger.

But the best thing about him was that he was a wonderful friend—kind, sincere, and understanding. The fact that he had money didn't hurt, but it wasn't a factor for Emma. René had been there for her, patiently waiting for the ghost of Trevor to disappear, trying to help her forget him. Emma knew that only she could do that. For some reason, she couldn't let go of Trevor and how he had made her feel. How he still made her feel.

As the music boomed in the background, Emma felt the room revolving around her, the mild evening air carrying the aroma of baked ham and seafood. Lobster canapés dotted small tables around the living room and dining room, enough food for fifty people. René had magically surprised her with this lovely party of family and friends. She turned and saw him talking with Katie and watched as her sister laughed and flirtatiously touched his arm. She understood what Katie was doing and wasn't angry about it. She remembered feeling the same way once. She knew her sister well—her ways, her boyfriends. Emma was not that surprised. She herself had admitted they looked good together. The song, "What I Did for Love," played in her head. She had done many things for many "loves," but they never turned out right. Maybe this time would be different. After all, she loved them both.

The cacophony of English and French voices flooded over her. The smell of pipe tobacco and *Gauloises* cigarettes forced her out onto the balcony. The sun had shifted slightly to the west, dipping behind the mountains. She looked up, searching for the first signs of the evening star and remembering what she used to do when she wished for something. She would close her eyes and see her wish coming to life in her mind. She'd done the same thing many times when she was nineteen and had wanted Trevor to call. She'd send him her wish telepathically, she thought. It usually worked. He would call her sometimes while she was still in the middle of her wish.

She took a deep breath, trying to inhale all of Provence into her. She loved it here, this place, this view. She was at home in the moment but wondered if she would be celebrating her fiftieth, sixtieth, or other birthdays here. She was uncomfortable thinking about a future she couldn't predict and probably couldn't change. Emma knew it was really her heart she longed for. She missed the passion of her heart. Could she find it again? She closed her eyes and made a wish.

23

Trevor — A Near Miss

IT WAS A BEAUTIFUL, clear afternoon when the horizon began to rock at odd angles and gasps surrounded him. On approach to the Miami airport, the small jet's engine sputtered and died. The plane pitched hard. His heart raced, and he wondered if he died now, would he be remembered and how? His name wouldn't appear on any war memorial, only on a stone slab in the Brooklyn Heights cemetery next to his family; a cold damp place with a one-word message on his tombstone; probably—DIED June 15, 1993.

He thought about Emma and how he had asked her once what she needed. Without hesitation, she told him, "You." He had been amazed at how certain she was. The answer was too simple and straightforward. Surely, she wanted more.

He'd thought she was too much of a romantic, unrealistic about relationships. Often, he had felt as if they were acting out roles in one of those romantic novels—those quickie paperback reads you take on trips to pass the time—maybe because he hadn't been sure what he wanted. Yes, he had found Emma exciting, but it had been too scary to make a lifetime commitment to one person. At the time, maybe he hadn't comprehended his own feelings. Had he feared the depths of his own passion, that helpless, out-of-control feeling that can't be contained, that aching want that's always there?

Was that love?

Sweat permeated his clothing as he reached for the oxygen mask, unsure he could inhale. Engine oil and puke hit his nostrils. He couldn't swallow. His body trembled with the feeling of a free fall.

He heard the man next to him praying aloud and saw his knuckles turning white as he grasped the seat in front of him. Why had it been easy for him to let go of so many things that were really important to him or could have been? He thought about this now as the plane sank closer to earth, wondering if he had ever really made the important, right choices when he needed to. Were men supposed to be this introspective? Emma had made him introspective, sometimes painfully so, without even knowing it. He had deliberately not made her any promises—to be faithful and marry her—afraid he couldn't keep them because he wasn't good enough. What a fool!

These things catapulted through his mind as the plane fell and bounced. When he gripped the armrests, he felt an odd inner peace. If it's my time, I'm ready, he thought . . . until Emma and unfinished goodbyes jarred him back to the edge of fear. The sensation of sinking, falling, and going down pushed against his chest and his brain.

As if someone had wrenched the guts from this metal bird, a loud roar exploded throughout the cabin as the landing gear unlocked, and the captain's voice snapped and popped over the loud speaker, "We're gliding in; our wheels are down. Hang on, folks." Knowing that he might only have a nanosecond, Trevor's body shook as he bent forward, grabbing his ankles and putting his head on his knees. *God, Em. What have we done? I'm sorry. I love you,* he whispered. No matter who or when, it had always been Emma and always would be, until the last breath was sucked out of him. He shut his eyes tight, searching for her face and her smile one last time.

THE NEXT DAY WHEN he woke up safe in his own bed, Trevor was still reeling from the jet experience, and weeks later, his stomach got queasy at the memory. He had begun to reevaluate the everyday motions of his life.

Did it matter that he had more money than he could spend, a house in the Hamptons, and an apartment in Paris? Were these important? Wasn't living what mattered, not owning or having, but doing and loving? He couldn't change the fact that his hair was going grey or his brow was lined with furrows, but he didn't want to awake someday haunted by a single miscommunication, missed opportunity, or choice that had changed everything for a lifetime. Regret came rushing toward him like a rock dropping from the sky.

24

Changing Course

THE OYSTER BAR AT Grand Central was one of Trevor's favorite places. He and his friend Louie often stopped there for lunch or after-work cocktails. Louie was a tall, blonde, handsome ad executive with a sexy smile who exuded charm and class without trying. He, Trevor, and Emma had spent more than one weekend together at boat shows, tennis matches, and the theater in New York early on when Trevor and Emma were dating. Louie had been married before Trevor ever thought about commitment, but like Trevor, had lost his young wife to cancer.

Tonight was a good night for oysters and beer. Light rain had been dousing Manhattan for the last couple of days. The city felt dreary. Trevor needed a break and wanted to be comforted by food and conversation. Oysters usually did that. They took him immediately to the shore and sun.

They sat in their customary seats at the long bar in the cavernous restaurant with its moody, terra cotta tile ceiling. The din of the crowd made it almost impossible to have a normal conversation.

"I'm living the wrong life," Trevor said. "I don't even know how I got here."

Louie smiled. "Wrong life? Look at everything you've achieved. You're successful, rich, and—"

"It's not about work. It's about living, really living." Trevor paused. "And it's about love."

"Love?" Louie asked. "You've been in love more times than I can count."

Trevor lowered his eyes and ran his hands over the cold marble of the bar. "I don't mean sex. It's about that love you find only once in a lifetime."

Confusion crawled across Louie's face. "You had that with Marianne, didn't you?"

Trevor thought about his wife—petite, muscular, and mercurial. He swallowed hard, forcing the raw oyster down his closed throat. "It wasn't the same kind of love. . ."

Louie's eyes widened, waiting for Trevor to say more. Nothing. But Trevor didn't have to say anything. "Emma?" Louie said. Her name tumbled through the air and landed awkwardly between them. Wasn't this the same Emma they both had sat waiting for in this very bar the year after Trevor graduated from Georgetown, the same Emma who had missed her train and arrived three hours later than scheduled? At the time, Louie wasn't even sure he liked her or thought Trevor should.

"Yeah, Emma."

Trevor reached for the hot sauce, but before he could speak, Louie said quietly, "Sometimes things don't add up . . . no matter how you count."

Trevor stared blankly at his friend. "If you mean things don't always work out, I'm the prime example where love is concerned."

"No," Louie said. "You're like everyone who has loved and lost but you try to fix it." Louie hesitated. "Maybe you need to let go."

Trevor looked into his beer, deep in thought. Let go? He took a deep breath. How could he let go of something he wanted so much? There is no lost love, he thought, until you lose the love you feel for your lover. As long as you remember that love, it never dies. He had read that somewhere. Let go? He didn't think he could.

The words of the woman next to them drifted into their conversation. "We want what we can't have," she said.

"She's right, you know." Louie motioned to the bartender. "Two more beers."

"And one very dry martini," Trevor said.

Louie frowned. "Just the beers," he told the bartender. "Trevor, no hard stuff, remember? It's not good for you . . . your heart."

"Do you know what *is* good for my heart?" Trevor glanced at Louie, not expecting an answer. He didn't know himself, so how could anyone else? "She's only partially right." Trevor gestured to the woman sitting at the table next to them. "We want what we can't have and can't have what we want."

"Wow, you really are depressed. And I thought oysters were supposed to stimulate your gonads, your sex drive . . . something." Louie laughed.

"Well, it must be true. I'm downing a couple of dozen and can't stop thinking of her."

Louie casually removed his wallet from his coat pocket and laid it on the bar. "How long have you felt this way?"

Trevor took a gulp of his beer, hesitated, then said, "Since the day I met her."

Louie's jaw hung open at hearing Trevor say these words after so many years. "I thought it was a college infatuation, a fling. God, Trev, you've been carrying a torch all this time?"

"That's about it."

"Why didn't you marry her, for Christ's sake?"

"I wanted to, but the timing never seemed right."

"I don't even know what that means." Louie stared at Trevor. "Is it ever right?"

Trevor didn't answer.

"Oh shit!" Louie checked his wallet. "I'm short of cash."

Trevor looked at him. "I'm spilling my guts, and you're counting your money?"

"Sorry." Louie fumbled through his wallet. "I can't believe you've felt this way all this time. You've never mentioned it. Why?"

"Why? Because I didn't want to admit I'd made such a huge mistake."

"This is about your near miss on that plane, isn't it?"

"Partly. When that plane was going down, do you know who I thought of? Emma. Doesn't that tell you something?"

"Maybe." Louie paused. "Maybe that you have unfinished business with Emma, not that—"

"I don't want to die without seeing her again."

"Huh? What are you going to do?"

Trevor shrugged. "Go to France and find her."

"France? She's in France?" Louie didn't wait for Trevor to respond. "Look, isn't it kind of late for that?"

Trevor fidgeted with his glass. "It's timing, not time, that matters."

Louie couldn't believe what he was hearing. "And you think now is good timing after what, twenty years? Come on. She's probably married."

Trevor smiled. "No, she isn't. She lives in Paris and still works for the magazine."

"God, Trev. You've been stalking her from afar?"

"I ran into someone from *Condé Nast* at a wine event. I asked about her."

"She knows you're married—were married—doesn't she?"

"Not that Marianne died, I don't think. Not about her miscarriage." Trevor's voice trailed off, thinking about the loss of his child.

Louie looked at the pain on Trevor's face. "I hate to ask this, but what makes you think she'll want you in her life now?"

"Nothing. It's about what I want. I can't fix the past, but maybe I can have a chance at the future." There was that word—chance. Trevor knew that most everything in life was accidental, by chance, even love.

"Well, I think you're crazy to pursue this." Louie handed his credit card to the bartender. "After your recent near plane crash, I don't know why or how you'd fly across the Atlantic."

"I think you do. Would you want to wake up one day knowing you missed that one fleeting opportunity to make everything right and chart a course you should have been on to begin with?"

Louie thought about Trevor's words before answering. "Probably not."

Trevor nodded. "I let her go without a fight. I was a stupid coward."

Louie turned pensive. He waited. "Aren't you being a little hard on yourself? Doesn't it take two?"

Trevor downed the rest of his beer. "Yes. And I'm half of that very equation. Besides, the greatest regret is not for things we did, but for things we chose not to do." Regret. The harshness of the word grated against his teeth. "All I know is that if you want something you've never had, then you've got to do something you've never done."

And he needed to tell her . . . everything.

25

The Hospital Visit

IT WAS ALMOST too quiet. Only the slight buzzing of a ceiling light distracted Emma as she walked down the long corridor. Not long ago, the hospital floor had been filled with frenzied nurses and doctors bustling around corners and peering in and out of the intensive care rooms.

Now, no one. Nothing but the echo of her footsteps as she followed the twists and turns of the walls, noticing for the first time they were pale blue, not the grey she remembered. Pale blue: a soft, calming spring-like color. To make everyone feel better amid sickness? Where was everyone? Emma felt uneasy. Maybe it was the time of day—after lunch—and the patients were resting comfortably. Or maybe many of them had returned home. She didn't like to think about the alternative.

Jacques was still here. It had been about two weeks, but seemed longer. He had been in intensive care for more than half of that time.

Family members still could visit only for short spurts during certain hours. Emma felt fortunate that she could visit him. René had made sure of that.

She turned the last corner and walked in the direction of the steady beep coming from his room. She rested her hand on the door frame and peeked inside. He lay perfectly still with his eyes open, resting. The ward-like room was sparse: no flowers, no TV, and no reading materials scattered about. The only personal touch was Margarite's white cotton shawl draped over a visitor's chair.

"Bonjour, Jacques." Emma moved to his beside.

He turned, looked up, and smiled faintly when he saw her. *"Asseyais-toi,"* he whispered.

Emma pulled up a chair and sat next to him. "It's good to see you."

"You just missed Margarite."

Margarite had been there two or three times a day from the beginning. Emma noticed that Jacques was thinner but had good color in his face.

Emma nodded and reached for his hand. "You're looking much better. You have some color."

The early afternoon light warmed the room with a pristine, almost spiritual, glow. Jacques was hooked up to a heart monitor and an IV drip. The air in the room was stuffy and still like someone waiting to exhale. Emma wanted to open the window, but that wasn't allowed.

Jacques spoke quietly. He wasn't one to complain about anything, but today he told Emma he wanted to go home. He felt useless. He needed to be behind the counter at the shop. The nurses were nice enough, but he didn't like being dependent. He wanted to take long walks with Margarite or sit in the garden and smell the flowers. He needed some chocolate, a croissant.

"I'm tired of this place." His voice cracked. "When can I go home?"

"Soon. You'll get your strength back. The doctor says so."

"Oh, who believes the doctor? What does he know?"

It was not like Jacques to be even a little depressed. "You're kidding, right? Thanks to the doctor you are here, alive and well."

He looked at Emma. *"Il etais toi, toi.* It was you, you. My dear Emma, you and I both know you were the one who saved my life."

Emma hesitated. "I was in the right place at the right time. Anyone would have done the same."

"You're not anyone, Emma. You're special. Like a daughter to me."

It was true there was something like a father-daughter bond between them. She had felt it from the first night she met him. She missed her own father and considered both Jacques and Margarite like second parents. She and Margarite had the pastries and garden in common. And with Jacques, it was the land. The land was as dear to Emma as it had been to her father and grandfather. She was grateful that Jacques felt the same.

Emma adjusted Jacques' pillow so he would be more comfortable and then reached for his hand.

Jacques began telling her how coming so close to death had brought him back to life. He had always enjoyed life to the fullest, but now he said he understood the value of every rain drop, blade of grass, flower, and person around him. He was determined to bring more meaning and joy to his days, his friends, and even strangers. Emma understood that these feelings were fairly common and that survivors often changed their lives for the better. She could relate. She knew about loss and the value of life. She knew how temporary life was.

Emma stared at the heart monitor and understood how delicate the heart was, how easily it could be damaged or break, but enough of this melancholy. She wanted to cheer up Jacques, so she changed the subject.

"Everyone asked about you at the party. I'm sorry you weren't there. René and Katie did a wonderful job. It was lovely."

"I heard. René told me. He also told me you have a charming sister, but . . ." Jacques began to cough. Emma reached for a glass and poured some water, then held the glass close to Jacques lips while he drank in small deliberate sips.

"Be careful," Jacques whispered, "with affairs of the heart."

Emma arched her brow, wondering what René might have said. She certainly didn't want his father worrying about them.

"Oh, Jacques," she laughed. "I'm not worried, and you shouldn't be either. Love takes care of itself one way or another." Her own self-fulfilling prophecy, she thought.

Jacques looked at her more seriously. "*Exactement.*"

Emma looked past Jacques, focusing on the doorway. How did he know or what did he know? Could he read Emma's feelings, or was it René who was sending out innuendos to his father or Katie? She squeezed his hand. "Don't worry. Just get better."

Jacques pressed his lips together in a smile. "There is something I want you to have." He proceeded to tell Emma about the stone shed behind the butcher shop. "The key is under the large rock below the window. Inside, you'll find a yellow box. Open it, and you'll understand. It's nothing extraordinary, but you will enjoy it."

Emma's eye widened as she listened to his instructions. She paused a long while, wondering about the mystery. "Jacques, that's not necessary. You don't owe me anything."

"You must accept it. It belongs to you."

His dark sincere eyes touched her heart. "Sounds mysterious." She smiled.

"I want it to be a surprise."

"This is all a surprise. I don't know what to—"

A nurse appeared. She interrupted and hovered over Jacques like a hawk watching its prey. "Mademoiselle, it's time to go. You can return tomorrow."

Emma looked at Jacques and then at her watch. "Yes, of course." Emma leaned over and kissed him on the forehead.

Jacques gave a slight wave. *"A la prochaine fois—a chez moi."* Until the next time—at home.

Emma blew him a kiss as she left the room.

26

The Gift

"HOW'S JACQUES?" KATIE inquired back at the house.

"On the mend. They'll move him to another room soon, I'm sure."

"Won't he be coming home soon? René said maybe in another week."

René, Emma thought. He and Katie had spent the morning riding in the vineyard. "How was your ride?" She had some minor pangs of guilt about getting them together too fast but believed they would be good for each other and that the chemistry was there. She wondered if they had gone to the stone bench and made out or maybe raced to the chapel. The thought stopped her. The chapel was the very last place she wanted Katie to explore. The chapel was hers, her dream, her secret.

Katie smiled. "We had a lovely time. I think I understand a little more about winemaking."

"Yes, René's passionate about wine." Emma wondered if his passion would extend to her little sister. Could she actually deal with René and Katie as a couple? She'd be alone again. Emma looked at her sister.

"I need to wash off the dust and horsey odor. Let me know if I can help with . . ." Katie's voice trailed off as she walked to the shower.

The late afternoon sun streamed through the open kitchen window, warming the yellow walls and red chairs with a cozy, golden glow. Emma loved this room. It reminded her so much of Evergreen and family.

The sound of the shower reminded her of the day René came to her Paris apartment with breakfast in tow to cheer her up after her relapse over Trevor. She thought about Katie and René as she rooted through the fridge for some salad fixings, pulling out lettuce, arugula, and goat cheese. Maybe a romance would blossom and she wouldn't lose René entirely the way she had her father—and Trevor.

Her hands tore at the greens, throwing them into the metal colander and rinsing them over and over in the farmer's sink. She could feel the tension rush out of her chest into her fingers as she began chopping the almonds with the precision of a master chef. Whack, whack, knock, knock, swish, swish echoed the large blade as it hit the marble cutting board. The names—René, Katie, René, Katie—bounced into the air, while Trevor's name slid alongside the knife.

Emma retrieved carrots and onions from the vegetable basket and began to surgically remove the skins. She wiped her arm across her eyes, hoping to stop the flow. It was the onions—fresh and warm— that were making her cry, she told herself as she stopped, washed her hands, and splashed cold water on her face.

What was it Jacques had said? Be careful with the heart?

She thought about Jacques' gift. Did he buy it for her birthday? Did René know about it?

She recognized that maybe she loved René's family more than René, something that had been more on her mind lately. Now the mysterious gift increased her concern about how Jacques would feel about her if she were no longer with René. Would he still care about her? Maybe she was living too close, too much in their world.

THE SUN WAS slowly yawning up the side of the Luberon when Emma placed the key into the lock and turned it until it clicked open. She had wondered about the shed for days, but an uneasiness about accepting an inexplicable gift from Jacques had kept her from coming here until now. What was it and what did it mean? Did he understand how she now felt about René or did he see her as a future daughter-in-law?

She grasped the door handle, hesitated, and stepped back, ready to leave. What was she doing? Crazy, snooping around in the wee hours of the morning like a thief casing her neighbor's property.

Jacques had made it seem rather mysterious, though. He hadn't told René, only her. "It belongs to you," he'd said. She was more than curious. She pushed open the large wooden door and stepped inside, waiting cautiously for the dark interior to meet her eyes. Vaguely, she could see junk, old milk cans, a worn butcher's table, ropes, meat grinders, and gadgets she didn't recognize. A faint smokey odor tickled her nose. An old smokehouse? She knew about smokehouses. Her grandfather had built a stone one at Evergreen. As a child, she had been scared of the vast, dark space holding the drying pig carcasses high above her. It took her breath away. She never went there without Shep or her father. She had feared she would end up dried, shriveled, smelly, and hanging from the rafters. Now Emma laughed at the thought as her eyes darted from corner to corner until they settled on the yellow box at the far end of the table.

She walked deliberately toward the box and opened it, pulling out

ANNE CROWN

some papers and a large key. She held up the key and read the inscription, then let out a squeal of surprise. Excited, she looked around the room again, searching until her eyes fixed on the large tarp in the far corner. It's under there, she thought. I know that's where it is! A glint of silver caught her eye as she pulled off the tarp. Sky blue. She ran her hands over the Vespa and the carry-all on the back. Really? She didn't understand why he had done this. Such a generous gift. Could she really accept it? Was it a bribe? A bribe to leave René alone or a bribe to make her stay? No, that wasn't Jacques' style, she thought. Emma paused a long while staring at the bike, running her hands over it again as if petting a new puppy. If it had been a gift from her father, what would it have meant? Maybe Jacques had understood all along and knew about her heart's desire. Did he also know about her special place? Maybe.

Emma straddled the scooter, holding the shiny metal handles, and then sat on the grey leather seat. She leaned forward in racing mode, imitating the "vrrrrrooom, vrrrooom" noise of a revving engine. She could feel the wind in her hair, and a sense of wanderlust came over her. She twisted her long hair around her fingers—she would need to buy a helmet. She got up, checked the back compartment, and found a grey helmet tucked inside. She swished her hair up on her head and pushed it up under the helmet, then fastened the chin strap. She removed the gas cap and looked in the tank. Voila! Half a tank. Perfect.

27

Emma

EMMA LEFT THE BIKE and put the key and papers in a box at the back of the top shelf of her bedroom closet. A safe place for now. It was almost 7:00 a.m. Katie was still asleep. In the kitchen, she filled her coffee mug and buttered a stale croissant, noticing how the subtle, early morning light hung over the rooms like gossamer—mysterious and romantic. What a lovely painting this would make, she thought.

It was the perfect time of day to do a little digging and weeding. In a couple of hours, it would be too bright and hot to work outside. The house itself was cool inside in the summer thanks to fourteen-inch-thick walls. Outside, the sun was intense this time of year. She retrieved her gardening gloves and tools from the worn green box on the steps, picked up her navy clogs, and grabbed her big straw hat from the old brass hook near the entryway.

The scent of lavender surrounded her right away—sweet, fresh, and relaxing. Emma took a deep breath and walked through and around the roses, deadheading, trimming, and then weeding the beds. Not as many as Margarite's garden but plenty to tend to. She focused on the tall, old world rose that came with the house. It was a lovely shade of deep pink with grey-green foliage, and each bud unfurled like a small cabbage—hence, the name cabbage rose. Bees and butterflies were attracted to its heady, sweet aroma.

Emma was happily distracted by a large yellow, black, and teal swallowtail weaving around the blossoms. It was such a beautiful and carefree insect content just to be.

Emma understood the meaning of content when she was outdoors surrounded by nature. Surely it had to do with the way she grew up at Evergreen with parents happy with their own lives. We all want that, she thought.

As she snipped and pruned the dead flowers and canes, her mind wandered to Jacques and his gift. All of her questions, she decided, didn't matter. What mattered was that it was a very special gift that Jacques wanted her to have because he cared for her. She was sure he would tell her more about the scooter when he was well and at home. Emma put aside any clandestine thoughts she might have had, believing Jacques was not the type to manipulate anyone. Perhaps he did know about the chapel, although she'd told no one she had bought it shortly after finding it.

She thought it normal to have questions or minor suspicions, or maybe she had a difficult time accepting gifts from men. She had to laugh at herself. She didn't have a hard time taking presents from Trevor, maybe because they were few and far between. His tokens of affection were more spontaneous, romantic, like the pink coral cameo he found in an antique store in Paris the first year she was there. She hadn't questioned his extravagance or his motives. She simply treasured it. If René were to give her something like that, she knew she'd be terrified it meant they were serious. Dear René. What to do about him without hurting him or her relationship with his family? Emma hoped Katie could be the answer.

"Ouch," Emma whined, pulling the long cane of thorns from her flesh. Focus, she thought. Focus on the work at hand. She pushed the trowel deep into the rich soil, turning it over and over and pulling out the weeds. The repetition and monotony of this exercise helped empty her mind. She sat back on her heels, picking up the weeds and tossing them into a nearby bucket. A light breeze stirred around her, cooling her.

Could she toss away the past, the memories, so effortlessly? What did she really want? Could she walk away from René? Would she be able to stay here if she did? Why couldn't love be simple, straightforward? It never was and wouldn't be, she knew that. Could Katie fall in love here? With René? Weren't they supposed to be going on a picnic somewhere today? To Joucas, she remembered. René had invited her as well, but she'd made up some excuse—she needed to work on a story for the magazine. And maybe she would.

One thing was certain. Emma knew how to smile when her heart ached and how to laugh through her tears. She knew what it meant to be head over heels. Or not. She knew how temporary life was and how it could change in a nanosecond. She knew when hours could escape her grasp and when to push time to its end. She knew she had lived a lifetime, but not lived enough. She knew that few things in life made sense or were fair. She knew she simply had to move forward.

Emma looked at all the fabulous flowers in her garden. She was surrounded by idyllic settings at every turn. This was her dream. She needed to live it even if she was unsure of what else she wanted for herself. Maybe she needed to take a different tack, immerse herself in nature, meditate, be more creative.

She thought of the pale blue Vespa in the shed. Now was the perfect opportunity.

28

Trevor Arrives in the Village

THE FLIGHT FROM PARIS to Marseilles was better than the transatlantic one from New York. This time, at least, Air France was on time. It was all too common that only by chance your flight would arrive or leave on time or that you would make your connection. Trevor knew this. As a New Yorker, though, it was sometimes hard to swallow this laissez-faire attitude. But wasn't that part of the problem? He couldn't merely let it be. And he didn't want to leave things up to chance anymore or let everything stay the way it was. Still, he couldn't help wondering if he was crazy to think he could do something about the past. He only knew that his near-death experience had made him obsessed with savoring each moment, each day, no matter what. Even if things didn't work out now, he would have given it a shot.

He hadn't remembered it being so hot in Provence in early July. There was always a fabulous breeze, but today, he felt out of place in his cotton dress shirt and chinos. He removed his tie, took off his socks, and shoved them into his leather duffle. Being sockless gave him a sense of youthful freedom as he slipped back into his loafers. He bemoaned the fact that there were no more automatics left at the car rental and he had to settle for a stick shift. They were out of Mercedes or anything larger, so he crammed his six-foot four-inch frame into the petite Peugeot 205 convertible and headed west. It wasn't until he was driving eighty miles per hour around mountainous curves that he realized his foot was too big for the clutch, leg room was sparse, and his knee hit the steering wheel each time he changed gears, causing him to spit out four-letter words cursing the French.

By the time he arrived in the village, it was late afternoon. The scent of lavender filled his senses, reminding him of the time he'd bought her a huge bouquet of lavender and sunflowers from the market in Apt. Adrenaline pumped through his veins, cleansing his exhaustion. He meandered through the narrow streets, excited yet fearful to be here. He saw a large yellow house on the corner where a couple of women were walking through a rose-covered archway into the street. His heart stammered as he stopped to ask if they knew Emma. Then he panicked, realizing he probably didn't speak very good French, especially the Provençal dialect, which he considered something of a phonetic mishmash. A photo, he thought, as he fumbled through his wallet looking for the old college photo, but his fingers trembled and couldn't grasp what he wanted.

In the next second, a shock of red hair got his attention. Could it be? Anxiety raced through his pores. Was it Katie? He couldn't remember the last time he'd seen her, but that hair—a hot drama of golden orange—flashed like a neon sign. It had to be Katie. Her profile blurred against the bright afternoon sun as she closed the garden gate. He wasn't sure, but when she turned and saw him walking toward her, he knew. She hadn't changed much—still tall, slender, and beautiful.

He saw her place her hand across her mouth, covering an outward gasp. Surprise and shock seized her face. He could imagine what she was thinking: Trevor? Here? Why? She stood motionless not knowing what to do or say.

Almost weak-kneed, Trevor approached her. "Katie? Remember, me? Trevor?"

"Yes, of course."

"Is she inside? Emma?"

Katie hesitated. "Not at the moment."

"Back soon I hope?"

"We don't know." Her back stiffened.

The worried look on Katie's face puzzled Trevor. "What do you mean?"

Before she could answer, a man stepped forward and introduced himself as Emma's neighbor, René. Trevor ignored him and instead spoke to Katie.

"Katie, I don't understand. What's going on? Is Emma okay?"

Katie's eyes pierced through Trevor as if he were a stranger. She reached for René's hand.

"Would someone tell me what's going on?"

Trevor was aware of René scrutinizing him and wondered what René knew.

Trevor fiddled with his car keys and then moved around Katie and René, trying to duck into the house, see for himself, find Emma, hold her, and tell her what he hadn't been able to until now.

René reached for Trevor's shoulder and said, "Perhaps you'd better come inside where we can talk."

Trevor pulled away, annoyed. Patience had never been his strong suit. "Look, I've just traveled four thousand miles. Someone give me a straight answer!"

Katie's eyes welled. "We haven't seen or heard from Emma in a couple of days. No note. No phone call. Nothing."

Trevor felt his heart shift into high gear. "Are you serious?"

"Very serious." Katie's lower lip quivered.

They're overreacting, he thought. She's just away somewhere. As they walked up the stairs and entered the kitchen, Trevor noticed the worn red tile floor aged like a fine wine and caught a glimpse of an old photo on the far countertop of Emma and her family at Evergreen. He walked over to it and held it, wishing he could touch the long dark hair he saw before him. The aroma of French espresso closed in on him. Exhausted, he took a deep breath and sighed, "I think I could use a cup of that." He thought about the first time they had coffee together in Paris at a little bistro on the West Bank that later became their favorite. She had laughed when he told her it tasted like "tar." It was all so long ago. They were so long ago. Had coming here been a mistake?

Katie poured Trevor a small café and waited as he slumped into the red high-back kitchen chair. When he picked up the white ceramic cup, he noticed immediately the green lettering for "Café de Flore" one of the places they frequented in Paris. His heart ached. He wished he were there now and it was 1977 again. He took a sip of the strong, hot coffee but maybe not strong enough to deal with what lay ahead. Katie's reaction to him made him wonder what they were thinking. It was as if she were trying to be kind yet remain aloof. He began to jiggle his spoon in the coffee and said, "So tell me. You don't you think she's missing, do you?"

The tears began to stream down Katie's face. She glanced at René, apparently unsure how to respond. "We really don't know. She left her phone and car keys behind. We've checked with the police and hospitals, but no luck."

Trevor glanced around the yellow and red kitchen, looking for signs of Emma, pieces of her life here. It was foreign to him, so very French. French colors, china, art, cookware. What had made him think he could fit in here, in her life, now? His eyes caught a glimpse of something familiar near the bottom of the door. Hadn't they bought that together at the flea market in Paris? Yes, of course, the white rooster doorstop was an early find one weekend there. He felt lost somewhere between the past and present. All of his memories of her were carried within him.

Trevor looked at Katie. "Well, it's only been a couple of days, right? Maybe she's just off somewhere." Even he realized how stupid it sounded. He didn't think Emma would go off without any word. Frustration churned inside him. He was upset that Emma wasn't here and upset that no one could give him the answers he wanted. He wondered if he deserved any answers at all?

Katie looked at René. "And her room was as she had left it—undisturbed. Her desk was cleared and her laptop was off."

Trevor felt a pain in his chest. He tightened his grip on his cup as if to squeeze the life out of it. He couldn't seem to process what was happening. The sound of Katie's voice seemed distant, muffled.

"We went through her things, and . . ." Katie paused, glanced at René, then back to Trevor. "We found a letter addressed to you in her papers, but it is only to be opened in the event of her . . . " Katie couldn't say the word.

She left me a letter. That must mean something. She has something she wanted to tell me. Maybe she still cares. But his hope waned at the thought he might not see her again. The fear of loss, not knowing where she was, exhaustion, and aggravation were swelling inside him, making him angry. His entire body was warm with the sweat streaming down his face and neck, making his shirt stick all over. He was worried no one knew anything, angry with himself he had not told her he was coming, and ticked off over his stupid expectations of a romantic reunion. What was he thinking? Unable to absorb what they were saying or contain his emotions, Trevor slammed his fist down on the table. "Oh, come on. She's not missing—dead. That's ridiculous!"

René stared at Trevor. "Take it easy. Katie's told you what she knows. Let's talk man to man."

Trevor gave René an intense look. Man to man? What was this 'kid' talking about? Who in the hell was he anyway? He was practically glued to Katie. Maybe he was Katie's boyfriend, but Trevor had noticed a small photo of him and Emma on the fridge. No, too young for Emma. But he couldn't be sure. Did Trevor still know the girl he had fallen in love with all those years ago? Had he ever known who she was and what she wanted? And how could he possibly know if she'd want him now? That was the heart of it: Would she want him now?

René recounted for Trevor the last night he had seen Emma four days before when she had cooked Margarite a lamb stew and brought it to her. René had been visiting his mother when Emma walked in. She stayed for an hour or so, René told him, helping his mother and inquiring about his father and when he would be coming home. René had noticed that Emma, although relaxed and conversational, seemed a little distracted about something.

"Well, you're friends, right? Did you ask her what was bothering her?"

René paused. "If she'd wanted me to know, I think she'd have said something." He glanced down. "Maybe she didn't like that I was spending more time with Katie even though she'd asked me to show her around and watch out for her. I don't know."

Trevor's brain was churning up all kinds of scenarios. Why would she have been jealous of René and Katie, unless she had strong feelings for René?

Trevor pressed his hand against his stomach, hoping to ease the queasiness he was feeling. He realized he hadn't eaten in hours. He was about to ask Katie for some crackers when she placed a plate of cheese, fruit, and bread on the table next to him. She refilled his coffee.

"I thought you might like to eat something," she told him. "I'm sorry I didn't think of it sooner. If you don't want coffee—"

"This is fine. Guess I didn't realize how hungry I was. Thank you."

René pulled a chair next to Trevor and sat down, continuing to describe the last few days. He treated Trevor like an older brother, talking with him and answering his questions. He told Trevor how he met Emma and how long they'd been dating. Trevor's heart sank. I don't know her. They are—were—lovers.

Trevor hid his emotions well, something he had learned from Emma herself, but he was determined to get to the bottom of this. The sooner the better. He needed to find her.

The more questions he asked—Who saw her last? Who she'd talked to? Was there a special place she liked to go to get away?—the more questions he had. But the overriding question he had was about René. Was he in love with her? Was Emma in love with him? It was too soon to ask. René definitely fit into her life and was the best connection Trevor had to finding Emma. He could hear René's voice in the background as he wondered what Emma had been thinking, where she could have gone, and why.

The Emma he knew rarely got depressed or despondent. Was that still true?

AT 2:00 A.M., TREVOR crawled into bed, exhausted but thankful he'd found her house and Katie had allowed him to stay there while looking for her. Trevor gazed at the soft night sky lighting one corner of the room. In the stillness of the moment, he wrestled with the fact that he had no claim on Emma anymore. Mostly, he felt stupid for coming all this way to find that what he was chasing might not even exist.

29

The Manuscript

WHEN KATIE AWOKE THE next morning, the coffee was already made, and Trevor was sitting at Emma's desk, hoping he might find something: a clue, a note, anything.

He gestured to Katie. "I hope you don't mind. I'm checking to see if there might be something here that stands out."

Katie nodded. "It's fine. Help yourself. How long have you been up?"

"A couple of hours. I didn't sleep well. Your local rooster alarm—"

Katie laughed. "Oh, yes. I forgot about him. He crows at five a.m. every day. You get used to it after a while."

Trevor didn't want to get used to it. The only sound he wanted to hear was Emma's voice.

He wanted to see her. That was all. He didn't understand why she'd take off without telling anyone. She had always played things close to the vest and liked a little intrigue. But she hadn't known he was coming to see her, so this wasn't about him. Maybe this was a charade for the benefit of René? Maybe it was her way of dumping him or making him jealous? Myriad thoughts raced through his mind, prompting him to dig deeper into her life.

"Did you check her computer?"

"Well, sort of," Katie said. "I'm not very good at that technical stuff, but René looked through her emails and didn't see anything unusual."

"Would you mind if I had a go at it?"

"Please," Katie said. "Another pair of eyes would be good. Oh, by the way, her password is Park Slope." She smiled and went to the kitchen and poured herself a cup of coffee.

"Thanks," he replied, hiding the nostalgia that crept over him and booting up her machine. Memories of Emma, the Battery, Clinton Avenue, and Chinatown flashed before him like an old black and white movie.

He began reading and searching through documents, looking for something, anything. Her letter to him lay on her desk, still unopened. He picked it up and looked at it, wondering what Emma had written to him. I refuse to accept this, he told himself, placed it in the top drawer of her desk, and continued searching.

The village was still quiet, but soon shutters would open and folks would trickle onto the streets. By 8:30 a.m., voices and the sound of feet scurrying across the cobblestones resonated through the narrow walkways.

Katie opened the shutters above Emma's desk and cranked out the windows. "You find anything?"

Trevor had found Emma's manuscript and was reading through it. "Maybe," he said. "A manuscript. Have you read it?"

"No. I'm computer illiterate. Wouldn't know what to look for. René didn't mention it either." Katie turned toward Trevor, lifting the coffee mug to her lips. She hesitated. "I have to ask, though. Why are you here?"

Trevor looked up from Emma's desk. He saw the younger Katie in her green eyes and fair skin. The faint laugh lines around her mouth were almost erased by her drawn, serious expression. There it was. He had wondered how long it would take her to ask. He took a sip of coffee, staring at the cup before answering. "I need Emma."

Katie's jaw dropped. "You need her? Now? I—I thought you were married?"

Silence filled the space between them. Trevor turned towards the computer. "My wife died."

"I'm sorry."

He felt her staring at him. Then she spoke, "Why didn't you let Emma know you were coming?"

"If I had, do you think it would have made a difference?" Hell, she left me, he thought. She could do it again, and she has without even knowing it!

"We won't know, will we? But you certainly have terrible timing."

Trevor thought about this. It was true. They both had had awful timing. For years. "Maybe not," he said quietly. "Maybe she needs me now more than ever."

At least he was hoping that would be the case.

"Oh, please. You show up after all these years and think she'll be here waiting for you? Emma's over you. She doesn't need you." Her voice sharpened. "She's in love with someone else."

Trevor let her words glide silently to the floor. "You mean René? I'm not so sure about that."

"Look at René. He's young, handsome, and wealthy. Why not?"

That was all true, he thought, but maybe she didn't need young. "Maybe too young," he said.

ANNE CROWN

"Oh, come on." Katie looked at Trevor. "I'm sorry, Trevor, but I never really understood what Emma saw in you."

Trevor rather expected this at some point. He, too, had wondered what Emma had seen in him. More often than not, he hadn't been there for her. Now, he had shown up out of the blue with great expectations. Although he realized it was inappropriate to play the steely lawyer now, that's what he knew; it was his comfort zone. He told himself to listen even if Katie didn't like him very much right now.

Katie slapped the top of the desk with her hand and leaned close to him. "Let me tell you something about my sister. You think she's strong and independent, but she has a fragile heart where you're concerned. You were the love of her life. Every decision she made was because of you—going to Georgetown, trying to move to New York—it was all about you."

Trevor's forehead creased. "Katie, she married someone else—"

"Of course she did, but she didn't want to. She wanted you. She wanted you to stop her, not hint at it. You told her that she shouldn't marry anyone but you, and then you told her to go ahead and marry Rick. You broke her heart, and she has never recovered or forgotten and didn't even try to love anyone else for a long time. Now that she has a chance at happiness with someone who will treat her right in a place she loves, you show up with your big ego and undying love to destroy everything once again. Do us all a favor and leave. Go!"

Trevor stared at the computer screen. Leave echoed in his brain. But he couldn't go now. He'd just arrived. He glanced at Katie, noticing her flushed cheeks. "It has taken me years to get here," he said, wishing he could open up and let her know how he felt about Emma. But he couldn't. Her anger, although justified, kept him silent. He looked at her, searching for Emma, but they were nothing alike. He noticed, though, the pain in her eyes. He'd seen that before. He'd seen that same pain the night he had shown Emma the sonogram. After a long pause, he said, "You're right. I'll leave . . . but only when I find Emma and she tells me to go. For now, let's try to get along." He reached for her hand.

Katie pulled away. "Don't—"

"I'm curious." Trevor raised his chin. "Why are you here?"

Katie huffed. "I'm her sister. I'm spending the summer here." A smile tugged at Trevor's lips. The little sister on the defensive, starting to boil. Maybe that's why Emma had gone; she'd run away from her sister, but he knew this wasn't the time for sarcasm. He had nothing to say. He returned to reading the pages of her novel.

After he left, the hum of les cigales lulled her to sleep. She slept deeply, the scent of him permeating her bed and body.

Katie ignored his dismissive attitude and continued. "If you know so much, tell me why she would leave her car and phone behind."

Trevor turned away from the manuscript. "The car doesn't puzzle me as much as the phone. She may not need the car, but the phone— that's her lifeline."

"*Lifeline.* Oh my god, she has no lifeline."

Trevor saw the worry in Katie's face, so he changed the subject by redirecting. "I don't understand why she didn't tell anyone where she was going. I assume you searched everywhere for a note?"

Katie's voice rose. "Of course! René, Margarite, and I searched the house. We talked with the neighbors, but no one saw anything."

No one saw anything. What about heard? Trevor wondered if anyone had heard anything. He could see the tears in Katie's eyes. He stood, walked over to her, and touched her gently on the shoulder. "It's going to be all right. We'll find her. I think she's okay."

Katie looked puzzled. "Why do you think that?" The question hung in the air, and Trevor wasn't sure how to respond.

"It's only a hunch, but her book—"

"A hunch? God, who are you? Sherlock Holmes?" Tears welled in her eyes and her cheeks flushed. "You have a lot of nerve showing up after all these years and telling me you have a hunch. A hunch? Do you even know anything about her? A hunch, my ass."

She slid onto the soft cushion of the kitchen chair, breathing slowly and deliberately, creating a rhythm to make her fear subside. After a long silence, she calmly asked Trevor, "So what did you find that makes you think she's okay?"

"I'm not sure yet. It's sort of intuition. I need to keep reading and digging."

"For what?"

"Answers—to her state of mind, what she was thinking."

A slight smile appeared on Katie's face. "Great. I guess you're more of a Watson after all."

Trevor turned toward Katie. "Did you go through her things?"

"Of course, but if you think you can do a better job, feel free. Search the whole house if it helps. In the meantime, I need to do something meaningless. I'm going out. Do you want anything from the market?"

"No, thanks." He didn't look up. He heard Katie walk through the kitchen and close the door. A couple of minutes later, he got up and walked into the room for more coffee. He stood by the window and watched Katie get into René's car, thinking they made a good-looking young couple. He didn't want to consider that Emma might have feelings for the young Frenchman. Trevor returned to Emma's desk and sat down. He knew he had good instincts and needed to follow them and search for answers. He knew Emma could be understated and subtle, like the spaces between the lines of her novel. Like a good investigative reporter, he needed to find the story behind the story.

Funny, he thought he always knew her story, their story, but now he felt like a detective of clandestine emotions and unresolved truths.

I've been walking on the mines I laid, resounded in Trevor's head as he read the manuscript. He didn't want to rush through the words. He took his time, slowly devouring the places and times described, all part of his own personal journey.

He wondered why she never called him back. Was it because she already knew his plan, understood him so well that no words were necessary?

He continued to read in, around, and between the lines of the dialogues of her characters, certain he would find the answer. And find her.

The ringing of church bells broke his concentration. Trevor stood up and walked toward the balcony in the dining room in time to see the young bride and groom leaving their wedding service. They shared a kiss and posed for the photographer and their friends.

Emma's kiss was forever burned into his memory—warm, seductive, and filled with intense emotion. He could see her smile and feel her fingers run gently over his lips like someone in the dark seeking reassurance, making sure he was there and real. He began to feel somewhat lost in the dark himself and needed to know she was safe. For a long time, he stood at the open glass doors and thought about what had brought him here, wondering what might play out in the end. He couldn't and wouldn't accept that Emma had disappeared. There had to be a logical explanation for what was going on. Besides, his heart felt that this was the beginning, not the end, of something.

30

Just a Drink

HE HAD NEEDED A break. Trevor thought a beer would help cool the warm summer evening. A quick drink and then he'd head back to Emma's computer. But at the local bar, he'd unexpectedly run into René at a small table in the back of the room. There was something about him, something familiar that Trevor couldn't put his finger on. Cigarette smoke hung like a hazy curtain over the cave-like room. He had decided he'd like to talk with René and maybe learn more about him and Emma. He would be gracious and charming and on his best behavior.

Instead, they had been sparring for the last hour, sitting in the corner of the crowded bar staring at each other and squabbling like teenagers.

Trevor pressed the bottle to his lips and wondered what Emma would think if she walked in right now and saw her two men together. Would she be shocked or worried, or would she smile with relief? He wished she would walk in so he could sweep her off her feet and leave this godforsaken place.

"It doesn't matter what happened years ago. You think she wants you now?" René was saying for the nth time.

Doubt flooded over Trevor. How would she feel seeing him again? "What do you know about it?" Trevor leaned across the table. "She needs a man, not a boy."

"I'm a man all right—her man."

Trevor raised his eyebrows. "Has she told you she loves you?"

"None of your business."

"I thought so!" Trevor shook his head. "You're simply a diversion—boy toy."

"A diversion, yes. Exactly what Emma was to you."

Trevor felt the blood rush into his face and neck. He grabbed René's arm. "You don't have a clue about my feelings."

René pulled away. "Well, here's a clue: You could have asked her to marry you more than once. You didn't."

Trevor squeezed the neck of his beer bottle. For a moment, he couldn't hear the lively French conversations, the rattling dishes, or clanging silverware. He was not in this smoke-filled, dimly lit bar listening to René. He was back on campus at Georgetown in the Tombs, having a beer and waiting for Emma. Waiting for the shock of his life, seeing the ring, telling her to go ahead and get married, that he didn't care. Hadn't he cared enough? No. He had cared too much, but the shock of it had left him wounded, angry, and speechless.

"You have no idea how much I love Emma. You have no idea." His chest tightened. "She married someone else."

"And you didn't try to stop her? Come on, man."

But he had made one feeble attempt. He told her she shouldn't marry anyone but him. But when she asked if he was proposing, he remained silent. He was in his first year of law school. He couldn't commit. He wasn't ready, but he could have at least been honest with her. He had been too young to know what to say or how to say it.

"What do you know about me or her? Nothing. Do you even know where she went to college? Do you know her favorite color?"

"What's her favorite wine?" René countered.

"What's her favorite car? Who taught her to drive a stick?"

"I know what's important." René glared at Trevor. "I know she's passionate about life and love."

"I suppose she's passionate about you too? Did you take her to her first college prom?"

René shot back. "Did you take her on her first horseback ride through a vineyard?"

"Your father's vineyard." Trevor sneered. "Not yours."

René's eyes narrowed. "What's your point?"

"My point? You inherited it; you didn't create it on your own."

"And I suppose you've done everything on your own—no help from anyone?"

"Pretty much."

"Well, maybe that's why you lost her, Mr. Big Shot who doesn't need anyone."

Was this true? Trevor wondered. Hadn't he needed her enough? But in the next breath, he thought, bullshit, and said, "Oh, for God's sake, gimme a break. Emma was so much like me—independent and self-sufficient, that—"

"That you didn't make the effort?" René's voice was calm.

Trevor tried to take a sip of beer but couldn't. His throat felt swollen. Maybe he hadn't made the effort. Maybe he had been careless with her love. He struggled for the right words in this conversation that had gone silent on one side. Only a little over a year ago, he had finished mourning his wife's death. He wondered what had held them together for the last five years. Had she simply needed him? Her illness had brought them closer together. He had grown accustomed to being attached. It had suited him. He had not yet begun to think about changing his life. He had no plan or direction. But his own near-death experience on that crippled plane a few weeks ago brought into focus again how tenuous life was and that everything revolved around time—time enjoyed and lost. Before that, the thought of coming to France and looking for Emma was unknown to him. But here he was in a crowded, smoke-filled bar in a remote village in the south of France surrounded by noisy locals who spoke no English.

"You couldn't even make the effort to tell her how you felt? Not much of a communicator."

"I'm a lawyer. Communicating is my fucking job. I told her how I felt every minute of every day we were together." But he hadn't. He hadn't wanted to be rejected. He hadn't told her that he never stopped thinking about her, wanted only her, and that she made him deliriously happy. He'd never told her how much he loved her.

Trevor realized he was letting this little French prick get to him. What had Emma told René about him?

"Look, all I know is that life is precious and Emma deserves someone who loves her and makes her happy. Not someone who makes her break down when she hears his name."

"You sound like a book of daily devotions. Life is precious," Trevor mocked. "Wait—What do you mean breaks down?"

"You don't remember me, do you?"

Trevor was confused. "Should I?" His brow furrowed.

"New York. Two years ago. The big society wine tasting at the Castelli Gallery."

That was it—the connection and familiarity. A chance thirty-second meeting at a tasting that René remembered, but he hadn't. Bizarre.

"You told her you'd met me?"

"Yes. And I had no idea that—"

"She still cared," Trevor said. The lines on either side of his smile deepened. "I love her. Always have. Always will."

René waited. "But you can't show it."

"The hell I can't! When I find her, I'm going to ask her to marry me." The word—*marry*—ricocheted inside him. Trevor couldn't believe how easily *marry* slipped through his lips and fell into the conversation without hesitation. Finally, he would follow his heart and be happy. He would marry her. Why hadn't he done it years ago?

René set his beer down. "Good luck with that. May the best man win."

"The best man will. I guarantee it—when I find her . . ." His voice trailed off.

He stared at René's boyish face, flawless olive skin, and dark eyes. A pretty boy—the perfect ladies' man—handsome. Then he noticed the scar that ran down the side of his neck near his hairline. Maybe not so perfect after all.

Trevor felt the dryness in his throat.

THE SOUND OF THE bar door slamming behind him faded as he walked into the clear night air. Thousands of stars seemed almost within his grasp, reminding him of his summers at Long Beach Island. He walked along the cobblestone street to Emma's house—Exactly like the old streets of Georgetown, he thought, where they would stroll after eating out or listening to jazz at Blues Alley. What he wouldn't give to have her beside him now. He'd thought of Emma every day since they had first met twenty-two years ago. That he was here now was like wandering in a dream, looking for a part of himself.

31

Looking For Her

TREVOR LAY IN THE large bed in the second guest room, starring at the ceiling fan, mesmerized by its whirring blades. The sun had shifted behind the house, leaving slender rays of light sneaking across the foot of his bed. He couldn't believe he'd slept so long—9:30 a.m.—but couldn't seem to move to get up. He'd never heard the rooster or Katie.

All was quiet, but he could smell coffee. He needed a drink, a series of good stiff ones, not coffee. He wanted to get drunk and stay drunk, something he hadn't done since college. The irony of being here so close to Emma, yet so far away, struck him. He was where he wanted to be but unsure if it if was where he should be. Was this the way it was going to be—out of sync, unsteady? If he'd only followed his heart years ago, would everything have worked out? But he couldn't change the past. He had to get his ass out of bed and focus on what he could do now.

He took a cold shower to revive his senses. When he looked in the mirror to shave, he rather liked the baby stubble that was beginning to cover his rough-hewn face. After, he rummaged through the kitchen looking for something hearty to eat and decided on the typical French ham and cheese on a baguette—the kind they used to take on picnics or shared at their favorite corner café. He pulled out the large blue coffee cup with the Van Gogh sunflowers and filled it to the brim. Trevor looked out the kitchen window. Where was everyone? What day was it? Sunday? Then he saw Katie's note on the countertop. Saturday. She and René were at the market.

He headed for Emma's desk, where the tall windows were open and the computer was on. Katie, he thought. The room was bright, and he liked that he could sit at the computer and see the mountains and valley spread out before him. What a great spot to think and write. He could see Emma here working and enjoying a landscape that surely had been painted thousands of times.

He bit off a large chunk of sandwich, opened her manuscript, and continued to read. He opened the desk drawer, reaching for a pen or pencil for quick notes and pulled out the envelope addressed to him. He couldn't believe he had been here only three days; it seemed so much longer. He swallowed hard and held the envelope up to the light. Not heavy, not thick, probably a single sheet of paper; not a will. He stared at it for a while, hesitating, and then placed it on top of her desk. Later. Maybe.

He delved into the manuscript where he'd left off. The more he read, the more he felt a connection with the lives of the characters in the book.

But there was something else he couldn't get his head around. It wasn't like her to write something that danced around the twilight zone. There appeared to be no happiness for the two lovers in the manuscript. The main character, a writer writing a story, entered the pages of her fictional characters and then lived content forever in southern France. Life imitating art?

A writer writing a story about a writer who enters her own novel to find the happiness she couldn't find elsewhere? How pathetic, almost juvenile, so unrealistic, Trevor thought. But he knew one thing: It was making him examine his own choices, his heart, and his happiness. Maybe that was the point. Hadn't he created his own fiction? Hadn't he convinced himself he was happy and content with his life? He hadn't fought for her; he'd let her go, and he didn't know why. Convinced they would "never get anything done" together except make love, he had traded passion for achievement. And yes, he was an accomplished lawyer, had been a loving husband, and had created his own perception of contentment. Maybe it was his life that had been pathetic and trite.

By mid-afternoon, Trevor had skimmed through half of the manuscript pages. The more he read, the less he knew what he was looking for. He was more curious to know what she was trying to say and why. He put his cup on top of her polished antique oak desk with its worn edges and random nicks. A metaphor for himself, he thought, except that the desk was obviously well cared for and treasured. He was not. A couple of photos, a small ceramic cicada, a Nantucket paperweight, and a Mont Blanc pen still in its box sat neatly along the back of the desk.

He stared at the large candid photo of Emma, her parents, and Katie in front of the big wraparound porch at Evergreen. Emma was probably nine or so, and a young Katie, maybe four, was in her mother's arms. Emma's long hair and light eyes drew him in. She had always been beautiful. He remembered being on that porch with Emma after Thanksgiving dinner. He could still feel her soft white angora sweater against his skin as he kissed the nape of her neck. He longed for that moment filled with youthful joy.

Another smaller photo showed Emma in her riding attire standing next to Star, holding the reins in one hand and a blue ribbon in the other. Shep was next to her, posing with a doggie grin. Emma must have been around twelve. He paused, picked up the photo, and studied it closely. A young girl between childhood and her teen years. Her teeth were too big for her small face and she would need braces, he noticed. He smiled as he returned the photo to its place.

He pushed Emma's letter to the side, pulled the paperweight closer, and held it tightly. Another memory rushed toward him. Out sailing, on the way back to the house, they had stopped in a little gift shop near Sag Harbor, where Emma bought the sea glass paperweight so she could always carry the ocean with her.

A lifetime ago.

He placed the paperweight on the desk and sat a few more minutes, his eyes tired from staring at the computer, and wondered whether her novel could really tell him anything. He grabbed his empty coffee cup and walked into the kitchen, searching for a beer and something more to eat, stretching as he moved, his shoulders tight. He discovered some roast chicken and half a bottle of white wine in the fridge, bread in the pantry, and in the freezer, two full cartons of chocolate ice cream with a dozen or so frozen Heath bars lying side by side. Definitely Emma's freezer unless Katie had a similar sweet tooth. He laughed to himself.

Trevor carried his sandwich and wine back to her desk and continued to read the manuscript on the screen while printing out the pages he had already read. He wanted to study them more closely, and Katie hadn't objected to his plan. He wondered how Emma would feel knowing he was snooping through her work, house, and things.

He hoped she would understand. He skimmed over the descriptions of lavender and wheat fields, searching for facts and details. The line about the New York lawyer with the boyish grin got his attention. He slowly focused on the next few sentences about Fire Island at night, the ferry, the kiss.

They caught the last ferry from Fire Island back to the city. She held on tightly to his arm as they walked around the deck. The end to a perfect July weekend, the ultramarine sky filled with luminous stars igniting the evening.

He felt his heart rise in his chest. It was about their first weekend away together early on in their relationship. Was this their story? He stared at the vivid computer screen and inhaled her words:

She felt safe and content. Laughter from those onboard seemed distant and faded into the background as he pulled her to his body and kissed her ever so slowly—a long, deliberate and passionate kiss, a melding of their souls.

Trevor sighed, recognizing the parallel lives of the characters in her book with their own love story, happiness, and loss.

This summer was different than any other she could remember. Their stays on the island now seemed to be a time of overwhelming beauty, laughter, and passion. They sailed, swam, biked, and enjoyed every moment together. Many nights ended with dinner and dancing at the Sandpiper. She thought of these times often, knowing that she would have these memories forever.

The tiny bits and pieces of a lifetime, some forgotten, made him wonder what else had been omitted from his own memory. He rapped the pen against his notepad, thinking back to the everyday happenings that had escaped him, like that day on a crowded elevator in Manhattan. He had picked her up at the *Condé Nast* office for lunch at the Brasserie. He had squeezed her hand as they stood huddled in a far corner of the elevator. When people exited floor by floor, she had kissed his lips firmly, yet tenderly, and so sweetly that he couldn't exhale, didn't want to, and only wanted to stay in her arms forever.

Trevor smiled to himself as he continued to study the pages of their story. He barely noticed that the more notes he jotted down, the smaller his handwriting got, so that by the end of the list of possible clues and double entries, the words were barely visible. They began to disappear, much like Emma herself. He continued to a new page, with a new list of ideas that might lead to a revelation he could live with.

32

Dinner for Jacques

TREVOR NOTICED KATIE scurrying around the kitchen and putting bread and vegetables in the green mesh sack that hung by the door. The rustling of paper and opening and closing of the fridge and cabinets distracted him. It was time for another cup of coffee. He'd been alone most of the day, reading and searching through Emma's computer and manuscript. He got up and poured a fresh cup.

"What are you doing?" Trevor asked.

"Getting some things together for dinner at René's."

He watched her put a box of pastries in the sac. "I see," he said. "You like him, don't you?"

Katie blushed. "Of course. He's nice. He's smart. He's Emma's—"

"Boyfriend?"

"Yes. Of course," she said softly. She glanced at him. "It's not what you think."

"Oh? What do I think it is?"

She laughed. "You know what I mean. René is cooking for Jacques' homecoming. He wants Margarite and Jacques to relax. I'm helping a little with the cooking."

A box of pastries doesn't a baker make, Trevor thought, wondering if she *could* cook. Emma was a wonderful cook, he remembered, and they had enjoyed cooking together on the weekends. "Jacques?"

"René's father. He's been in the hospital for almost a month. An aortic aneurism. Emma saved his life."

Trevor was speechless with disbelief. He stood staring at Katie, wondering what had happened. Hearing it for the first time was shocking, but he guessed it was possible Emma did something extraordinary to help. "Really?" he said. "I'm glad his father is okay. Maybe you can fill me in sometime on what happened."

"I wasn't here when it happened, but Emma and René both mentioned it to me. You may want to talk with René to get the specifics."

Trevor was silent. That'll be the day, he thought.

"You're welcome to come to dinner with us if you like. Sometime later this evening or tomorrow, René will tell Jacques about Emma. He doesn't know she's not here."

No, she's not here. Where in the hell could she be? Trevor wondered.

"René said they were—are—close," Katie said.

Trevor thought about this. The past tense had already slipped out. "How close?"

"She's like a daughter."

"Oh." Trevor realized that Emma had become part of René's family, making it harder for him to see her still caring about him. But maybe Jacques knew something that no one else did. No, that couldn't be. He's been in the hospital. Trevor looked at Katie. "Do you need help with anything?"

"No, but thanks for asking." She smiled. "So, are you coming?"

Trevor paused, then said, "I think I'll stay here. It might be too much for Jacques; I'm sort of the complicating factor in this." Old flame, lover, he thought. He also was sure he didn't want to be there if or when René told Jacques about Emma. "Besides, I had a big sandwich not long ago,"

"Okay then. I'm off. See you in a couple of hours."

Trevor watched her walk out the door and down the stairs to the street. He poured himself another cup of coffee and returned to Emma's desk. It was that time of day in Provence when the sun was getting a little closer to the mountains. Although the sun didn't set here until nine or ten, the light at early evening had a subtle golden hue that brought with it an uplifting sense of possibilities.

33

The Letter

TREVOR STARED AT THE unopened letter on Emma's desk. He picked it up slowly. He held it again and felt its thickness. If he opened it, would it mean he thought the worst and had given up? Or would it help him understand her more? He tapped the envelope on the desk, causing the contents to settle. A single cut with the letter opener and perhaps he'd find a clue to her whereabouts.

No, that wouldn't help; the envelope was dated 1989.

He tried to recall four years back and then it hit him—of course, the last time they had seen each other. The only thing opening it now might do would be to bring some closure to what they were or who they used to be. Trevor pulled the ebony and ivory letter opener from its case. Ebony and ivory. Wasn't that a song? *Ebony and Ivory live together in perfect harmony* ran through his head. Paul McCartney and Stevie Wonder, he remembered, but could anyone live in perfect harmony?

The letter opener sliced a straight line through the parchment envelope. Trevor's hands shook as he unfolded the typed pages and began to read.

My dearest Trevor,

If you're reading this, I guess it's not good news for me. This is not the way I wanted to say goodbye. God knows I've longed for you every day of my life and only wished and hoped I would see you again before my time ended.

Goodbye. They'd said goodbye many times—after dates, weekends, and dinners—but it had usually meant something hopeful. It meant "see you." Trevor wished he had a glass of scotch in his hand. He shouldn't be reading this. God, he didn't want to go there. He paused, swallowed hard, and read on.

There are so many things that have been left unsaid, hanging like the loose ends of a frayed sweater, often leaving me exposed to a life somewhat in disarray and filled with guilt over wrong choices and bad timing.

Guilt. He'd had plenty but never considered she had. Why should she? She'd played it cool and close. But maybe too much so. He took a deep breath, trying to calm his hands, his heart.

Supposedly, everything happens for a reason; there are no chance meetings or coincidences, but rather deliberate, if not divine, interventions in one's life. I don't know if I believe that, but I do believe timing is important and is perhaps everything. If you don't choose what is presented to you when it happens, then it races along the continuum of time beyond your grasp, never to reappear.

Trevor felt the pain of her words. He understood. Timing could be everything and often it was, especially for them. They seemed to have had the worst possible timing. Even now, Trevor wondered if his timing was all wrong and maybe too late.

It doesn't seem fair that everything can change in a second and that

what was once a fleeting moment is forever and permanently removed.
So, forgive me for not choosing you when I should have, just as I have
forgiven you.

Trevor read the lines again. The words cut through his heart. It
hurt to breathe. "Fuck," he said to himself.

I have justified my choices, knowing that "loving someone means being
able to let them go." I know you understand that. For us, fate intervened
in a nanosecond, changing our lives forever.

"Shit." Trevor shifted his eyes to the open window. Yes, fate had
intervened more than once, but he wasn't sure what she meant now.

Remember the day you came to Georgetown and I was taking grad
classes? We'd planned to meet after my class in front of the 1789. We
hadn't seen each other in a while, and you didn't know I'd gotten engaged
to Rick a couple of months earlier.

After class, I headed down the street to meet you. I saw you standing
in front of the Tombs. I knew in that moment 'you were the one' and that
I loved you. I decided then to break off my engagement. I stood staring out
at you, hoping to catch your eye. Instead, the coxswain of your old crew
began talking with you. You looked somewhat startled and upset. After
he left, you went into the Tombs.

Trevor looked away from Emma's words, trying to remember that
day. He had been 'the one' and never knew it. Sadness came over
him as he played the scene over in his mind. He had been shocked
and angry with her before she'd even gotten a chance to tell him. He
remembered. He hadn't wanted to hear anything she had to say. He
had told her to get lost. Now he was angry with himself. Another
screw-up. But why in the hell hadn't Emma ever told him any of this
before? He got up from the desk and began pacing back and forth.
He needed a goddamn drink. He opened the fridge and pulled out
a bottle of French beer. It would have to do. He couldn't believe he

was reading this. How could they both have been so fucking stupid? He threw himself into the big chair by her desk and downed half the bottle before his eyes scanned the next paragraph.

I thought it was odd that you didn't wait for me that day, but I knew where you were and headed downstairs. I made my way into the noisy rathskeller where I found you sitting at the bar having a drink. I was so excited and happy to see you. Quickly, I tried to remove my ring, but no amount of twisting and tugging loosened it from my finger. My entire being was flooded with emotion and our physical connection. Everything else melted away. But on that day our encounter was brief. You bombarded me with "So, you're engaged. Let me see the ring. Who is he?" It only took a few minutes for the mood to change. Before I could say anything to you, you said, "Go on, get out of here. Go ahead and marry the guy. I don't care."

Trevor's stomach churned. He felt nauseous. He had never thought about her feelings. He had been pissed that she'd ever consider marrying someone else. But sometime later, he had told her she shouldn't marry anyone but him. That he remembered. He knew now the words hadn't been enough. He hadn't shown her. He simply hadn't shown her, and he regretted that. He looked beyond the things on her desk—the computer, the manuscript—to the mountains, realizing he had never heard any of this from Emma's own lips and wondering if he ever would. He was angry and sad that he hadn't done more at the time, but he hadn't known what to do.

I worshipped you but didn't understand what you were really saying to me. I took you so literally. I left. I called Rick, he comforted me, or so I thought. But now I know that he took advantage of the situation.

She worshipped me? She'd hid that well, he thought. Was she scared? As scared as he had been of getting hurt, being rejected? When you're afraid, isn't that when you know you're in love? You have that fear of losing each other? They'd created their own self-fulfilling prophecy. They didn't trust each other enough. Maybe they hadn't wanted to risk not being loved in return.

What you don't know is that right up until my wedding day, I didn't want to marry him. But I didn't know how to get out of it. I let loyalty and my word rule my heart and have regretted it ever since. During the wedding ceremony, I prayed you would show up and object. That just shows you how out of it I was. You didn't even know where or when I was getting married! Crazy! All the years we were together, I just never found the right moment to tell you this.

Oh my god! He couldn't believe what he was reading. His heart was in his throat. She never loved Rick. Never. She loved me, but he had blown it. Why hadn't she said something, yelled at him, said anything? This is nuts. Emma had seen it all as a big rejection. She hadn't understood his anger, and he hadn't understood her reaction. They'd both chosen their actions but not their consequences,

After my divorce years later when I was in New York, I had planned to tell you then. But you told me you were married, and I knew all was lost. I cried for three days. When we had dinner in Brooklyn later that week, I wanted to tell you, but my head kept screaming, why didn't he ask me? Remember I asked you if you were deliriously happy? That was my way of wanting you to say that only I had ever made you feel that way. And in a way, you did. Your answer was, "I'm content."

Yes, he'd said that. What he'd meant was he was at peace with his decision because he had felt it was the only one left then. It became a choice of attitude. After all, she'd married someone else.

Trevor, I'm so very sorry things didn't work out for us. I never wanted anyone but you. I'll always love you.

Emma

Trevor buried his face in his hands, trying to check his emotions.

If only she were here now, he'd tell her how he felt, that he was sorry, and that they needed to be together. He folded the letter, placed it back in the envelope, and shoved it to the back of the drawer but not to the back of his mind. He felt drained, tired, and confused. She couldn't tell me. Why didn't she ever tell me? Was there more she never told me? He felt numb. What a fucking waste, he thought, but didn't he already know that and feel that way? Hadn't her letter told him what he wanted to know and hear—that she loved him still. Was it too late again?

He had to find her now more than ever.

34

Alone in the Chapel

EMMA SAT WITH HER knees pulled close to her chest, cradling her thoughts in her arms. For the first time in a long time, she could see things clearly. She was able to breathe deeply, free from the anxiety of the past.

After the last couple of days, she knew it had been a wonderful idea to come here, immerse herself in the solitude she had longed for, and do something different. The timing was good. Her book was finished, René would entertain Katie, and she could spend some time rejuvenating her artistic senses. Maybe it had been impulsive—even a little crazy—but she had been longing to stay here from the very first time she had seen the chapel with René. It had been for sale, and she purchased it shortly before renting her house in the village.

Bit by bit, she had been getting it ready. Now almost eighteen months later, she had created this special place known only to her. An artist friend in Apt had helped her choose the right brushes, paints, and canvases over the last year. She wanted it to be exclusively hers, a place where no one would look for her. Redundant, silly in some ways, because Provence itself was a retreat from the universe.

She wondered how things at the house were going without her, especially with Katie. She was frustrated that she had accidentally left her little flip phone on the kitchen table and couldn't call her, but she knew Katie wouldn't worry. Her note that she had been called away suddenly to write a brief travel piece and would be back on the weekend would keep them from worrying. She didn't like lying, but she would write something about the hamlet of Croagnes and had been gathering information about the chapel for months to satisfy her own curiosity.

For the moment, Emma had done what she'd promised herself—spend some time with her canvasses and brushes to try and recapture the creativity that had been dormant since high school and college. It was more difficult than she had thought to switch gears and creative endeavors in an instant. Her writer's mind was racing with stories of who had lived here before, who had built the chapel, and why and how had it come to be her own private residence. She had created her own parallel universe. Yet, when she wrote she thought of her art, and when she painted she thought of her writing, both intrinsically linked, intertwined. Would she always be caught this way? In between one desire and another, one man and another, one world and . . .

A soft breeze whispered across the top of the mountain. Emma continued to sit in the garden behind the chapel courtyard, sipping her coffee and sketching the datura, fountain, and statuary. She had been up since dawn, taking photos of the sunrise from the chapel's garden wall and doing some preliminary sketches for another painting. She finished some value studies, something she usually skipped in her hurry to get concepts on paper. But this time, she wanted to focus on the darkest darks and lightest lights to find a good focal point, much like finding her own focal point and compass in a faded life.

The noon sun was now melding these values into a bright glaring white, forcing her inside to the coolness of her studio. Emma walked across the stone patio, stopping briefly at the far wall to examine her pink rugosa roses and look at the valley from the hilltop. This time of year made her think of Cezanne and how he hadn't wandered far from home to create some of his best works—like those of Mount St. Victoire and the riverbanks near his studio at Jas de Bouffan. We only have to look in our own backyards to find what we are searching for, she reminded herself. She loved the height of this place and wondered how her own house looked from the sky. Was it merely a small dot on the world map? At night, the view was glorious. The sky and stars hung low, casting a glimmering net over the village.

Once inside, Emma headed upstairs to the vast light-filled studio with its many oversized windows. An expanse of old hand-carved beams stretched along the entire length of the ceiling. She moved the large wooden easel near the open studio window. Old and worn, she had confiscated the easel from a derelict art building in Apt. Big and heavy like Monet's easel in his Giverny studio.

Emma fingered through the many canvases looking for the right surface, the right size. She pulled a linen panel from the rack near the far wall and placed it on her easel. She had created a retreat within a retreat and was quite happy with herself, but generating art of any kind was hard work, both mental and physical. She ran her hands over the smooth canvas and adjusted its height. She looked out the window at the landscape below and pretended to sketch on the linen panel—a warm-up exercise she always did, much like a pitcher in the bullpen before heading out to the mound.

She held the charcoal at arm's length from the canvas and made some gestural marks to identify the hills, roads, and small buildings in the landscape before applying any paint. She had painted the same scene of the valley three times now and was able to calm her disappointment and frustration at not being able to immediately translate her vision into a readable painting. She was trying a new way, a little more abstract, by responding to the scene with touches of pure color. She knew it was like anything else—practice, practice, practice, and patience. She hadn't painted in years and knew she would have to take her time, go slow, and do what she could. It didn't have to be realistic or beautiful. She was simply trying to get the right amount of paint on the brush and use a simple, direct stroke onto the canvas, alla prima, like a true plein air painter.

The vivid local color stirred her emotions, making her eager to dip into her paints and let them speak for her. Most folks could see and appreciate the blue mountains, green olive trees, and rows of golden wheat and purple lavender, but Emma saw every color of the color wheel—the triads, the complementary and analogous colors—all bound up in form and shape. She knew in her heart that none could be replicated and that great art was merely a response to that natural splendor. She understood what Cezanne had meant about nature: "I can't seem to express the intensity that beats in upon my senses. I haven't at my command the magnificent richness of color that enlivens nature . . . look at that cloud, I should like to be able to paint that!" Indeed, Provence had the most fabulous azure skies and whipped cream clouds of anywhere in the world.

She saturated her brush in the ultramarine, permanent rose, and viridian to create a deep, dark hue that would shape the forms of shadows cast from the trees and mountains. She struggled to interpret what her eyes believed to be true, but it was foolhardy to attempt to create something so beautiful, so perfect. She remembered that someone once said, "into a painting love starts." She smiled. How ironic, she thought, that she simply couldn't get away from it—love. Was her painting a metaphor for the man she didn't marry, complex and unfinished, or the beginning of something new and unknown? The answer, she thought, was still a long ways off.

35

A Flicker of Light

TREVOR STOOD AND PACED around the kitchen and dining room, pausing briefly to admire the vineyards and the mountains beyond. The sun shifted to the west, pushing richer colors across the valley. His train of thought drifted to that late afternoon in Dumbarton Oaks when they had a picnic and lay side by side on the blanket, telling each other their young dreams. Back then she wanted to paint; he was pre-med. He knew his dreams had changed and wondered what she would tell him now about hers.

He thought about what he would tell her when he saw her, how he'd read her novel, how he'd thought she was truly lost, and he couldn't live without her. He walked toward her bedroom and stood in the doorway, scanning its contents. The white walls were accented by hues of blue from the sky to the ocean, with occasional touches of lavender in the linens and chairs. It was feminine but sophisticated. Everything was in its place—tidy, like a small hotel room. A few family photos sat on an old French dresser and one of her mother and father was on a nightstand near her bed, along with a small photo of her and René standing next to two horses, perhaps in the vineyard. He stared at it, saddened that he was not the one in the photo, not part of her life.

Trevor moved next to the small bookcase on the other side of the bed and knelt down, pulling each book from the shelves, flipping their pages, looking for notes, letters, or lists. Nothing except underlined words and notes in the margins, a writer's way of reading. The books on Cezanne, Van Gogh, and Matisse had sticky tabs identifying colors, techniques, and painting locations used by the masters. He focused on her handwriting—graceful and artistic but strong like her. He remembered the large collection of philosophy, art, and music books she'd had in Georgetown and wondered if she'd kept them and still loved them as she had once loved him.

As he carefully pushed each book back in its place, he noticed a magazine jutting out at the end of a row of books on the bottom shelf. He pulled it out to straighten it and saw Emma's name on the cover by one of the articles, *P.S. I Love You*. It was an old issue of the *Harvard Review* from the 1970s. He wondered why she'd kept this for so long; maybe it was her first published story. He turned to the middle of the magazine and began to read.

Perfect moments surrounded us—summer evenings window shopping on Wisconsin Avenue, afternoon picnics near Dumbarton Oaks, smelling the roses at the Brooklyn Botanic Gardens, dining at the Italian restaurant on Flatbush Avenue, weekends at Fire Island, and that first year in France, relaxing at the Paris apartment and sharing des cafés at Montparnesse.

There was so much about you that changed me. You helped me grow into a woman. The line between black and white blurred. I became more open to different ways of seeing. I could think more abstractly.

Huh? This was about him and it was published. Another unknown about her, he thought. He skipped down.

You said you never understood me, but that I was the most exciting woman you had ever known. And there was much about you I didn't comprehend. In fact, you had a favorite saying: "To be great is to be mis-understood." (Emerson, on Self Reliance, I later learned) So perhaps you deliberately tried to keep me in suspense as well.

Sometimes I wonder if either of us really understood what happened— why it didn't work. There's another Emerson quote I've learned since: "Give all to love; obey your heart."

It seems simple, obvious, but it wasn't. It still isn't, but I am better at trying and searching for the right connection. And . . . P.S. I love you.

Dumbfounded, Trevor closed the magazine and put it on the shelf. He was confused. He wasn't sure he knew who she was; maybe he never did. Maybe keeping secrets was a part of who she was. Maybe she's keeping a secret now, he thought, not wanting to be found.

He stood slowly and walked toward a small closet, then hesitated, wondering whether he should continue looking through her things. They were too personal. He was an intruder, an outsider, but when he opened the door, something red on an upper shelf caught his eye. He reached and pulled down a red box. He opened it, revealing the Pashmina cashmere scarf folded carefully inside. It was the one he had spent Christmas Eve shopping for in New York many years ago. He had wanted something sophisticated but delicate, something soft to the touch that would feel good against the skin. The salesgirl at Neiman's had suggested it, and he chose the color—deep red—red for Christmas, love, and passion.

He ran his fingers over the scarf, remembering her smile and lips He held the box close to his face, trying to capture her scent. *Emma.* He thought she is like this red scarf, standing out in the crowd, easily noticed. Like the presence of the lone, red cardinal tucked into the branches of the winter pine that brightens up everything around it. She had that quality and charisma of making a lasting impression with her splash of color against a grey world.

He folded the scarf, put it back in its place, and fumbled through an old shoebox at the back of the shelf. He was surprised to find letters and cards he had sent her from Long Beach Island and Manhattan the first year they dated, things he'd forgotten. These were little romantic gestures he didn't realize had meant so much to her. When he read them, his words surprised even him. His invitation to the shore: "I miss you. Please come and spend a lovely weekend with me in September. I'll be all alone. It will be just the two of us in the sun and sand." There was some relief in knowing he *had* tried to reach out to her in his own boyish way, but it had been too soon, too misunderstood.

He was especially shocked to find a note from his mother to Emma inviting her to lunch in Brooklyn whenever she was back in the city. He knew they had talked on the phone a couple of times, but he had no idea about this. I wonder if she went, if they met. She had never mentioned it. More mystery. What else hadn't she told him? He couldn't believe she had kept these letters. She obviously cared about him. What had gone so wrong? But deep down he knew. They simply couldn't or wouldn't meet each other's needs. And probably still couldn't. He didn't know anymore. He placed the lid on the box and shoved it gently back on the shelf where it belonged—closed, hidden, and past. He didn't want to look anymore or think about the past dreams, all gone to a different time and place.

He was here now.

Every place has a season, like love, Trevor thought. Love put him here looking through Emma's things, still searching, trying to find the right answers. Love and heartbreak had left their scars. Reminders of the right choices at the wrong time and the wrong choices never at the right time. He wondered if now he was finally in the right place at the right time. He needed to know that everything would work out okay. He wanted a happy ending for them both.

Trevor thought her manuscript might yet provide some answers. At least he would know what she had been writing or thinking about before she left. He returned to the study, sat down at her desk, picked up his half sandwich, and began reading more pages. He sat and stared at the computer screen. For the first time, he noticed something different on the screen saver. He saw a small, terracotta shape in the background. He glanced up and looked at the view out the balcony window. It was the same view. Why hadn't he noticed this before? What was it, and where was it, he wondered? He stared at the mountains, and his eyes told him something was out there. Lights flickered in the distance atop the petit Luberon. He hadn't noticed any houses there, but this tiny flicker piqued his curiosity and hope. It was worth investigating.

By 2:00 a.m., Trevor had finished re-reading all of Emma's pages, unsure if he'd really learned anything more about where she could be. Katie had come home hours ago and brought him some leftover dinner. They talked briefly. He couldn't remember when he'd experienced a night so quiet and dead that even the songs of the cicada were silent. New York was never this still. Cynicism swept over him. What if this is what remains for me without her—silence and emptiness. He didn't want to go there and quickly approached the doors to the balcony to shake himself out of this mood. He stepped outside to a stunning full moon backlit by a pitch-black sky glistening with millions of stars.

36

A Revelation

TREVOR AWOKE EARLY AND walked onto the balcony again to search in the daylight for what he had seen in the distance last night. Each morning, he felt disappointed at not having made progress in finding Emma. He had read her manuscript through twice but wasn't any closer to what he thought might be the truth. He'd been here four days now and hoped today might be different.

He squinted into the distance, anticipating seeing something, but he needed binoculars to better focus on what was there or what was not. So many things needed to be in focus for him. Why had he come here and what were his plans?

He thought he'd known before he read her pages, but now he was tormented with a variety of feelings. Was he here by way of guilt, love, or loss? Maybe all. Maybe just regret. He stared out at the vineyards, amazed at how the vines thrived in the rocky soil and hot sun. Perhaps this meant that even barren dreams could morph into happiness. Maybe that was the whole point. Maybe this was an exercise he had to go through to cleanse his soul from guilt and regret. Maybe this was his revelation.

Last night, the lights in the distance told him someone else was out there in the mountains. It was possible the lights had always been there and he hadn't noticed. It was strange that Emma's screen saver mirrored the view from her house with something—a shape—in the distance. Maybe it was a clue. He felt a little like Colonel Mustard in the study with the candlestick, but he was beginning to believe there were no coincidences. He would ask René.

KATIE WAS STILL ASLEEP when he walked down the main street to Margarite's patisserie, where he learned René was in Paris. It was his first time meeting Margarite, who was warm and welcoming. René had told her he was an old friend of Emma's. Trevor learned from Margarite that Jacques knew everything about the area and to talk with him. Trevor bought a bag of croissants and brioche to take with him. An hour later, he was approaching Margarite and Jacques' house, hoping Jacques would feel well enough to talk.

A light breeze pushed along the cool, mid-morning air, but by noon the Provençal sun would beat down. He opened the garden gate and immediately succumbed to the aroma of Margarite's roses and lavender. Trevor stopped and looked at the varieties of flowers and the well-kept beds: a gardener's garden. It reminded him of the rows of Jackson Perkins' bare-root roses he'd helped his mother plant in their long, narrow backyard in Park Slope. He was a boy who loved to dig; he didn't know anything about flowers. She had enlisted his help in spading a dozen holes and then showed him how to enrich the soil with peat moss, compost, and dehydrated manure. Later, when the roses matured, he was the one who pruned and deadheaded the plants. When he sold the house after her death ten years ago, the roses had transformed the yard into a small park of perfumed blossoms. He always thought of her love of roses whenever he bought them or savored their fragrance.

Trevor nervously knocked on the front door, but no one answered. He called Jacques' name, but no one came. Maybe he was still asleep. Trevor walked toward the gate but decided to wander the yard to see what else Margarite's green thumb had nurtured. He saw a man out back on the patio having coffee. His blue striped pajamas and cotton robe hung loosely from his large frame. Trevor moved toward him. "Bonjour, Jacques?"

"*Qui est-il?*"

"It's Trevor. A friend of Emma's." Trevor walked toward the patio and was taken aback by Jacques' pallid appearance—as if he'd never seen the sun—which Trevor figured had been as long as his hospital stay at least. He felt as if he was invading Jacques' privacy. "I'm sorry," he said, turning to leave.

"Come." Jacques waved him to the table.

Trevor reluctantly walked over to this obviously once large man who looked drawn and tired and meekly held out the bag of pastries as a casual greeting. Jacques shook his head and tapped his heart with his hand. Of course, Trevor thought, he can't eat this stuff. Stupid.

Trevor gave a half shrug. "Sorry, *désolé.*"

Jacques reached for a chair and motioned for Trevor to sit. "*Asseyez-vous.*"

Trevor wondered if this was a good idea without René or someone to translate for them. Jacques' English was about as good as Trevor's French, which wasn't saying much. He was having second thoughts.

"I'm Trevor, Emma's friend." He put the bag of pastries on the table. Trevor noticed the worn and frayed slippers adorning Jacques' feet and felt like a true outsider. Now what? Would he have to use gestures and pantomime to ask his questions? He was anxious. How would this work, exactly?

"*Je sais, je sais.* I know. Good to meet you."

"Likewise; *moi aussi?*" Trevor said, questioning his French, but he realized Jacques had a much better grasp of English than he had thought. He declined Jacques' offer of coffee, and before he could say anything else, Emma's name rolled off Jacques' lips.

"Emma? I haven't seen . . ."

That was it. Apparently, no one had said anything to Jacques. He didn't know Emma was gone and probably for good reason. Trevor wasn't going to be the one to send him back to the hospital. Instead, he tried, "*En voyage?*" hoping that it meant she might be away on travel.

"*Peut être.*" Maybe. He smiled. "*Se cacher?* Hiding?"

A look of surprise crossed Trevor's face. So, they *had* told him . . . or did he know where she was?

"Don't worry. Emma's okay." It was as if Jacques had read his mind.

"Where is she?"

"Oh, *je suis désolé*, don't know."

"Why do you think she's okay?"

Jacques shrugged. "*Un sentiment.*"

Trevor thought for a moment. A sentiment—a feeling. Oh, for crying out loud, why did everyone feel that she was okay? But he remembered he'd said the same thing to Katie. Was this like one of those games where you repeat something often enough that you believe it to be true, or did those who knew her well assume she could take care of herself?

But Jacques told him a little more. He told him about the bike he'd given Emma and when he checked the shed this morning, it was gone. He had tried to reach Margarite to tell her but hadn't been able to get through at the shop.

Jacques poured a cup of coffee for Trevor and then pointed at the cream and sugar. Trevor shook his head. "*Noir, pour moi.*" That much he'd remembered from the times he'd spent with Emma at the cafés in Paris.

"Black," like the night, like the depths of despair, the end. Emma once told him that many artists, including herself, mixed myriad colors to produce a beautiful black. Black had its own depth and richness. He liked thinking about it that way.

Jacques sipped his coffee and then continued. "Emma is like a daughter. The Vespa was a birthday gift."

Trevor thought it odd that Jacques hadn't told anyone about the Vespa but realized he'd been in the hospital and probably didn't know until recently that Emma wasn't around. Strange. He hadn't told René or Katie either, but maybe he hadn't made the connection until he went to the shed and found the scooter gone.

Trevor looked at Jacques. "I have a question."

Jacques waited. "Okay."

Trevor pulled out his pen and a piece of folded paper and drew an outline of the mountains in the distance. He put some little stars and rays of light around the spot he was interested in and showed it to Jacques, who studied it carefully, tracing the mountains with his fingers.

"You've seen lights there." Jacques pointed to the mountains.

"Yes, yes." Trevor nodded.

"*C'est Croagnes . . . un hameau.*"

"*Croagnes? Un hameau?*" Trevor repeated.

"A hamlet."

Trevor got the message: a small community named Croagnes.

Jacques took Trevor's pen and wrote the name on his drawing. Beside it, he wrote *24 kms par voiture.*

Okay. Now he was getting somewhere. "What is there?" he asked. *"Qu'y-a-til?"*

"Ce qui?" Jacques repeated. He rubbed his chin. "What is there? *Une chapelle,*" he said. *"Une maison."*

A chapel. A house.

Trevor sat with Jacques for a while longer, enjoying his coffee and one of Margarite's buttery croissants. He thought Jacques seemed in good spirits. This small encounter with Jacques helped him understand that Emma had people around her who cared about her and loved her. He could see Jacques as a father figure for her and wished he'd been able to sit with his own father and share coffee and conversation. Maybe this *was* the right place for Emma at the right time. Maybe René was right as well. Trevor continued to question himself as he thanked Jacques and left him in the garden.

Maybe it was best to leave things the way they were and not pursue—No! What was he thinking? He had to know the truth. Emma could decide.

It was all up to Emma.

37

Croagnes

TREVOR PULLED HIS Michelin map from the glove compartment and unfolded it on the hood of the car. His finger traced the South of France from Marseilles through Aix to Vaucluse and Apt, and Bonnieux. No Croagnes. It was too small. Jacques had told him it was northwest of the village about ten miles. He'd head in that general direction.

Trevor abandoned his pessimism as he drove out of the village. His senses heightened with the excitement of his mission. Even the delicate fragrance of lavender that drifted across his face and permeated his nostrils didn't distract him. Near Bonnieux, he was surprised to see a trickle of water under the old Roman bridge. He didn't stop but made a mental note to come back sometime.

The Peugeot Cabriolet convertible made him feel young and free again as he zipped along the narrow, winding roads. The nostalgic image of his old Healey popped into his head, and he was a college student at Georgetown, driving the country roads of Virginia with Emma on their way to Evergreen. Their relationship had never been simple, but they had loved each other deeply once, and any past hurt melted away when they were together. He pushed his foot against the accelerator to shed the sense of helplessness that had overshadowed him for the last couple of days.

After several wrong twists and turns, the road began to narrow until it ended at the bottom of the mountain. This couldn't be the only way to get to the hamlet, he thought. He got out of the car and walked around for a long while until he found what he thought was a path. Trees and brush almost hid it, but it looked like it led upward. Although somewhat uneven from lack of use, it was definitely walkable. He decided to take a chance and not waste any more time searching for another driving route. He trudged up the rocky trail, pushing through the silvery-green olive shrubs, the sun pressing against his shoulders and back. After twenty minutes, Trevor realized he was out of shape for this kind of exercise, but he had come to a clearing and a rocky ledge overlooking the valley. It was a sight to behold. Yellow, green, and purple squares, rectangles, and semi-circles reached across the valley as far as the eye could see. When he looked back, he was certain that the rows of vines far below were René's. Somehow he knew he was on the right track.

He stood there for a moment, getting his bearings. His heart pounded, his breath shortened, and sweat dripped from his forehead. He took a long drink from his bottle of water. Excited, he turned one-hundred and eighty degrees, searching for a road, a house, some sign of life. And then he saw a cross, a steeple, and a terracotta chapel. Was this the shape he'd seen on her computer? It must be the hamlet. As he got closer, he saw about seven white and adobe-colored houses scattered about the top of the mountain. His heart raced—Croagnes.

He caught his breath and walked up the cobblestone street toward the chapel. The front door was locked. Anxious, he walked behind the building and down a slight grade toward a walled patio area. Something caught his eye. Propped up in the corner of the back wall was a light blue Vespa. His heart was in his throat. The one Jacques had given her? Beyond the roses and cherub fountain in the center of walled courtyard, he noticed a pair of leather sandals in the corner. His eyes followed the curve of the wall past the archway to the other side of the patio, where she was sitting on the end of the far wall facing the valley. His stomach felt raw inside, deprived. Her back was to him, but he knew he had found her. She had deliberately hidden herself away in this remote place and worried everyone. Why? The relief that had gripped him turned to anger. "Emma! Emma! Emma!"

Deep in thought and focused on her sketch, Emma didn't respond or turn around. Trevor's voice grew louder. When she turned toward the strange, deep voice, she was blinded by the late morning sun. She shielded her eyes and tried to focus on the figure before her. She watched his lips move. She heard nothing. She studied the dark, aviator sunglasses framing his unshaven face, looking for clues. Her heart leaped. No! It couldn't be. She couldn't believe her eyes. An angry-faced Trevor was there in front of her. He held her gaze.

Emma felt a shiver through her body. She looked hard at the tan face and slightly greying temples. She noticed his strong arms glistening from the heat of the day. She was in the middle of her own dream, unable to move forward, daring herself to wake up. Didn't she want to run to him, throw herself into his arms, and kiss him until drained of all passion? Isn't this what she had always wanted? Trevor on her own terms? She wanted to laugh and cry at the same time, but mostly, she didn't want this dream to disappear, dissolve into nothingness.

She couldn't move.

She couldn't speak.

"Emma, what in the hell are you doing? What's this about?"

Her eyes widened. She stood slowly, trying to steady her legs. Her sketch book slid from her trembling hands. She began walking toward him slowly in a trance-like state, somewhat off balance, her mind awash with images of the past: the mixer where they met, the play they went to on their first date, and the first time they made love in his Brooklyn brownstone. It was as if her entire relationship with him passed before her in a matter of seconds. She was elated to see him, yet terrified. This wasn't real. *Real.* If she could say it with enough conviction, maybe it would be true. Her ears strained to understand his words. What was he saying? He was yelling at her for not being dead, for having found her. What?

Her heart threw itself into high gear. "Trevor? Is that—why—how—are you here? Why? How did you find me?"

"I've been at your house with Katie."

"I don't understand." She swallowed hard. "Why are you here?"

Trevor hesitated, thinking how to answer. He looked at her paint-laden shorts and torn T-shirt. "Because I need you." The words slipped from his mouth, unplanned, natural.

The blood rushed to her face, colliding with her confusion. She stammered. "You need me?"

"I've always needed you. I don't want to waste any more time." He noticed the red paint on her knee, like dried blood from an old wound—like one of many he had inflicted. "I made a mistake."

"Mistake? And which mistake was that?" Her voice was gentle.

"Okay, *mistakes* then." Trevor paused, gathering his courage. "The first one was letting you marry someone else; the second was getting married when I was in love with you."

He had surprised her. Was he really saying this? What did it mean now? Emma took a deep breath. She felt the tears against her cheeks. "I don't think—" Caught off guard, she stopped, not knowing what to say or how to say it.

Trevor's heart sank. He waited to hear more, something positive, encouraging. "What? Have I made another mistake? Was it a mistake for me to come here and find you?"

Mistake rang in her ears. She wiped her hands on her shorts and waited for the pain in her head and the ringing in her ears to stop. Hadn't she made the same mistakes? Was she determined to repeat them? What about René? Did she love him? Was he a mistake too? Would Trevor wipe away all of her remorse or only remind her of it? Frightened and confused about how to respond, she said, "I don't know what to say."

"I know it must be a shock seeing me here, but I need to know. Do you still love me or want me? Could we . . ."

Emma looked through him. "I've loved no one more." She sighed. "But I've met someone."

Trevor's shoulders fell. "You mean René ?" He took a couple of steps toward her, feeling an impulse to hold her.

"You've met him?"

"Yes." What else was he going to say? He's too young for you. "And?"

Trevor felt his stomach churn. He couldn't believe they were talking about this guy. Did she really love this kid? Finally, he said, "And what?" He faltered. "He's charming. *Young.* Too young." His jaw tightened. "He's not for you."

"What do you mean? You don't know anything about him! About me, my—my life." Unsure of her feelings for either of them, Emma stood still, trying to unravel her emotions.

Trevor's heart hurt. She was right, of course. He had no right at all to her or her life. He'd given that up years ago. Still, he had come all this way. "You're right," he said. "I have no rights, no claims on you." He waited. "But you are the love of my life, and I believe in my heart you feel the same way."

Her eyes flooded; her vision blurred. She couldn't believe this was happening. He was everything she wanted but her mind was racing. She stammered, "You—you told me to marry someone else." She was surprised at how easily her wounds had ripped open the sutures of denial she had carefully placed over them. The hurt was as sharp as the day it had happened.

He inched forward. "It was a reaction. I was caught off-guard, shocked that you were engaged to someone other than me."

She studied the sincere worry lines across his brow.

He reached for her hand. "I've regretted it, but I can't change it." He studied her light blue eyes, searching for the woman he once had known. "Please forgive me. Love me now."

Love me now. His words crashed like an avalanche inside her. He was giving her what she had always wanted. Wasn't that enough?

"I'm sorry too." Tears filled her eyes. "I'm sorry I married someone I didn't love, trying to force your hand when you weren't ready. I'm sorry."

He put his arms around her. "Let's not do this again, Em. I know you love me." She nuzzled her face against his neck, savoring the musky scent of his skin. She felt safe.

"You do?"

Trevor smiled. "Yes. I read your letter."

Emma stood back. "What letter?"

Trevor removed the letter from his pants pocket. "This letter. The one I found in your desk."

Emma's face reddened. "You were in my desk?"

"In your desk and on your computer, looking for you . . . worried you were missing or worse. We all were."

"You were in my things?" She pushed him away but only half-heartedly. Did this really surprise her? Weren't they always in each other's lives, thoughts, stuff?

"How'd you think I found you? Your computer . . . your screen saver . . . and Jacques."

"Oh my god, you bothered Jacques? You went to the hospital?"

"It's okay. He's fine. He's at home. We talked. That's all. He told me about Croagnes."

"But he didn't know where—"

"No, Emma. Nobody did. Just as you planned. What in the hell were you thinking?" He eyed her charcoal-smudged face and her hair tied back from her face. She looked so young and girlish.

Emma's jaw dropped. "What are you saying? I left a note. I really didn't plan to stay here more than a couple of days . . ."

Trevor gestured with a sweep of his arm. "But what? It was too perfect, too beautiful to leave all this solitude? No one found a note. Katie and Margarite turned your house upside down. Nothing."

"I left it on the dry sink near the door."

"Well, it wasn't there."

"Oh my god. I never meant for this to happen. I had planned to call also, but—"

"But you didn't have this." He handed her her phone. "Did you mean to leave it behind?"

Emma looked at the phone. "Of course not. I need to call them."

After she called Katie, then René, leaving apologetic messages with them both and promising a full explanation upon her return, she glanced again at Trevor, her heart echoing in her chest, and then she tenderly pressed her mouth over his and put her arms under his.

Trevor let go of his anger. He put his arms around her waist and pulled her close to him, his chest, his entire body. The kiss, the long embrace, brought them back to the moment when they'd never been apart. "Damn it," he said, his voice low. "I'm not letting you go this time."

"Hold me," she whispered in his ear. "Hold me tight."

All the longing and wanting came together in mere seconds. It was Brooklyn 1978, and they were kissing, holding hands, and walking along the Brooklyn Promenade. It was junior prom; it was a sweet embrace in Georgetown near the 1789. It was every hello they had said to each other for the last twenty years, relived and rolled out before them.

THE DIMNESS OF THE ROOM startled him awake. Dusk. The afternoon sunlight had crept along the bottom of the terrace wall. He studied her lying next to him and then began to kiss her and hold her. He pulled her on top of him and looked into her eyes, blue like the Mediterranean, and said, "I love you, Emma."

She smiled. The words she had longed to hear rang throughout her body. She wanted to say I love you too but couldn't form the words, afraid he might disappear into thin air. She couldn't say how she felt because she couldn't put her elation into words.

"I'm curious," he said after a moment. "Why are you hiding out here?"

Emma didn't want to have to explain herself, not sure it would make sense to anyone but her. "I'm sorry everyone worried. That was never my intention."

She pushed herself up and sat on the edge of the bed, putting on his shirt. She handed him his khakis, fingering the torn pocket. "Come with me. There's something I want to show you." She wanted him to understand.

He was definitely curious. He took her hand, and she led him out a door on the other side of the room and up some circular stairs to a large loft area at the north end of the chapel. Emma explained how René had shown her the chapel when she first came to the village. She fell in love with it and bought it almost right away as a refuge of sorts. "I wanted a place where I could have some solitude and get away, even from writing."

"But isn't the village your hideaway? And I thought writing made you happy."

"Yes, but writing is my work, and I wanted someplace special where I could simply play."

"Can you buy a chapel? I mean, isn't it consecrated or something? Have we committed some kind of sacrilege by—you know?"

"You're right." Emma laughed. "When I bought it, I had to declare that I'd never have sex here."

Trevor grinned.

The loft ceiling stretched toward six skylights that brought in the best north light. Canvases rested in several racks around the room, and large easels rested near windows and under skylights. Paints, brushes, and paper were all neatly organized in containers and bins. An old hearth jutted from the exposed stone wall at one end of the room. At the other end was a music nook complete with a piano and guitar.

Trevor's eyes lit up. "A great place for a party. But I can see why you would want to keep it all to yourself." It was beautiful and comfortable, well-worn. "You haven't quit writing, have you?" Trevor wondered if there was something more, something she wasn't telling him. A mid-life crisis, perhaps.

"No, but I needed to do something else for a while. Not that painting is easier. It's just that I might not have another chance like this to indulge myself, to paint."

Trevor's eyes scanned the vast space and the rows of paintings leaning against the walls. He was amazed at how talented she was, how diverse. He loved her for that. "Why won't you have another chance?"

"I'm traveling more, doing more stories for the magazine. And I've written a book that I'll probably need to revise."

The book. Trevor hesitated. "I've read it. I'm sorry. I wasn't trying to pry, but we were all looking for hints as to where you were."

Emma realized Trevor had been extensive in his search for her, but she wasn't sure whether to be pleased or worried. "Oh my god. You read it. Tell me. What did you think?"

"Honestly? I found it interesting but complicated."

Emma began laughing. The irony of finding their own story complicated.

"It's us, isn't it?" he said.

Emma nodded through her laughter and hugged him hard.

THEY SPENT THE REST OF the evening lying in bed, making love and talking about everything, absolutely everything. There were no secrets and no regrets. The sun vanished behind the mountains, and Emma pulled the soft cotton sheets over both of them as she nestled beside him.

She thought about where they were now, settled in bed together in each other's arms and no longer felt haunted by his absence. She was deliriously happy.

How do you measure a miracle? Emma wondered. It was a miracle he was here, that he had found her, and that time had only intensified their feelings. It was an unanticipated, unexpected reward.

This time, timing was their own miracle.

38

To Dream

STILL ASLEEP, EMMA COULD feel a gentle massage across her shoulders. She stretched out her arm, reaching for Trevor. His name became a soft moan from her lips, and she turned on her side, searching in her mind for his warm body. She thought she heard someone saying her name, but her eyelids were drowning in a deep sleep and her senses were lost to the real world. She wrapped her arms and legs around Trevor and pulled herself into him. Emma lay quiet, but her body continued to move under the hands pressing against her shoulders and back. Her name. Someone was calling her.

"Trevor, I'm here." She smiled, still asleep.

"Em, Em. It's me," Katie said softly.

Emma let out a slight groan. She thought she heard distant voices speaking French. She was in a haze, trying to respond. She didn't want to get up and leave Trevor. She had been without him for too long.

"Em, it's me, Katie."

Emma moved ever so slightly, trying to pull Trevor closer. "Katie, I'm sorry, so sorry," she whispered.

"Sorry? Em, it's time to wake up. You fell asleep at your desk. You've been here all night. Emma it's me, Katie. Please wake up."

Emma turned her head, opening one eye. Gone were the beautiful white linens and musky scent of a man, her man. Her neck and back hurt. When she raised her head and opened her eyes, Katie was kneeling beside her, rubbing her shoulders and back.

"Huh? Where—Trevor?"

"You were sound asleep, Em. You're here at Evergreen," Katie said. "I'm sorry to wake you."

Emma sat up slowly, trying to remember where she was and why. The distant voices were now more distinct. She looked around and saw the BBC broadcast on TV in the far corner. A short clip of the French president and one of his cabinet members flashed on the screen.

"Oh no. God! No!"

Katie's mouth fell open. "Are you okay? I think you need some coffee." She headed for the kitchen.

Emma, dazed and disappointed, had been living her dream, her only dream, and now it had evaporated in seconds. She wished she could go back in time to Provence and into Trevor's arms.

Her computer and desk lamp still on, Emma glanced at the screen. The words "deliriously happy" leapt out at her. She wasn't. Would she ever be again? She wondered but knew she had to write it all down and get it out of her mind, heart, and being.

"I'm sorry I had to wake you," Katie repeated. "Can I get you anything else? How about some breakfast?"

Emma sat up and looked at her sister. "What I really need is lost in time. I need that one special moment again. That moment with Trevor. In love for the first time. I need to be in love again."

Emma could read that soulful look in Katie's eyes and knew exactly what she was thinking—what to say and how to say it? No, Trevor would never go away, she thought.

"Sis, you're lucky. You know what that one true love *is* even if it didn't end the way you wanted it to." She paused. "I've never been in love like that."

Emma smiled knowingly. Katie was younger and certainly would experience real love eventually. "You will, sweetheart. You will." Emma believed everyone should know a total love once in their lifetime and she wanted that for Katie.

Katie handed Emma a large mug of black coffee and sat down next to her. "Do you want to talk about it?"

Emma didn't answer. She reached across the desk, turned off the lamp, and logged off her computer. "I think I need a hot shower and a soft bed for a little while. You don't mind, do you? Maybe we can talk later."

Katie nodded. "Can I ask you something?"

"What is it?"

"What did you mean when you told me you were sorry?"

"Huh?"

"When you were waking up just now, you said, 'Katie, I'm sorry, so sorry.'"

"Oh, that." Emma gave half a shrug. "It was part of a dream. Nothing important."

But Emma knew dreams were important, especially her dreams. Dreams were wishes from the heart, she remembered.

What was that song? How did it go? She began humming and then mouthed the words: *Dreams are nothing more than wishes, and a wish is a dream you wish could come true.* Oh, yes. Harry Nilsson, so long ago. But her favorite Nilsson song was *Remember: Dream.*

Love is only in a dream. Remember, life is never as it seems. Dream . . .
Close your eyes.

She loved the words to that one especially. She had to agree. For her, love was only in a dream now. Emma continued to try to sing the words "d - r - e - a - m . . . " as she walked upstairs to bed. Maybe she would dream again when her head hit the pillow.

39

The Last Chapter

NEXT MORNING, EMMA had already downed three cups of coffee. She'd been at her computer since 5:00 a.m. She wanted to write it all down, everything she remembered, including Trevor finding her and loving her. She had entered the pages of her own novel without even knowing it, like the writer in her book. She could tie it all together now in the last chapter.

She noticed how the morning light was already changing from the bright intensity of summer to a softer, more translucent quality. It seemed tempered, cooler, but nonetheless spectacular. She understood why her grandfather and father loved this place so much, the land, farming, all of it. When she looked out the window toward Cedar Run, she could see each season change before her eyes. Nature let you see what was ahead if you let it, Emma thought, and she could feel change already coming. Soon, it would be Indian summer. She let these thoughts sift through her mind, knowing that soon she'd be leaving here. She didn't hear Katie come into the room or notice she was standing behind her.

"You're up early. What are you doing?" Katie asked, sipping her coffee.

"Oh, trying to finish up here."

"Finish? The book?"

"Hopefully, this is the last chapter."

"Really? That's wonderful. How do you know it's the end?

"Because there's nothing more to say." Emma knew that writers wrote not to say something but because they had something to say.

"Is this book going to set the world on fire?"

Emma looked quizzically at her sister. "I hadn't really thought about that. I just needed to tell this story." The truth was she often wondered why she had bothered to write this at all. Who would care? Trevor? Frequently, she overanalyzed her motives only to be pushed aside by the voice of her characters, their nagging and explaining. She was compelled to tell their story even if no one ever read the words.

"It's fiction, right? A love story?"

"Yes. Definitely fiction." But Emma believed that writers write about what they know or think they know, even in fiction. Besides, her desire to finish telling the story was with the hope it would mend her frayed heart.

"Is it about Trevor?"

Emma delayed her response. Wasn't everything about him? At fifty, wasn't she still waiting, hoping, wanting, dreaming? How could she write about love without writing about Trevor?

"Yes," she said quietly. "He's in the book."

"So, how does it end?"

The only certainty was that no ending was formulated in Emma's mind. As she gazed at the text on her computer screen, she began to question if there is only one right person in the world for each of us. And what did happy ending mean anyway? Shouldn't it be the beginning, not the ending of love?

"I'm not sure yet how it will end," she told Katie, "but I'm hoping the characters will do the right thing for themselves."

"The characters?" Katie asked. "Isn't all that up to you?"

Emma chuckled. "Sometimes the characters take us where we should go, not where we want to go."

"Really? I thought every writer had a plan from beginning to end."

Every now and then, Emma felt stuck between the pages of her own book, squeezed around and between the words and lines, pressed hard against her characters, looking close up and analyzing their every move, unable to write her way out of a scene or their lives. Her characters were conflicted about what to do and how to move on in their own words and across the page. They could be annoying—urging her to go places and do things against her intuition, but she did listen and consider certain requests, allowing insight into their thinking and ways to broaden their depth. This time, though, she believed they had let her desires drift into a dreamlike reality that helped her through to the conclusion.

Emma glanced at her sister. "It's hard to explain how the creative process works." Emma knew that although each writer had a unique style and method, writing was a mystery to most of them. She often wondered where the words were before they were written. Were they in the head or the heart, in the past, the present, or future? Were they simply part of the cosmic universe, waiting to land in an open mind or on a blank sheet of paper? She loved that in a single moment in time, they became a sentence, a paragraph, a story, a novel, a play, a memory of something heartfelt and true . . . or not.

"So, Katie wondered, have you found your style?"

Emma thought for a moment. "It's more like a work in progress. I'm finding my way slowly. That's why it's taking so long." Three years to be exact. Three years that she should have been here with her mother. Emma glanced at the calendar on her desk—almost five months since the funeral, burial, and reading of the will. It wasn't a shock that their mother had died. She was in her early eighties, but she and Katie were saddened they had not been here for her instead of so many miles away. Emma had learned more about her mother's life and dreams after her death than during her life. She had found old letters, poems, and a manuscript that revealed a talent Emma didn't know existed. Maybe she had inherited her mother's gift for writing.

"I can't help but think that maybe there was something I could have done to make things easier for her." Emma let out a deep sigh. "I should have come back for longer visits. I should have called more often."

"You don't know that." Katie turned toward her sister. "Mom raised us to be on our own, and she knew where we were. She could have called more too. You can't change the past; it is what it is. She would want us to go on, be happy, and live full lives."

Katie's words surprised Emma even though over the past few months, she had realized her sister had become more confident, determined.

"Did you ever think we'd wind up here again?" Katie glanced around.

Emma paused. "We knew they'd die, but I didn't expect to spend so much time here, let alone finish my novel here."

"So you're really near the end," Katie said. "Only this one chapter?"

"Hopefully."

"Then what?"

"You already know—back to Paris."

Emma felt Katie watching her peck at the keyboard.

"It's difficult starting over, isn't it, Em?" Katie hesitated, then shook her head. "Never mind. Don't keep your characters waiting. Get busy and finish this thing."

"Right!" Emma turned in her desk chair, watching the late morning light slide across the window sill and fall onto the dark hardwood floor. It left her breathless, inspired. Nothing is written in stone, she thought, as she began to hone in on the final scenes. The beauty and unexpectedness of life, especially writing, was what excited her, a wonderful mystery that unfolded in her own words. She used her sister's question as the beginning of the very last chapter, for her characters also wanted to know: *"Did you ever think we'd wind up here?"*

40

Leaving Evergreen

IN A FEW WEEKS, SUMMER had closed its doors all too quickly, and shorter days diminished into a palette of reds, rusts, and browns. The smell of change was in the air. Mid-September brought a season of crisper air, burning leaves, dried cornstalks, apples, and the start of something new. The book was finished, done. Emma felt relieved and drained at the same time. Perhaps writing had filled some void, some hope deep inside her that now was empty again. She didn't know why she wrote, only that she had to. She believed that no writers want to die with their stories inside, unwritten.

Emma stood at her desk looking through her favorite window and remembered how one of her teachers had told her that when you look out, you are really looking in. She thought about this now as she realized she was about to embark on a new adventure, a new time in her life. She would go to Brooklyn before returning to Paris, and of course, there were friends she needed to say goodbye to. She looked out at the hills of Evergreen and knew that, yes, she was truly look-ing in—into her mind and heart. She also knew that sometimes you need to look back before moving forward.

She tuned out Katie's voice and looked intently around the dining room, saying her mental goodbyes to her childhood home. She focused on every detail, from the dark hardwood floor to the tin ceiling, absorb-ing every last memory there—the tiger oak table and chairs where everyone came together, the corner where the old wood stove once stood, and the mirrored oak buffet that always held a glass jar filled with her grandfather's coconut and nougat candies. But her favorite spot was the window above her desk. She wanted to always remem-ber the view for its light, green pastures, flowers, and trees, to keep them close inside her, ready to recall them when she needed to or felt homesick.

Katie turned off the kitchen lights. "Em, are you ready? What are you doing?"

"I'm coming." She picked up her laptop and carry-on and headed for the door. She didn't look back as she walked out into the sunlight to the car.

"There you are." Katie opened the back door. "Is that all you're taking?"

Emma nodded. "Downsizing."

"Do you have everything?" Katie walked to the car and slid behind the wheel.

Emma went over her mental checklist. She had deliberately decided to take only the bare essentials. "Yes, I have everything I *need*," she said, but not everything I *want*, she thought.

The early fall air was mildly crisp, not a cloud in the sky. The trees were beginning to show tinges of burnt orange, cadmium red, and yellow. As they drove to National Airport, Emma watched the lines of the highway dissolve into hypnotic yellow flashes of light and the long stretches of farmland turn into housing developments, apartments, and office buildings.

"You never told me. How does it end?"

I wish I knew how it really ends, Emma thought, but answered instead, "I wrote us a happy ending. You end up with René, a lovely young Frenchman, and I get the love of my life."

"Trevor?" Katie smiled. "Did you change our names?"

"No. It's fiction. It doesn't really matter now." The only character with an alias was Rick. She didn't want to be reminded of that one critical mistake.

"I can't wait to read it. I'll put it in every room in the B and B." With the money she inherited, Katie was going to stay and transform Evergreen back into a beautiful Bed and Breakfast and horse farm.

Emma glanced at her sister, sad that she wouldn't be here to see the changes, but she knew Katie would do fine and could take care of herself. Emma smiled at Katie. "I'll miss the farm and you."

"I'm going to miss you, too."

"I'm very proud of you," Emma said.

Katie beamed. "There will always be a place for you whenever you want to come. I'm proud of both of us, though, for putting a little risk in our lives. We're lucky to have these choices to make."

Choices, Emma thought. Choices made or not made. So many choices. Do we really choose our destiny or future, or is it already chosen for us? Emma sometimes questioned why she had made certain choices, only to conclude that it was about forces at work at a particular moment in time. She couldn't really call these regrets. They were more like minuses chalked up unexpectedly. She knew that the many pluses in her life certainly outweighed them, but still they were there, and she wondered how her path might have been different if she could have erased them. She thought change now would be a good thing, bringing renewal and refocus. She believed both of them hoped for this. As they approached the terminal, Emma told Katie that she'd likely be in New York for a couple of days before heading to Paris.

"You'll be seeing Trevor, then?" Katie asked.

"Yes, that'll be my last stop."

OUT OF THE CORNER OF her eye, Emma watched the landscape blur into abstract lines and colors as the plane sped down the runway. She hated take-offs and landings. This noon flight from National to La Guardia was less than an hour, less time than it took to drive to the airport. She remembered when she lived here how she took the shuttle almost every other weekend to see Trevor. The anticipation of those weekends together meant she didn't eat or sleep for days before or after. She was always up in the air even when not on a plane, up in the air with Trevor, their relationship, and where it would ultimately land.

These memories played over in her mind as the nation's capital disappeared from sight and the multicolored trees of the Alleghenies came into focus. Oh my God, she wanted that life back in so many ways. So many years ago. What had really happened between them? She pulled down the shade and rested her forehead against the small window. Why had they made such stupid choices? If only she could have been honest with him back then, honest with herself. Honesty was a trait she admired or thought she had. But she didn't. She hadn't been honest with Rick or Trevor. She hadn't wanted to hurt anyone, but she'd hurt them all, maybe herself the most—a hurt that still sent pangs of sadness and regret to her innermost depths. She had always been a romantic and still was. She believed in "true" love. The trouble was when she'd found it, she'd bailed; she'd hid. It takes courage to let someone love you, and she guessed she hadn't had it then. And now, she thought, maybe it was time to be fearless. She could no longer carry the baggage of regret.

She glanced at her gold watch to doublecheck how close they were to landing. It had stopped. Time had stopped. She almost laughed out loud. She was able to stop time now when she didn't want or need to but couldn't make time work for her when she was most desperate. She closed her eyes tight and tried to imagine turning back the clock to when they first met, when she was engaged, and then married. She realized that it wasn't about time at all, but about timing. Bad timing, poor timing. Eyes closed, she felt herself tumble into a great white void. There was no sound. Stillness surrounded her. She stretched out her arms, reaching, looking for something to hang onto. She felt her chest rise and fall in a relaxed rhythm. Was this what it was like? To die?

Or to live without him?

As the wheels of the plane touched the tarmac, Emma opened her eyes and looked at her outstretched arms. She realized she wasn't reaching for something to hang onto. She was letting go. Finally letting go.

41

Saying Goodbye

EMMA'S FIRST STOP WAS Manhattan and the Roosevelt Hotel, a place she had stayed often and was comfortable with, where she could relax a little and make some phone calls before heading to Brooklyn. If she had time, she thought she might head out to Long Island for a last look at the old summer place.

She took her time unpacking her small carry-on and then sat on the large bed with the red satin coverlet and dialed Katie to let her know she had gotten here safely.

The answering machine picked up and Emma left a message. "Hey, sis. I'm here at the Roosevelt. It was a quick flight and I'm about to go out and walk around a bit and shop. I'll call you later."

Emma hung up the phone and looked out the hotel window. Had it really been so very long ago that she was here with Trevor? The hotel had been renovated since her last visit, a time of confusion and uncertainty when she had left Rick, had to get away, so she came here.

Now, she took a cab up to the Museum of Modern Art to see what the new exhibitions were, but even that reminded her of her weekends with Trevor. She used to come to the museum during the days when he was at work. She remembered the grand traveling King Tut extravaganza and how thrilling it was to see the Egyptian artifacts; she knew she would never visit Egypt. She was more of a Mediterranean girl at heart.

Whether it was Central Park, Brooklyn Heights, or Long Island, Emma knew she couldn't live here because she would always be looking for him around each corner and remembering his hazel-green eyes, freckles, laughter, and love. In some ways, her heart was still there, but time had moved on.

She visited with some old friends the next day and had lunch at the Brasserie and then drove out to Long Island. Emma wanted to have one last look, sit out on the dock, and take in the view. His old friend Louie had bought the house from Trevor some years ago. It was particularly stunning in the fall when the foliage reflected in the mirror-like water. Emma had spent little time there but found it peaceful and calming. Louie was a tall, handsome self-made millionaire who had been married at least twice but was now batching it in this mini-estate. Emma imagined wild weekends *a la Hefner* with babes in bikinis, but when she saw Louie, he looked much older, greyer, and a bit out of shape.

Louie held out his arms. "Welcome." He hugged her. "Em, you look terrific. It's been forever, hasn't it?"

"Yes. A long time." She looked as his blond hair, paler, and thinner now, but those sky-blue eyes still sparkled. "As I told you on the phone, I've been visiting friends before heading back to Paris. I haven't been here in a very long time, and thought I'd stop by and say hello."

Louie's whole face lit up. "I'm glad you did. Can I get you a drink or something?"

"Maybe some iced tea. I just had lunch in the city."

Emma walked up the stone steps in the front of the house and out onto a fabulous patio that wrapped all the way around to the back. The backyard, with its water view and dock, was what she loved most about this house. She and Trevor would sit out here after tennis or boating and stay until dark when they would see the moon and the stars drift overhead. It was a favorite place besides Provence.

Louie's backlit silhouette approached her with hands outstretched, carrying tall crystal glasses. For a brief moment, it was Trevor. Her heart raced, then came to a crashing halt as she caught her breath, smiled, and reached for the glass. "Thank you."

"Emma, I'm sorry about your mother. How are you holding up with all of this?"

"There are still times I want to tell her something I know she'd enjoy. I can't. I miss that. I miss hearing her voice." Emma stared out at the water for a moment, then turned to him. "What about you? Still working hard? Any love interests?"

"Love interests? Well, you know me. I haven't been lucky in that area. I've always wondered, though, what it would have been like if I'd met you first—instead of Trev," he said half-joking.

Emma didn't know what to say. She certainly found him attractive and had always liked tall, blond beach-boy types, but it had always been Trevor and no one else. "I guess we have that in common—the unlucky-in-love syndrome." She laughed.

"Believe me, he loved you. He just didn't handle it very well. As far as work is concerned," he went on, "I don't have to work that hard anymore."

"We had some fun, didn't we, Louie? We all lived life to the fullest."

There was a long pause. She waited for him to agree.

"We all loved each other, Em, and that's what made our lives full. I guess I'm hoping there will be more of that in the future. More love."

She had to give him credit for being an optimist, but Emma knew she was already full of all the love she could handle.

After an hour or so, Emma leaned next to him, took his hand, and said, "I really must be going. I need to get to back to the city. "

"You could stay here if you like." Louie smiled.

Nostalgia washed over her. "I wish I could stay longer, but it's a long drive and you know how New York traffic is."

"Will you see Trevor before you leave?"

"Yes. He's my last stop. My plane leaves tomorrow evening and . . ."

She couldn't finish that sentence. And what? She had to get back to Paris? She knew Paris would be there, but she felt caught somehow between this moment and tomorrow. She couldn't stay here and her heart wasn't in Paris.

42

Hello Again

EMMA FELT A SENSE OF happiness at being back in Brooklyn. Not on Clinton Avenue or at the Botanic Garden, but on Bushwick Avenue walking toward the past. The smell of shortened days, of Copely Hall, the palette of fall burnt around the edges—oranges, golds, browns— like those early days on campus when they were in their twenties.

Fall always carried her back to Georgetown, Dumbarton Oaks, Wisconsin Avenue, to the very first time they met, their first time at the Brickskellar, parties, football, and beer kegs. Fall evoked a return to school, a familiar change that came with the cooler days and parti-colored leaves. She hadn't realized all those years ago that this is what it would come to—another new beginning, another chance at making it right.

She knew what she had to do.

It was mid-afternoon, two days after his birthday, when she walked down the tree-lined street to see him. She loved the large park-like setting right in the heart of Brooklyn. In the spring, tourists, picnickers, and bird watchers poured into the area, enjoying the picturesque landscape filled with tulips, daffodils, and dogwoods surrounding the four large ponds. Cherry blossoms burst forth like those around the Tidal Basin in Washington. Diverse architecture from gothic to Corinthian columns and Roman gods and goddesses dotted the grounds. It was a treasured oasis in the very center of the daily hustle and bustle. She took a deep, relaxing breath of the fall air and walked into the center of the park.

As she continued along the path, the afternoon light began to push long shadows from the bottoms of the trees, stretching them over the grass like gentle arrows pointing the way. She had found her direction and was moving closer to it. The dashing young man with the boyish smile she had loved for so long was not far away.

She turned the corner and cut across the manicured lawn, walking deeper into yesterday. There was a stillness around her. The birds were asleep, no people, no cars. A strange, eerie feeling crept over her as she listened to the beating of her heart.

Emma slowed her pace as if anticipating footsteps behind her. Her imagination. Was she in the right place?

She stopped and fumbled for the miniature map in her jacket pocket. She wasn't sure whether she had made the right turn. She looked at the street map, turning it around and upside down. She traced the map and directions with her forefinger, mouthing the names of the streets around her and checking her direction. For a moment, she had lost her bearings, just as she and Katie had done in the woods at Evergreen, and as she had done many times with Trevor. She looked around. Finally, she continued along the sidewalk, walking with an unhurried, steady pace, in a rhythm of reluctance. She pushed up the collar of her leather coat to warm her neck and ears. She felt a chill throughout her body. She didn't understand why she was cold and her hands were shivering. Nerves, only nerves. She wanted to be here, but didn't. She had to be here but wanted to turn and run.

This was going to be harder than she had thought, but she had no choice. She had to break the ties of the past or at least erase the most painful ones.

She pictured the last time she had seen him, remembering how he had looked and what they had done. It had been longer than she realized—thirteen years. They had had dinner at Dominique's on Pennsylvania Avenue in Washington, D.C. She couldn't eat. She drank Merlot instead. She had learned three months earlier that he was married. She had been divorced for almost three years. They talked about work and travel. His wife was going to have a baby. She had a pain in her gut at the thought of it. They had danced around their own love story, afraid to turn a page, afraid someone would get hurt. But Emma was already devastated. She wanted to ask him why he didn't choose her but thought it was too late to matter. For her own peace of mind, she should have, but she didn't take the chance. Instead, she had tormented herself with the unknown.

A siren in the distance brought her back to the moment. She knew she should be angry with him like she had been when he told her he was married. It had been like a death. She had spent three days in bed wearing only an old shirt of his, surrounded by his old letters and photos, crying her way through to a new anger. But she was really angry with herself. Angry for marrying Rick, not understanding how Trevor had felt, not talking to him about it, assuming he didn't want her, and didn't choose her when he would have chosen her if she'd let him. She was furious with herself. She took a deep breath. Maybe it didn't matter now, but she needed to tell him so he could forgive her and she could forgive herself.

She walked past the grand marble lion's head and followed the path around the lavish pond shaded by bare dogwoods and cherry trees until it narrowed down a small hill into a cul-de-sac. This is it, she thought. Another couple hundred yards. Her forehead broke out in a sweat; she unbuttoned her coat. She felt nauseous. Then, a few feet away, she saw Trevor, her Trevor. She walked slowly, deliberately toward him.

She moved closer and looked hard at his name: Trevor M. Kinney. My Trevor, she thought. This is my Trevor: 1950–2000. "Damn you, Trevor. Damn you for dying on me."

She couldn't forgive the reality of it, the tragedy of his heart attack. He had a great heart. There was nothing wrong with his heart, she told herself.

She stood for a long while fixated on the black granite headstone. The etched letters were real, not to be erased, carved in cold stone forever. So unlike him. He was warm, tender. She carefully placed the long-stemmed red rose on the ground in front of her and sat down slowly on the nearby bench, studying the words before her. She remembered seeing his name on his desk in his New York office. One of those wooden nameplates lawyers have, one that wasn't permanent. More suitable, more fitting. We are all impermanent. This is how it ends for all of us. What's the sense of it? What's the meaning? She sat asking herself why she had come here. She couldn't speak. Tears of disbelief, relief, and regret streamed down her cheeks.

Finally, Emma whispered a faint, "Hello again. I've missed you. I've missed you every day of my life." Emma paused, remembering all the times they'd spent hanging out in Brooklyn, dining out in Manhattan, and summering at the shore. In her mind, it was only yesterday. Yet, it had gone by so quickly. It only takes an instant for an entire lifetime to go by.

"I'm sorry it's taken me so long to get here." She ran her hand over the sharply carved stone, fingering the letters of his name. "I miss you, Trev, I miss you." She hadn't been in the cemetery since his mother died many years ago. She couldn't bear going to his funeral and seeing their old friends, especially his wife. She didn't want to see his wife. Emma had been jealous of the woman who had her life, the life she had wanted and could have had but didn't. No, she couldn't put herself through that.

Emma closed her eyes and took several deep breaths, calming her emotions enough to speak again. "I saw Louie. He sends his love. He looks the same, a little greyer. He's taking good care of the place. And Katie sends her regards. Mother died, and we've been at the farm for months wrapping up things. Katie is staying there, reviving the B and B and plans to have her horse farm after all. It's funny how things turn out. I was the one crazy over horses who wanted to move to Arizona and have a ranch."

Emma paused as if she were waiting for a response. "There's something else. I've written a book, a novel, about us, our story. We're alive on the pages. I gave us the happy ending we deserved. I think it's good. And my editor thinks so too. I wrote what I knew and remembered from those many years ago. I told the truth, and you know it now. I think you know everything. I believe you are always with me, watching over me, and forgiving me." Emma put her face in her hands and wept quietly. "I'm sorry. Sorry I didn't trust you, trust me, trust us enough to let things take their own course. I had too much self-doubt to follow my own heart, my own voice."

The old adage about knowing then what you know now popped into her head. It had taken so long to figure it out and then come to terms with the regret and stupid choices. "Trevor, I'm so very sorry. I screwed up. I didn't understand what you meant or what you wanted.

I take the blame. I'm sorry." Emma knew that if he could, he would say the same to her. "Rick was there. That's all. I never intended to marry him. You were the one, the one I loved, the one I still love. I didn't know how to get out of the engagement or the marriage. I stayed. I tried to learn to love him. I'm sorry. Please forgive me."

By the time she was finished, Emma felt as if she were having an out of body experience, detached from herself, trying to make sense of it all and wondering if any of it mattered. She was saying what had been hidden inside her for years.

She wiped the tears from her cheeks and closed her eyes, trying to see his face, hoping he'd be there when she looked again. Emma sat silently. She wanted to see her life as one of reflection and remembrance not as fragments of moments lost in time. She wanted only the present to focus on, live in. The past was the past, and she didn't want to carry it into her future. She loved him. She forgave him.

Could she forgive herself? Could she have hope for something new, something real? No more strangled dreams. This time she wanted to get it right.

Emma shifted her weight on the stone bench, feeling cold again. A light breeze zigzagged through the tree limbs, and the sun moved more to the west. She looked at her watch. She had been there two hours. She would have to leave soon.

"Trev, I'm going home tomorrow, back to Paris, my job at *Condé Nast*, and my apartment. I'm going to look for a weekend place in a small village, maybe near Joucas." Like the one in her novel, she thought. "You remember Joucas? Charming and quaint. You know how I feel about Provence. To me, it's the most beautiful place on earth. I know what you're thinking. No, it's not New York, but it's unique. I have a special connection to the place. I'm myself there."

Emma leaned over and kissed the stone, reading the inscription.

"Time won't change the meaning of one love." She smiled, completing the Streisand lyric she knew: "ageless and evergreen." She stood, turned away from Trevor, and began walking back to her car. She didn't look back.

The air was thin like the last breath of Indian summer, the last breath of life. As she came out of the cemetery, Emma watched the sun slowly sink behind Manhattan. She would be in the beginning of rush hour traffic. Rush hour traffic. Why does everyone rush to work, rush home, rush to shop, rush, rush, rush? We all come full circle anyway. We all end up in the same place. The idea of full circle hit her head on. She had completed her own circle from Evergreen farm in Virginia to Evergreen Cemetery in Brooklyn.

She had ended where she had begun.

Epilogue

LIFE HAD A CERTAIN ORDER without him. A quick run in the morning, coffee at Café Tournon, a movie Sunday afternoon alone or with friends. But when she had been with him, it was about spontaneity, lovemaking, and sex. For Emma, sex was intimately and irretrievably connected to passion and love, or at least it had been with him. As she thought about it now, perhaps that was part of the problem, maybe not enough routine for a lasting relationship. Not enough to hold on to. She'd always dropped everything for him, put off dates, changed her plans to spend moments in his arms, watching him sleep, his chest rising and falling with each breath taken.

Why had she done it? It was her heart. Her heart compelled her to ward off the misery of his absence.

Even now, if she could, she would do it all over again. *Listen to your heart,* she thought. Something she knew she had to do now more than ever.

Emma turned the page of her desk calendar, realizing that today marked a year since her mother's death. It had gone by so quickly. But Paris had remained unchanged, still filled with the old-world charm and romanticism that had drawn her here in the first place. April had burst forth with all the magic and flowers she'd imagined in her manuscript, poems, and travel articles. It was a city for dreamers and lovers, old and young. It didn't matter. Paris would always be the same—just herself—inspiring writers, artists, lovers, or anyone who succumbed to her.

When Emma looked at her calendar she also thought of Evergreen, her mother's gardens, and Katie. She would call her sister today. They had been in close contact via email since Emma's return. She knew that things were shaping up at the farm. She would definitely plan a visit there sometime in the near future, but now she felt a desire to travel south to Provence. There had been no time to explore the possibility of a small apartment where she could go during *les vacances* in August. Maybe that's what she should do for a few weekends—explore and find where she might fit in.

Her boss had deliberately kept her busy in and around the city with weekend sojourns here and there to focus on the tourist havens for the spring issue. Now that it was on the stands, Emma wanted to spend some time on her own, visiting those places she'd only read about. Her book was published now, freeing up her thoughts about what to do next, where to go, what to write.

She looked at her computer and scanned the list of assignments for the week, then typed in Avignon, someplace she'd always wanted to go. Next, her fingers punched in Aix-en-Provence. She'd always thought it would be great fun to tour Cezanne's old haunts and maybe do a story on the journey. Maybe she could. She thought of pitching this to her boss to see what might transpire. If it worked, she could look in the area for a possible weekend retreat. Her thoughts drifted to Provence and the places she had imagined in her novel and wondered if there might be a small village for her somewhere that met all of her requirements for tranquility, inspiration, and even romance. She had begun to daydream her way there when her boss, Paul, tapped on her door and walked in.

"A penny?" he said.

Emma turned and looked up at him. He had barely aged since his arrival in Paris ten years ago. A slight bit of grey peaked out from beneath the sides of his jet black hair, but it was his eyes that captivated Emma and most women. They were cat eyes—peridot and playful. He was a few years younger than Emma, but she was beginning to feel that everyone was younger than her fifty years. The insecurity of aging, she supposed.

"Oh, thinking about possible stories." That was partially true, she thought

"Good. I just got this from the tourism office in Aix and thought you might be interested."

Emma looked at the release—a wine festival in Tholonet. "It looks interesting, but it's not until July."

"I know, but it's almost May. You'd have time to do some research on the winery and vineyard. You know it's always better to have a longer lead time than not."

Emma tilted her head and studied his face. No five o'clock shadow; it was as smooth as a baby's bottom. She smiled. "I've been wanting to go to Aix and actually was thinking more about a story on Cezanne and the area."

Paul hesitated. "I think that's been overdone, but if you can tie it to wine and feature the festival, I'll take a look at it." He handed her the information.

Emma took the paper and started to put it in her inbox.

"There's a contact for the vineyard listed at the bottom. You may want to begin there. Let me know what you think. I'll be back later."

Emma's eyes scrolled to the bottom of the page. *Family-owned and operated, La Palette vineyard has been producing superb wines for 100 years. La Palette*, she thought. An artist's palette? Unusual. She looked again. No, it was the small appellation of the wine region. She read on—*Contact: Jacques-René at. . .*

Emma's eyes froze on the name of the vintner. She laughed. Truth really was stranger than fiction. Already, her new book was coming back to haunt her. Maybe she should pass this on to her agent in New York. She'd appreciate the serendipity.

Serendipity. Didn't the word come from a Persian fairy tale? Emma wasn't sure she even believed in those anymore or ever did after the age of seven. Still, who was she to tempt the hand of fate this time around. *La Palette*, she smiled to herself. Life imitating art? She twirled her chair around to face her computer and started looking for the town of Tholonet.

CPSIA information can be obtained
at www.ICGtesting.com
Printed in the USA
BVHW050428170922
647299BV00004B/6